SEEING STARS

"Get over here," Patel said wearily as he pulled a set of handcuffs off his belt. "And you'd better not start mouthing me. I'm not in the mood."

James stepped forward and held out his wrists. Patel snapped on the cuffs and read James his rights in a monotone as they walked to a police car parked on the double yellow lines outside the gate.

"You do not have to answer any questions, but anything you do say will be taken down and used in evidence. . . ."

James had been arrested before and knew the words off by heart, but this particular reading had a surprise ending. As he ducked down to get in the back of the car, Patel grabbed James's head and thumped it hard against the edge of the car roof.

James was seeing stars as he collapsed across the rear seat.

"We'll sort you out," Patel snarled as he slammed the car door. "You've got no idea how sick I get of nicking dumb little brats like you."

Look for all the books in the

 series:

mission 1: *THE RECRUIT*
mission 2: *THE DEALER*
mission 3: *MAXIMUM SECURITY*
mission 4: *THE KILLING*

by Robert Muchamore

Published by Simon Pulse

CHERUB
a division of MI5

THE
KILLING

R O B E R T   M U C H A M O R E

Simon Pulse
New York London Toronto Sydney

SIMON PULSE
An imprint of Simon & Schuster Children's Publishing Division
1230 Avenue of the Americas, New York, NY 10020
Copyright © 2005 by Robert Muchamore
Originally published in Great Britain in 2005 by Hodder Children's Books
Published by arrangement with Hodder and Stoughton Limited
First U.S. edition 2006
All rights reserved, including the right of reproduction in whole or in part in any form.
SIMON PULSE and colophon are registered trademarks of Simon & Schuster, Inc.
Designed by Christopher Grassi
The text of this book was set in Apollo MT.
Manufactured in the United States of America
First Simon Pulse edition August 2006
10 9 8 7 6 5 4 3 2 1
Library of Congress Control Number 2005935208
ISBN-13: 978-1-4169-2459-3
ISBN-10: 1-4169-2459-0

What Is
CHERUB?

CHERUB is a branch of British Intelligence. Its agents are aged between ten and seventeen years. Cherubs are mainly orphans who have been taken out of care homes and trained to work undercover. They live on CHERUB campus, a secret facility hidden in the English countryside.

What Use
Are Kids?

Quite a lot. Nobody realizes kids do undercover missions, which means they can get away with all kinds of stuff that adults can't.

Who Are
They?

About three hundred children live on CHERUB campus. JAMES ADAMS is our thirteen-year-old hero. He's a well-respected CHERUB agent, with three successful missions under his belt. James's ten-year-old sister, LAUREN ADAMS, is a less experienced CHERUB agent. KERRY CHANG is a Hong Kong–born karate champion and James's girlfriend.

Amongst James's closest friends on campus are BRUCE NORRIS, GABRIELLE O'BRIEN, SHAKEEL DAJANI, and the twins, CALLUM and CONNOR REILLY. His best friend is KYLE BLUEMAN, who is fifteen.

And the
T-Shirts?

Cherubs are ranked according to the color of the T-shirts they wear on campus. ORANGE is for visitors. RED is for kids who live on CHERUB campus but are too young to qualify as agents. BLUE is for kids undergoing CHERUB's tough one-hundred-day basic training regime. A GRAY T-shirt means you're qualified for missions. NAVY—the T-shirt James wears—is a reward for outstanding performance on a single mission. If you do well, you'll end your CHERUB career wearing a BLACK T-shirt, the ultimate recognition for outstanding achievement over a number of missions. When you retire, you get the WHITE T-shirt, which is also worn by staff.

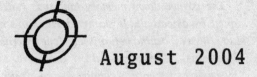

August 2004

The two thirteen-year-olds wore nylon shorts, sleeveless tops, and flip-flops. Jane leaned against the concrete wall of the housing block where she lived, peeling away strands of hair stuck to her sweaty face. Hannah was sprawled over the paved steps a couple of meters in front of her.

"I dunno," Jane huffed.

The words were meaningless, but Hannah understood. It was the middle of the summer holidays and the hottest day of the year so far. The two best friends were broke, irritated by the heat, and weary of each other's company.

"Makes me sweat just looking at 'em," Hannah said, staring at the preteen boys kicking a football around a tarmac pitch less than twenty meters away.

"We used to run around like that," Jane said. "Not football. I mean, racing our bikes and stuff."

Hannah allowed herself to smile as her brain drifted into the past. "Barbie bike grand prix." She nodded, remembering herself on a little pink bike, the white spokes blurring as she juddered over the gaps between paving slabs. Jane's nan always sat out in a deck chair keeping an eye on them.

"You and me had to have everything the exact same." Jane nodded as she curled her toes, making her sandal clap against her foot.

The voyage down memory lane was rudely inter-rupted by a football. It skimmed Hannah's hair and stung the wall behind her, missing Jane by centimeters. "Jeeeeeesus," Hannah gasped.

She dived forward, wrapping her body over the ball as it bobbled down the steps alongside her. A boy ran up to the bottom of the staircase. Nine years old, with a Chelsea shirt tied around his waist, he displayed a rack of skinny ribs every time he breathed out.

"Give us," the kid panted, putting out his hands to catch.

"You nearly whacked me in the face," Jane yelled furiously. "You might at least say sorry."

"We didn't mean it."

The other lads who'd been playing football were closing in, irritated by the break in play. Hannah appreciated that the kick was an accident and she'd been set to give the ball back until one of the kids gave her lip. He was the biggest lad there, ten years old with cropped red hair.

"Come on, you fat cow, get us our ball."

Hannah barged between a couple of sweaty torsos and faced the redhead, squeezing the football between her palms. "You wanna repeat that, Ginger?"

Hannah was three years older than the kid she was facing off, with height and weight on her side. All Ginger could do was stare dumbly at his Nikes, while his mates waited for him to come out with something clever.

"Cat got your tongue?" Hannah glowered, enjoying the way Ginger was squirming.

"I just want our ball," he said weakly.

"Go fetch it then."

Hannah let the ball drop and booted it before it hit the ground. It would have been OK in trainers, but as the ball soared towards the goalpost on the opposite side of the pitch, her sandal flew after it.

Ginger quickly backed up and picked the sandal out of the air. Enjoying his newfound power, he smirked as he held the sandal up to his nose and took a sniff.

"Your feet stink, girl. Don't you wash?"

Hannah made a grab for her sandal as the young footballers jeered. Ginger ducked out of the way before throwing the shoe underarm to one of his mates. Lumps of gravel dug into Hannah's sole as she stepped unevenly toward her new tormentor. She felt like a total wally for letting this gang of runts get one over on her.

"Give us that shoe or I'm gonna batter you," she snarled.

The shoe changed hands again as Jane stepped into the fray to help her mate. "Give it back," she steamed.

The angrier the girls got, the harder the boys laughed. They were spreading out, anticipating an extended game of piggy in the middle, when Jane noticed changing expressions on the young faces.

Hannah sensed something was wrong too. She turned sharply, catching a fast-moving object out of the corner of her eye a second before it smashed into the ground. It hit the staircase in the exact spot where she'd been sitting a minute earlier.

Hannah froze in shock as the metal banister crumpled. By the time her brain got up to speed, the terrified young footballers had abandoned her sandal and were shooting off in all directions. She found her eyes focused on the well-worn tread of a boy's trainer. His denim-clad

7

bum poked out of the crumpled metal and dust. The adrenalin hit hard as Hannah recognized the mangled body and screamed out.

"Will . . . No, for God's sake . . ."

He looked dead, but this couldn't be for real. She covered her face with her hands and screamed so hard, she felt her tonsils dance in the back of her throat. She tried to tell herself it was all a dream. Stuff like this didn't happen in real life. She'd wake up in a minute and everything would be back to normal. . . .

Uniform

For the past three years George Stein has worked as an economics teacher at the exclusive Trinity Day School near Cambridge. Recently, information has come to light suggesting that Stein may have links with the environmental terrorist group Help Earth. (Excerpt from CHERUB mission briefing for Callum Reilly and Shakeel "Shak" Dajani.)

JUNE 2005

It was a fine day and this part of Cambridge had the whiff of serious money. The immaculate lawns were coiffured by professional gardeners, and James drooled over the expensive lumps of German metal parked on the driveways. He was walking with Shakeel, and both boys felt self-conscious in the summer uniform of Trinity School. It consisted of a white shirt, a tie, gray trousers with orange piping, an orange and gray blazer, and matching felt cap.

"I'm telling you," James moaned, "even if you sat down and tried *really* hard, I don't think you could come up with a way to make this uniform look any dumber."

"I dunno, James. Maybe we could have partridge

feathers sticking out of the hats or something."

"And these trousers were meant for Callum's skinny butt. They're killing my balls."

Shak couldn't help seeing the funny side of James's discomfort. "You can't blame Callum for pulling out of the mission at the last minute. It's that stomach bug that's going around campus."

James nodded. "I had it last week. I was barely off the bog for two whole days."

Shak looked at his watch for the millionth time. "We need to up the pace."

"What's the big deal?" James asked.

"This isn't some London comprehensive full up with scummy little Arsenal fans like you," Shak explained. "Trinity is one of the top fee-paying schools in the country, and the pupils aren't allowed to wander around the corridors whenever it suits them. Our arrival's got to coincide with the change-over between third and fourth periods, when there's hundreds of other kids moving around."

James nodded. "Gotcha."

Shak looked at his watch for the millionth and first time as they cut into a cobbled alleyway that was barely wide enough for a single car.

"Come *on*, James."

"I'm trying," James said. "But I'm seriously gonna rip the arse out of these trousers if I'm not careful."

Once they'd cut between two large houses, the alleyway opened out into a run-down park with knee-high grass and a set of tangled swings. To the boys' left stood a chain-link fence topped with barbed wire, behind which lay the grounds of Trinity

Day. The main gates were carefully monitored during school hours, so this was their only way in.

Shak wandered through the long grass next to the fence, placing his shoe carefully to avoid turds and litter, as he searched for an entry point made by an MI5 operative the previous night. He found the flap cut in the wire behind the trunk of a large tree. Shak lifted it, doffed his cap, and attempted a snooty accent. "After you, James, my good man."

James fed his backpack and hat through the gap before sliding under. He stood with his back against the tree and brushed dirt off his uniform while Shak followed.

"All set?" James asked as he slung his backpack over his shoulder. It weighed a ton and the equipment inside clattered around.

"Cap," Shak reminded him.

James let out a little gasp as he leaned forward and picked the cap out of the grass. A claxon sounded inside the school building a couple of hundred meters away, indicating a lesson change.

"OK, let's shift," Shak said.

The boys broke out from behind the tree and began jogging across a rugby pitch towards the school building. As they did, they noticed a groundskeeper striding purposefully towards them from the opposite end of the field.

"You two," he bellowed.

Because James had been pulled onto the mission at the last minute to replace Callum, he'd only had time to skim through the mission briefing. He looked uneasily at Shak for guidance.

"Don't sweat it," Shak whispered. "I've got it covered."

The groundskeeper intercepted the boys near a set of rugby posts. He was a fit looking fellow with thinning gray hair, dressed in workman's boots and a grubby overall.

"Exactly *what* do you think you're doing out here?" he demanded pompously.

"I was reading under the tree at lunchtime," Shak explained, pointing backwards with his thumb. "I left my cap behind."

"You know the rules of the school, don't you?"

Shak and James both looked confused.

"Don't try playing the fool with me, you *know* as well as I do. If you're not attending a lesson, a match, or an official practice, you do not set foot on the games pitches because it causes unnecessary wear and tear."

"Yes," Shak nodded. "Sorry, sir. I was in a hurry to get to my lesson, that's all."

"Sorry," James added. "But it's not like the pitches are muddy or anything. We're not really tearing them up."

The groundskeeper took James's comment as a threat to his authority. He swooped down and showered James with spit as he spoke. "I make the rules here, young man. *You* don't decide when you can and can't set foot on *my* pitches. Got that?"

"Yes, sir," James said.

"What's your name and house?"

"Joseph Mail, King Henry House," James lied, recalling one of the few elements of his background story he'd managed to remember from the mission briefing.

"Faisal Asmal, same house," Shak said.

"Right," the groundskeeper said, bouncing smugly on the balls of his feet. "I'll be reporting both of you to your housemaster and I expect your cheek will have earned you both a detention. Now, you'd better get yourselves to your next lesson."

"Why'd you answer back?" Shak asked irritably as the boys walked towards the back entrance of the school.

"I know I shouldn't have," James said, raising his palms defensively. "But he was *so* full of himself."

They passed through a set of double doors into the main school building, then up a short flight of steps and into the busy thoroughfare that ran the length of the ground floor. There was plenty of noise, but the Trinity boys walked purposefully, nodding politely to the teachers standing in the doorways as they entered their classrooms.

"What a bunch of geeks," James whispered. "I bet these dudes don't even fart."

Shak explained the situation as they headed up the stairs to the second floor. "Every kid has to pass special exams and an interview to get into Trinity. There's always a humungous waiting list, so they can afford to boot out anyone who doesn't toe the line."

"Bet I wouldn't last long," James grinned.

By the time they reached the second floor, most kids had found their way to lessons and the classroom doors had been pulled shut. Shak pulled a lock gun from the pocket of his blazer as they passed by a couple of classroom doors. He stopped at the door of an office with a nameplate on it: *Dr. George Stein BSc, PhD, Head of Economics and Politics.*

Shak pushed the tip of the lock gun into the keyhole. James stood close by, blocking the view of a bunch of kids waiting outside a classroom fifteen meters away.

The lock had a simple single-lever mechanism, meaning Shak only had to give the lock gun a brief wiggle and pull on the trigger to open the door. The pair hurriedly stepped into the office and put the latch down so that nobody could burst in on them, even with a key.

"Stein should be teaching two floors up," Shak said. "We've got until the next lesson change in thirty-six minutes; let's get to work."

Technique

While Shak stepped behind Stein's desk and dropped the venetian blind, James surveyed the office. It contained nothing exciting: basic desk and chairs, two filing cabinets, and a coat rack. Shak used the lock gun to undo the metal cabinets, then began sifting through the files. He was looking for any papers relating to George Stein's personal life, especially anything to do with his campaigning for environmentalist groups.

James sat at the desk and switched on Stein's PC. While the computer booted up, he pulled a miniature JVC notebook from his backpack and ran a network lead between the two computers. Stein's machine demanded a password, but James wasn't flustered. He started up a suite of hacking tools on his computer and used it to run system diagnostics on Stein's machine.

Once the system had gleaned basic information about Stein's hard drive and operating system, James opened another module of the hacking software, which allowed him to view all of Stein's files.

"Candy from a baby," James smiled confidently.

Now that he could see the files, James clicked the

Clone icon and the notebook began copying the entire contents of Stein's PC on to its hard drive.

"How much data's he got?" Shak asked as he pulled out the second drawer of the cabinet.

"Eight-point-two gigabytes. The progress bar says it'll take six minutes to copy it all across."

While the computers went about their business, James shifted some papers and stood on the desk. He reached up and pulled out the metal reflector covering the ceiling-mounted light fitting. The resulting cloud of dust tickled his nostrils as he studied the line of fluorescent tubes above his head.

"Cut them off, Shak."

Shak leaned across and flipped the light switch. James reached into the fitting and pulled the starter plug from one of the fluorescent tubes before jumping down. He rummaged briefly inside his rucksack, emerging with an apparently identical plastic fitting. But whereas the starter unit James had removed cost less than a pound, the replacement cost three thousand. It was a listening device, consisting of a pinhead-sized microphone, a transmitter, and a chip that could store five hours of sound.

Light fittings are perfect for locating listening devices. First because they're usually located in open space high above a room, where it's easy to pick up sound. Second because the device can easily be wired up to source electricity from the mains.

As James went up at full stretch to replace the grille, he heard the ripping noise he'd been dreading all morning. His trousers had cracked open around the crotch seam, revealing a garish set of boxers.

Shak couldn't help smiling as he flipped the lights back on. "Nice shorts, J."

"Man, that feels *good*," James gasped. "I might be able to have children after all. What's next?"

"Keys," Shak reminded him.

"Assuming he's left them in here," James said as he walked towards the jacket hanging up by the door.

He fished a bunch of keys from Stein's pocket, then grabbed a packet of wax tablets from his rucksack. Meanwhile, Shak had found some interesting documents in one of the filing cabinets and was copying the pages with a handheld scanner.

The wax tablets separated into two biscuit-sized pieces. James sandwiched each of Stein's keys between a tablet, creating impressions that could be used to make duplicates. By the time James had worked his way through the whole bunch, the laptop had chimed, indicating that it had finished cloning.

James sat back in front of the laptop and used the hacking suite to install spyware on Stein's machine. The spyware program would record every keystroke Stein typed and then transmit it covertly over the Internet to the MI5 monitoring station at Caversham.

Shak had finished rummaging through the file cabinets. He grabbed a small metal box out of his backpack. It was held together with bits of insulating tape and looked like the creation of a mad professor. In fact, it had been built specifically to capture and replicate the radio signal from the plipper that worked Stein's car alarm.

Shak turned the device on by taping a wire to the top of an AA battery. He flipped a switch on the front of the box to the receive position and asked James to press the plipper on Stein's car key. It took a couple of attempts before a green LED on the front of the gadget flickered, indicating that the signal had been successfully recorded.

"Is that everything?" James asked.

Shak nodded as he checked the time. "In the bag with six minutes to spare."

James and Shak did a final check, making sure they'd picked up their equipment and repositioned everything exactly the way they'd found it. When the claxon sounded for the lesson change, the boys darted outside and began heading down to the ground floor. James was conscious of the growing split in his trousers, but none of the Trinity pupils seemed to notice.

At the main entrance of the school building the boys stepped outdoors and turned left, heading down a gentle ramp towards a recently built sports complex that had a teachers' car park beneath it.

The boys caught a whiff of sweat as they passed the entrance to a changing area where a group of Year Ten boys were getting ready for PE. They headed down a corridor lined with historic photos of Trinity rugby teams. After reaching the door leading into the teachers' car park, James did a full three-sixty check before they passed under the STAFF ONLY sign and down a flight of bare concrete steps. Everything looked new, with scarcely a tire mark on the yellow lines dividing up the parking bays.

The boys quickly identified Stein's silver hatchback. Shak pulled the metal box out of his blazer and flipped the switch across to transmit mode. James slotted a dealer's key in the driver's side door. This key was designed to open any car of this model, but it didn't contain the embedded microchip necessary to silence the alarm.

"Ready?" James asked, waiting for Shak to nod. "Three, two, one—turn."

There was a fleeting squeal from the alarm in the instant between James turning the key and Shak canceling it with the gadget. James dived into the driver's seat and reached across to pull up the little door lock on the passenger door. By the time Shak climbed in, James had reclined in his seat. He pulled the clear cover off the vanity light and unscrewed the tiny bulb and the silver plastic fitting in which it was mounted. Shak reached up and pushed in a specially constructed replacement that contained a listening device. Once it was clipped into place, James replaced the bulb and the outer cover.

Shak briefly rummaged inside the glove box, checking out the various receipts and scraps of paper for anything interesting. He laid a couple of bits out flat on the glove box lid and copied them with the handheld scanner. James searched over in the rear seats and in the driver's door cubby, but all he found was a road atlas and a mass of crumpled paper cups.

"Is that it?" James asked as he hit the recline lever, making his seat spring back up.

Shak nodded. "Now we just have to make it out of here without getting busted."

James opened the car door, but as he stepped out,

he noticed a reedy female outline emerging at the bottom of the staircase.

"Damn," James whispered, as he quietly pulled shut the car door.

Shak sneaked a glance at the beanpole woman as she lit up a cigarette and puffed as though her life depended on it. The boys had no option but to crouch down low in their seats until she went back upstairs.

They gave it a couple of minutes before following after her. The mission plan called for the boys to hide in a desolate area behind the sports center for the remaining half hour of the school day, when they'd be able to walk out of the front gates alongside the real pupils.

As they passed the changing rooms again, James noticed that the PE teacher hadn't locked the door again when the kids had gone into the gym. Tantalizingly, more than a dozen pairs of the orange-piped Trinity trousers were scattered about the room.

"Keep an eye out," James said. "I'm gonna whip me some trousers."

Shak wasn't exactly happy about James taking an unnecessary risk, but realized that he wouldn't have wanted to travel back to campus with a giant crack in his trousers either.

James passed by the first few pairs. He was slightly above average size for thirteen, but these Year Ten kids were still bigger. James eventually found a pair that looked right. He ripped off his shoes and quickly slipped into them. Realizing that there wasn't time to transfer everything between the two pairs of trousers, he balled up the ripped pair and crammed them into his backpack on top of everything else.

James stepped out of the changing room and started walking back the way they'd come.

"Wait," Shak said.

James turned back. "What's up?"

"Nothing. It's just, while you were changing, I looked through the window and realized what's on the other side of that door. Instead of walking out the front and all the way around the edge of the building, we can go out through there."

James stepped across the corridor and peered through the frosted glass in the door. It clearly led directly to the back of the building.

James shrugged. "Why not?"

He pushed down on the handle and nudged the door open with his shoulder. As he did, a loud buzzing sound broke out from a plastic box above their heads. The boys exchanged a shocked look as a burly PE teacher came steaming out of the gymnasium towards them.

"What the *hell* are you two playing at?"

"Run?" James asked.

Shak didn't answer; James just heard a squeal of shoe leather as his friend set off towards the entrance at full pelt.

Hair

James's sister Lauren had wanted to dye her hair black since she was six years old, but her mum wouldn't let her, no matter how much she whined. The only thing that stopped Lauren doing it in the two years since her mum had died was a sense that it would have been disrespecting her memory.

In the end it took heavy persuasion from Lauren's best friend, Bethany Parker, who claimed she'd bought black hair dye by mistake. Lauren couldn't understand how you *accidentally* bought hair dye and didn't believe Bethany's claim for a millisecond; but once the dye was right there, on the bathroom shelf, she couldn't resist.

Lauren was fairly happy with the result, especially when she put on her black Linkin Park T-shirt and ripped jeans, and mussed her hair up so that it looked punky. But she wasn't totally confident and she couldn't help staring at herself every time she passed something reflective, as though the thousandth glance would reveal some miraculous truth not imparted by the previous nine hundred and ninety-nine.

She was in a sore mood as she walked along a corridor toward the Pre-Training Briefing (PTB) classroom, because four lads had ganged up on her in the last lesson of the afternoon and spent the whole time taking the mickey out of her hair. It didn't hurt her feelings, because they were the sort of idiots who would have made fun of anything she'd done, but they'd been in her face for the best part of an hour and it ended up severely getting on her nerves. The worst part was having to sit there with a tight grin, taking whatever they threw at her, because she knew any sign that they were getting under her skin would only encourage them.

Lauren checked her watch as she passed through an open door into the PTB classroom and headed for a long table marked with a plastic sign saying TEAM D. Teams A–C, each five strong, were gathered noisily around some of the other tables. Team C was jointly led by James's girlfriend, Kerry, and her best friend, Gabrielle, while Team A was led by James's best friend, Kyle.

Lauren sat down next to Bethany Parker. Bethany's little brother, Jake, sat opposite and Dana "Cheesy" Smith was at the other end of the table, as far from everyone else as she could get.

Jake was nine years old. He wouldn't be able to enter basic training until he turned ten, but his education was already being geared towards becoming a CHERUB agent. On top of normal lessons, Jake had daily karate and judo sessions and was almost fluent in Spanish and French. Now he was set for his first taste of outdoor CHERUB training, as the most junior member of Team D.

Dana was a fourteen-year-old tomboy who'd been recruited to CHERUB from an Australian children's home. She sat with her legs out straight and her arms folded over a filthy combat jacket. Dana had been a qualified CHERUB agent for four years, but while an imposing physique had taken her to numerous karate trophies and three wins in CHERUB's annual triathlon, her mission performance had been unspectacular and she still wore a gray shirt.

Lauren half-smiled as she grabbed a chair. "Hello, Dana."

"Hello, *boss*," Dana sneered in her Australian accent, without bothering to changer her *No one likes me, I don't care* scowl.

Lauren had discovered that being one of the youngest navy shirts on campus was a mixed blessing. It was cool in a way, but it was awkward when she found herself outranking kids who were several years older.

"Where's your big bro?" Dana asked as Lauren dragged her chair up to the table.

"James won't make it to this briefing," Lauren said. "I'll have to make notes for him. He should be back by eight o'clock."

Jake butted in. "Your hair looks ridiculous."

Lauren bunched a fist. "Not as ridiculous as your face will in a minute."

Jake tutted contemptuously. "I'm *so* scared."

Lauren looked at Bethany and shook her head. "Boys are *such* morons."

"Tell me about it," Bethany said, giving her brother a withering look.

The classroom went silent as CHERUB's most ruthless training instructor stepped in. Mr. Large was tailed by two of his assistants, Mr. Pike and Mr. Greaves. The two younger men perfectly fitted the

CHERUB instructor mold: tall, fit, in their late twenties with the physiques of heavyweight boxers. Greaves and Pike were both ex-CHERUB agents who had pursued careers in elite military units after they'd retired.

Everyone was scared of Mr. Large, but Lauren had more cause than most. Mr. Large still held a monster grudge against her for knocking him into a muddy hole with a spade.

"Silence, you pigs," Mr. Large yelled as he slammed the classroom door.

Bethany leaned over and whispered in Lauren's ear. "His mustache has got bigger. It looks like he's got a gerbil taped to his lip."

Lauren was tickled by the image of Mr. Large sticking a rodent to his face. She couldn't help giggling and a second later Mr. Large was screaming at her.

"What's so amusing, young lady?"

"Nothing, sir," Lauren said, grinding her teeth as she realized that attracting Mr. Large's attention was the absolute worst thing she could have done.

"So you're laughing at nothing? What's the matter? Have you gone mad? Get to your feet, girl. Everyone stands to attention when they're talking to me."

Lauren stood up sharply.

"I see you've earned a navy T-shirt already," Mr. Large spat. "And the black hair to suit your black little heart. I still think of you every morning, Lauren Adams, when I wake up with that pain in my back where you hit me. I should be in Norway with Mr. Speaks and Miss Smoke right now, running basic training. But my bad back means I'm stuck here, looking at your disgusting, fat, little face. You're puke, Adams. What are you?"

"Puke, sir," Lauren answered, brimming with rage as she remembered the hours of torture Mr. Large had put her through during basic training. She would have felt guilty if she'd injured anyone except him.

"Stand up front by the blackboard. You can help me with a little demonstration in a moment."

Lauren took a stroppy walk towards the blackboard while Mr. Large looked around the room. "Is everyone here?"

After a pause he answered his own question. "Where is the elder brother of Puke?"

"He got called on to a mission early this morning," Bethany explained. "But he should be back by eight o'clock."

"Perfect," Mr. Large steamed, scowling at Lauren as if she was somehow to blame for this.

Lauren propped herself against the blackboard. Gabrielle and Kerry both looked at her sympathetically and shrugged, as if to say, *What can you do?*

"So, my little cupcakes," Large said. "This exercise is designed to give you all experience of working as a team in a *highly* pressurized environment. For some of you it will be your first experience of mission training, while the older members will have their leadership and team-building skills put to the test.

"The basic rules are as follows. There are four teams of five. Each team is led by an experienced agent ranked navy T-shirt or higher. They will be accompanied by three other qualified agents ranked gray or navy. Finally, each team contains a nine-year-old red shirt who will be getting their first taste of advanced CHERUB training. Every team member will be given six eggs with their names written on the shells—that's thirty eggs per team. You must carry these eggs about your person at all times.

"After a short drive to the SAS training center down the road, the four teams will be released into the urban warfare training compound at twenty hundred hours this evening. The winners will be whichever team is in possession of the largest number of their own unbroken eggs twelve hours later. That's zero eight hundred hours tomorrow morning. To help focus your tiny minds, the team or teams finishing up with the lowest number of unbroken eggs will enjoy an extra-long cold shower, before accompanying me on a cross-country run with heavy packs immediately after the training session is over.

"The team leaders must decide on strategy. You can be passive, by hiding yourselves. Or aggressive by going out and hunting down members of other teams to destroy their eggs. You'll find useful equipment scattered around the training area. The only rules are that you must release any prisoners you capture as soon as they have surrendered their eggs. Also, you can't remove anyone's protective clothing, use physical torture, shoot your weapons at targets less than three meters away—oh, and you can't kick the boys in the balls."

The girls all groaned.

"You will be wearing tracking devices fitted with emergency buttons. That means I know where you are at all times and I can come into the compound and pluck you out if you break the rules, or if there's an accident. There are also surveillance cameras throughout the compound. A siren will go off to signal the end of the exercise, or if we need to suspend the exercise while we deal with an emergency.

"You will all be armed with the latest in combat simulation technology. It's a system of synthetic ammunition that was designed for training the United States Marines. In order to demonstrate the difference between this system and conventional paintballing, I'm going to use my unbeautiful assistant, Miss Puke."

Mr. Large handed Lauren a wooden tile thirty centimeters square and two thick.

"Hold it in front of your chest and move across to the opposite side of the room."

When Lauren was in place, Mr. Large grabbed a paintball gun off a desk and fired a shot. It hit the wood with a loud crack and Lauren felt a mist of lilac paint spatter her bare arms.

"Almost no power, short range, and limited accuracy," Large explained, throwing the gun down with contempt. "Now we'll try one of these."

He picked an assault rifle off the desk.

"This is a proper weapon. A Hungarian-made AK-M assault rifle. There hasn't been a war fought in the last fifty years where soldiers on one side or both haven't used some variant of the Kalashnikov. That's because they are compact, lightweight, and extraordinarily robust."

Mr. Large picked a banana-shaped magazine off the table, clipped it into the underside of the gun, and set it to fire single shots.

"As much as I'd enjoy using live ammunition on Puke, this AK is loaded with a training and simulation round. This ammunition has been designed to provide the most realistic combat training you can get, short of actually letting you fire live bullets at one another."

Mr. Large took aim at the square of wood. The noise was similar to that made by the paintball gun, but when the round hit and the paint exploded, Lauren stumbled backwards and the plant erupted into a mass of splinters. When she regained her composure, Lauren noticed that the bullet had torn a huge hunk from the center of the paint-splattered wood.

"Because of the power of these simulated rounds, you'll each have to wear helmets and full body armor," Mr. Large explained. "Do *not* remove them unless you absolutely have to. You will be provided with special water canisters with straws that can pass through your visors. If you need to urinate, make sure you're in a safe position and get one of your teammates to cover you. There is a serious risk of being blinded, so you must keep your helmets and visors in place at all times."

Kerry raised her hand.

"Yes, Kerrykins."

"Sir, what are the rules if we get hit? Do we have to lie dead for ten minutes or something?"

The gerbil bristled as Mr. Large grinned one of his most evil grins. "The underlying principle behind this new generation of simulated ammunition is simple: If trainees are scared of getting shot by something painful, they will act in a fashion similar to how they would act in a live combat zone. There are no fancy electronics telling you where you've been shot, or regulations saying how long you've got to lie down on the ground. The rules are very simple: If you get shot, it hurts like hell."

Escape

James and Shak broke outside on to the concrete ramp, with the PE teacher hurtling after them. The front gates of the school were less than fifty meters away, but the lock was controlled from indoors via an intercom and there was no way they'd be able to clamber over before the teacher grabbed hold of them. Their only option was the flap in the wire fence they'd arrived through, but that was on the opposite side of the school grounds.

James took a glance over his shoulder as they charged back into the main school building. The PE teacher was over two meters tall with a rugby player's build, and he was closing up rapidly. To make matters worse, the boys wore flat-soled shoes that skidded hopelessly on the polished floor.

By the time James and Shak made it to the flight of stairs leading down to the playing fields, the PE teacher was almost within touching distance. The boys gained ground by sliding down the metal banister in the middle of the staircase, but this trick nearly backfired: James picked up so much speed that he couldn't stop himself when he slid off at the bottom and he ended up crashing painfully through the doors.

It took a second for James's eyes to adjust to the afternoon sunlight. His heart sank as he looked out on to two pitches covered with Year Eleven kids. They were playing soccer, and he got a nasty feeling that they'd try and bundle him if he charged into the middle of their game with an angry teacher in hot pursuit.

While James hesitated, Shak had sprinted onwards, displaying an impressive turn of speed. James jerked violently and stumbled forwards as the PE teacher ploughed into his back and wrapped a hairy arm around his chest.

"You lot, get that other one," the teacher shouted, his mouth almost in James's ear as he pointed towards Shak.

The teacher thought he'd captured James the moment he got an arm around him. But he'd assumed he was chasing after a pupil of Trinity Day, not a CHERUB agent who'd done advanced self-defense training. James ducked down and used a simple judo throw, taking advantage of their forward momentum to roll his much heavier opponent over his back and slam him against the sunbaked grass.

There was a chance the throw had injured the teacher, but James reckoned he looked tougher than that. It had probably just made him extremely angry and James didn't want him getting up and coming after him again, so he drove a hard punch into the base of his nose.

While the PE teacher wrapped his hands over his face and yelled out in pain, James looked up and rapidly tried to assess his chances of escape. Shak had nearly made it across the pitch. He had an entire football team on his tail, but it looked like he was going to make it to the hole in the fence and out of the school. The trouble was, once Shak had revealed the location of the flap, the kids chasing him would easily be able to block it off. James realized his only way out now was over the fence, barbed wire and all.

The nearest stretch of perimeter backed on to the gardens of some houses. It was less than fifty meters away, but there were three kids closing him down. James picked the smallest one—who was still bigger than he was—and charged straight at him. The kid dropped low and spread out wide to make a tackle. James dummied, before spinning out to the right and avoiding him. He stumbled a couple of paces, before clattering into another kid who shoved him flat on to the grass. Using a technique learned in karate training, James managed to roll head over heels and spring explosively back to his feet. He now had a clear path to the fence.

Ideally, James would have had time to throw his blazer over the barbed wire topping the fence, but the heavy pack hooked around his shoulders made it impossible to get the jacket off quickly. He launched himself at the fence at full speed. The gaps in the wire mesh were too narrow to get a toehold, so he had to rely on upper body strength to haul himself up four meters. By the time he was within reach of the barbed wire, his shoulders were in agony and his fingers felt like they were set to pop out of their sockets.

James swung his leg up on to the top of a concrete fence post, narrowly missing the grasping hand of a footballer trying to get hold of his ankle. He had second thoughts about the four-meter leap awaiting him as he tried to position a hand on the barbed wire without getting spiked; but the prospect of giving up and getting on the wrong end of a group of angry sixteen-year-olds was hardly more attractive.

As he tried to perch atop the wire to make his jump, the kids down below gave up trying to grab him and adopted a new tactic: violently rocking the wire mesh in an attempt to knock him down.

As James swayed precariously back and forth, the teacher who'd been giving the football lesson was practically foaming at the mouth, still convinced that he was looking at a genuine Trinity Day pupil. "Come down this instant, boy. You *will* be expelled for this."

James gasped in pain as one of the barbs tore into his thigh. He took a quick breath before hurling himself clumsily off the fence. He'd hoped to jump clear of the shrubs edging the garden and collapse sideways on to the lawn, paratrooper style, but the violent swaying of the fence made the jump impossible to judge. He ended up landing on his side, with his feet tangled in a hydrangea bush. Only the heavily padded backpack saved him from injury.

After scrambling up, James couldn't resist an opportunity to triumphantly flick off the Trinity boys.

He kept low as he jogged across the lawn towards the house. The TV was on and there were some little kids running around inside. Fortunately there was a wooden gate at the side of the house that opened with a simple latch.

He crunched down a gravel driveway between two houses, inhaling the stench of overflowing plastic rubbish bags as he caught his breath. When James stepped out onto the pavement, he leaned against a low wall and burrowed into the mobile phone pocket on the side of his backpack, trying not to think about the growing circle of blood soaking into his trousers.

He flipped the phone open and frantically dialed his mission controller.

"Ewart," James gasped into the handset. "I'm outside number thirty-four Pollack Street. I think we might have screwed up. You've got to get me out of here fast."

"I'm on my way to get Shak," Ewart answered. "I'll meet you by the postbox at the top of the road."

James's heart thumped as a police siren wailed in the distance. "You'd better hurry up about it," he gasped, feeling a sharp pain in his injured thigh as he broke into a jog.

Ewart Asker jammed down the brake pedal of a black Mercedes. Shak threw the back door open before it came to a full halt, then scooted across to the other side of the rear seat, allowing James to dive into the car.

James looked at Shak as Ewart accelerated away from the curb. "How far did those guys chase you?"

"Only two followed me through the fence," Shak said. "I belted one over the head with a garden gnome and the other one backed off."

James smiled, rubbing streaks of sweat onto his cuff as he took his first breath of the chilled air inside the car.

"So what went wrong?" Ewart asked sharply.

James was worried how Ewart would react. Despite having the air of a laid-back guy, with his baggy cargos, tongue stud, and bleached hair, Ewart had a reputation as one of CHERUB's strictest mission controllers.

"We set off an alarm, passing through a fire door leading out to the back of the gym," James explained.

"*You* set it off," Shak said as he threw down his tie and started unbuttoning his shirt.

"Yeah," James said irritably as he wriggled out of his blazer. "But *you* looked out the window and said we should go that way."

The two boys exchanged scowls. Now the car was a couple of streets away from Trinity School, Ewart cooled down his driving to blend in with the ordinary traffic.

"Fire doors are often linked to alarms," Ewart said. "Didn't either of you remember that from your infiltration and surveillance training?"

"Actually, now that you mention it . . . ," James said, nodding sheepishly.

"I suppose it *is* mostly my fault," Shak admitted.

"We can play the blame game later," Ewart said as he took a sharp turn into a main road. "Right now I need to know *exactly* what happened and see if we've got a mess that needs cleaning up. Did you get the bugs into position?"

James nodded. "Both of them; that bit of the plan worked fine."

"Nobody saw you in Stein's car or office?"

"No," Shak said. "We only got rumbled after we came upstairs from the car park."

"And you didn't leave any equipment behind?"

Both boys shook their heads. "Nope."

"Good," Ewart said. "So the bugs are in place and there's nothing linking you to Stein."

"But they still saw us," Shak said.

"Use your loaf," Ewart replied. "They saw two boys dressed in Trinity uniform. They'll assume you're a couple of local lads playing a prank, or trying to break in and steal stuff."

"They found us around the changing area," James said. "And there's a wallet in the back pocket of these trousers I nicked."

"Bonus," Ewart nodded enthusiastically. "In that case they'll think you were thieves trying to rob the changing rooms."

"What about us wearing Trinity uniforms, though?" Shak asked.

Ewart shrugged. "Maybe you picked them up at a local jumble sale or something. . . . Actually, I think we did buy them in a charity shop in town. Besides, a couple of kids breaking into a school are hardly headline news. The cops might dust for fingerprints and show a few mug shots of the local yobbos to the people who saw you, but unless the school kicks up a huge stink, they probably won't even bother with that."

"So the mission was basically a success?" Shak asked.

James caught Ewart's wry smile in the driver's mirror. "Despite the misjudgement with the fire door, I guess you boys did OK."

James was greatly relieved that Ewart wasn't going to go psycho at them. He lifted his bum off the seat and pushed his bloody trousers down as far as his knees.

"Is there a first-aid kit around?" he asked.

Ewart nodded. "Under the front passenger seat."

"Does it hurt?" Shak asked, as James grabbed the green plastic box from between his feet.

"Course," James said as he ripped open an antiseptic wipe and cleaned away the blood, revealing a small puncture wound that was already showing signs of scabbing over.

"It's minute," Shak said, looking at the injury with contempt.

"Yeah, but it's deep," James said defensively. "I think it almost went through to the bone."

"Oh *give* over," Shak giggled. "I've seen paper cuts worse than that."

"Yeah, well," James moaned. "With an injury like this, I still don't think I'll be up to going out on training tonight. Ewart, can you write me an excuse note?"

Ewart shook his head. "James, you know the rules. If you think your injury is serious, go and see the nurse in campus and she'll write one for you."

"Come on, Ewart," James beggede. "I bailed you out this morning when you found out Callum was glued to the toilet."

"Give over," Ewart grinned. "You practically begged me to let you come. Didn't this job already get you out of some physics test? As far as I'm concerned, you're scheduled for a training exercise tonight, and unless you have a legitimate excuse, you're going to do it."

James kicked the back of the passenger seat. "Bloody hell," he muttered, making sure it wasn't loud enough for Ewart to hear.

Eggs

James got back to campus shortly before seven o'clock, giving him an hour to clean up, change into uniform, and down some food. He was already knackered from the mission, and while he knew the adrenaline rush would keep him alert through the overnight training exercise, the loss of a night's sleep would leave his body out of sync over the upcoming weekend.

Kerry was taking her tray across to scrape when James arrived in the canteen. She'd eaten with Gabrielle and the rest of her team, and they'd clearly been discussing their strategy for the exercise. She gave James a peck on the cheek as she passed by.

"Good luck tonight, sweetie," she said, grinning sarcastically. "It'd be so sad if your team ended up finishing with no eggs and getting that punishment run."

"What punishment run?" James asked.

"Ten kilometers with heavy packs. Sounds like fun, eh?"

"Really?" James asked. "Oh man, I don't know any of this stuff. I tried to get hold of Lauren, but she's not in her room and her mobile's off."

"You mean to say . . ." Kerry giggled, shaking her head. "James, have you even met up with all the members of your team yet?"

Kerry looked back at Gabrielle and the three other kids on her team, who were lined up behind her, holding their dinner trays. They exchanged knowing glances and shook their heads.

"I wouldn't get too cocky," James said, trying to sound like he wasn't ruffled. "Ewart told me some stuff about the egg battle on the drive back and he gave me a few pointers."

As Kerry's team filed away, James realized he had to find Lauren fast. If they arrived at the combat training area without having studied the maps and made a plan, they'd get wiped out. He grabbed a burger and fries, sat at the nearest table, and started wolfing them down.

"Yo, bro."

James was relieved to look over his shoulder and find Lauren, Bethany, and Jake heading towards him; but the training exercise went clean out of his mind.

"Oh my *God*. What have you done to your head?"

Lauren grinned. "Like it?"

"It's um . . . black. I bet Mum's spinning in her grave."

Lauren was wounded by James's remark. "Do you really think she'd be upset?"

James sensed he'd hit a nerve and changed tack. "Nah, don't sweat it. Mum would probably be surprised you waited as long as you did. You must have asked her fifty billion times. Just don't get that nose ring you were after as well."

Lauren shook her head. "We're not allowed to pierce anything except our ears before we're sixteen— so does it look OK, or what?"

"It's not terrible," James shrugged. "But most boys *prefer* blondes, you know."

Lauren looked at Bethany. "That's the best reason I've heard yet for dying it black."

James grinned. "I can't wait until you get your first boyfriend. I'm gonna have so much fun teasing you."

"Don't hold your breath," Lauren sneered.

"So what's happened to Dana?" James asked.

Bethany shrugged. "Cheesy went back to her room."

"Why do they call her Cheesy?" Jake asked.

"'Cos she doesn't wash," Bethany grinned.

James smiled. "She's not a girly girl and she's a loner, so some of the others take the mickey. I know she wears a scruffy uniform and that, but I've sparred with her in the dojo and she smells as fresh as anyone else."

"James fancies her," Bethany giggled.

Bethany severely got on James's nerves at times and this was one of them. He shot her a furious look. "God, Bethany, I really wish you'd grow up."

"Did you beat her?" Jake asked.

Lauren laughed. "James couldn't beat Dana. He got nailed by Bethany and she's ten."

Jake nodded. "Yeah, James. You're strong, but you're really slow."

"Bethany didn't pin me, I slipped," James huffed. He was anxious to steer the conversation away from humiliating reminders of losing a fight to a ten-year-old girl. "Anyhow, we've got less than fifteen minutes to plan our strategy."

Bethany unrolled a map of the combat training area. Lauren and Jake held down the corners to stop it curling up. James swallowed his last couple of chips and rubbed his salty fingertips on his trousers as he tried to sound like leadership material.

"OK, here's what we'll do . . . ," James said, walking his fingers across the map. "Um . . . there's the drop point, so as soon as the mission starts we'll head for this high ground here. We can station scouts here and here and pick off anyone who tried to come near us."

"Good plan," Lauren said. "Just one *teensy* problem."

"What?"

"That particular piece of high ground is in the middle of a lake."

"Is it?" James gasped.

Lauren nodded slowly. "As a rule, the blue bits on a map indicate water."

"Good point," James grinned weakly. "You passed my test."

Jake thumped his palm against his forehead. "Why do I *always* get put on the rubbish team?"

The cherubs all gathered on the stretch of road outside the main building to find that twenty sets of appropriately sized kit had been laid out behind an army truck: body armor, weapons, and a backpack for each trainee. The sun was starting to drop, but it was still warm.

"The truck leaves in eight minutes," Mr. Large shouted. "Let's move it, muffins."

James sat on the tarmac and pulled off his boots before stepping into a chunky, Kevlar-lined overall. By the time he'd pulled on the heavy gloves, strapped on the helmet, and pushed down the visor, he was boiling hot.

Jake was struggling to load his gun with his gloved hands, so James walked over to help him out.

"Five minutes," Large shouted. "Fifty punishment laps for any kid who holds up the truck."

James clipped the ammunition onto his gun, then looked at Jake. "Are you OK? You look like a ghost."

Jake grinned uneasily. "How bad do you think it hurts when those bullets hit you?"

"Pretty bad, but don't worry; there's four of us looking out for you."

James held the loaded weapon out for Jake, but Jake backed away and scowled at the ground. "I don't wanna go," he said anxiously, tugging at the chinstrap of his helmet to unbuckle it. "I changed my mind."

James groaned with frustration. Until Jake turned ten and committed himself to becoming a CHERUB agent, he didn't have to go on any training exercises if he didn't want to; but James knew he'd catch hell from Mr. Large if a member of his team dropped out minutes before the exercise was due to start.

James desperately tried to think up a way to talk Jake around. "You're lucky, you know, coming to CHERUB before you're ten. I only got three weeks before they put me into basic training. I was unfit and I could barely even swim."

"I'm sorry, James," Jake sniffled. "I'm tired. I wanna go to bed."

"Don't back out now. You're a tough little guy."

"What's the holdup?" Dana asked. "We need to get on that truck."

James shrugged hopelessly. "Jake doesn't want to go."

"Doesn't he?" Dana grinned. She flipped up her visor and pressed her beefy hands down on Jake's shoulders. "What's your dysfunction, brat? Are you chicken?"

"No," Jake said defiantly.

"Do you know how bad your mates are gonna flame you when they find out that you bottled it?"

Jake couldn't think of an answer.

"Do you really want to go back to the junior block?" Dana asked. "They'll laugh their socks off when you walk around that corner into the rec room."

"I just . . . ," Jake said meekly.

"Don't give me *I just,* brat," Dana said. "Take your gun from James and put your helmet back on. You're gonna go out there and show everyone what you're made of. I'll cover your back, OK?"

Jake was a little scared of Dana, but the idea of this imposing girl looking out for him was reassuring. He nodded obediently at her before taking his gun from James.

"OK, soldier." Dana grinned, giving Jake a friendly pat on the back. "Grab your pack and go climb into the truck."

James smiled at Dana as Jake headed towards the truck. "Thanks."

Dana returned a look of contempt as she pushed her visor back down over her face. "You should study the tricks the instructors use to motivate us," she said harshly. "What little boy wants to get teased by his mates?"

James nodded. "Look, Dana. I know it's awkward me being in charge when you're older and more experienced than me."

"It's not awkward, James, it's idiotic. So spare me your stupid pep talk and let's get this over with."

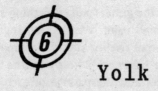

Yolk

The urban warfare compound was a rectangle one kilometer by one and a half. It was designed for soldiers training in attacking or defending built-up areas. Teams A–C had already been dropped at their starting points. Mr. Large pulled the canvas-covered truck up sharply and Mr. Pike—who'd ridden in the back alongside the kids—slid a bolt, allowing the rear flap of the truck to slam down.

"Team D," Pike shouted. "What are you waiting for?"

Pike handed each kid a box containing six unbroken eggs before they jumped down. James was out first, followed by Jake, Lauren, Bethany, and Dana.

James glanced around as the truck pulled away and Bethany unfurled the map. The artificial town had a surreal air. Rusted cars lined the streets, with all their windows removed to avoid any danger from flying glass. The buildings were finished in bare concrete and were designed to simulate different kinds of environments: shops, homes, offices, and warehouses. Some were as much as four stories tall.

The legacy of thousands of mock battles lay everywhere: black scorch marks on the walls, metal shell casings in the gutters and everything spattered in brightly colored paint. With no moving vehicles and a population of twenty kids, the compound was eerily quiet. All James could hear were the footsteps of his teammates and the passage of each nervous breath around the inside of his helmet.

"Any bright ideas?" James asked.

Lauren pointed at a building a few hundred meters into the distance. "I like that one," she said. "It backs onto the corner of the compound, meaning we only have to defend it from two sides. It's also nice and high, so we can station a lookout on the roof."

Dana tutted. "Yeah, microbrain, but it's also blindingly obvious."

Lauren reared up. "Who are you calling microbrain, Cheesy?"

"You try calling me Cheesy again," Dana screamed, facing Lauren off, "and I'll rip your head off and spit down your neck."

James placed himself between the two girls. "Calm down and stop yelling. We're supposed to be killing everyone else, not each other."

"Suppose someone comes after us," Dana spat. "They know we were dropped in this area and that's the first place they'll come looking."

"Well that's where I think we should go," Lauren said, sounding narked.

"OK, OK," James said, feeling the pressure of being in charge. "What if we station a sniper on the roof of Lauren's building, then we'll barricade the door so that it looks like we're all in there? But really, all except one of us are in the low building opposite."

"That might just work," Dana nodded. "If anyone comes by and tries to storm the building with the sniper inside, you lot can steam out from behind and ambush them."

James looked at Dana. "Do you want to go up the stairs and be the sniper? Are you a good shot?"

"Better than any of you, I expect," Dana said. "Though it'll be pitch dark soon and we haven't got night scopes."

"If you hear anyone, start shooting so that they think we're in there."

"What if it's one of you guys?" Dana asked.

James looked blank.

"We need a signal," Bethany said. "Meow like a cat or something, then you'll know it's one of us."

James nodded. "But if you hear a meow, return with a bark, like a dog. That way we know it's not someone ripping off our noise. And remember, once it gets dark, sound is the best way of tracking us. Only call out if you absolutely must."

"OK," said Dana as she set off towards the high building. "You'd better not make a mess of this. I'll see you losers later."

Lauren waited until Dana was out of earshot before responding, "Not if I see you first, Cheesy. . . . And thanks for taking *her* side, James."

James tutted. "It's not a question of taking sides, Lauren. Face facts, Dana was right."

"This is all very well *if* your plan to lure the opposition towards the big building works," Lauren sniped. "But what if they see through it?"

"Will you shut up and let me think?" James said.

"We need to get under cover. Kerry's team was only dropped a few hundred meters from here. They could be on our backs any second."

James led Lauren, Bethany, and Jake towards a single-level structure with a canopy, designed to resemble a fast-food stand. He opened the aluminum door and stepped inside, surprised by how cramped the space was.

"Bethany and Lauren, keep the chatter down and watch out of the window. Me and Jake will cover the rear."

"There's a duffel bag behind this table," Bethany said excitedly as she crouched down near the back window.

James turned towards her. "Large said we'd find extra equipment scattered around the training area."

The team gathered in a semicircle. Bethany undid the buckle and opened the bag, revealing five pairs of night-vision goggles. The sets were specifically designed to clip on to their helmets.

"Sweet," James grinned. "These will give us a massive advantage once it starts getting dark."

"Hang on though," Lauren said. "This is the first building we've been in and we've already found some valuable equipment. For all we know, there's something useful in every building."

Bethany finished her thought. "And if we hole up here while the other teams grab a load of fancy equipment, we could end up being totally outgunned."

James, Lauren, and Bethany looked at each other. "Lauren," James said, "you stay here with Jake. Be ready to start shooting if someone attacks Dana's building. Me and Bethany can head out onto the street. We're gonna check all the other buildings and see what we can find."

"What am I, an octopus?" Lauren gasped. "I can't do all that on my own."

"You'll have to try your best," James said stiffly. "You've got Jake with you."

"Great, a red shirt," Lauren sneered. "What's he gonna do?"

"I don't wanna stay with *her*," Jake said. "Can I go outside with you, James?"

"James," Lauren said. "This isn't a strategy, this is a disaster. One minute we're all holing up here waiting for an ambush. Now you want us all to split up. If someone comes after us we'll get picked off one at a time."

"Well, what do you want me to do, sis?" James whispered angrily. "I'm the team leader. Being my sister doesn't give you the right to start an argument over every single decision I make. Now, I know this isn't ideal, but we can't let the other teams get hold of all the equipment."

"How about I stay here with Bethany and you go out hunting with Jake?"

"Fine, whatever," James said angrily. "I'll go out with Jake. You stay here and play dolls' houses with your little friend."

It was hard to read Lauren's expression through the visor over her face, but James was fairly sure she was glowering at him. He spun on his heel and crashed out of the aluminum door. Before realizing how stupid it was to make so much noise, James felt a loud crack against the side of his helmet. As he stumbled sideways, a second shot tore painfully into his ribs. The paint dribbling down his side was yellow, indicating that he'd been shot by a member of Kyle's team.

James had been hit hundreds of times by paintballs. It wasn't nice, but the stinging went away ten minutes later. The simulated ammunition was in a different league. James could hardly draw breath as he collapsed against the side of the building. Luckily, the third shot skimmed past his shoulder and clanged into the metal door behind him.

As James gasped, he spotted the eleven-year-old twin girls from Kyle's team ducking down behind a car. James reached for his gun, but the pain in his chest made him clumsy.

"Don't think so," the girls chanted as they came out of cover with their weapons aimed at James. "Drop your gun, and throw us the pack with your eggs in."

James didn't want to surrender his eggs, but the girls were standing at the regulation three-meter minimum shooting distance, and he'd already found out how painful the simulated rounds could be from much farther out.

As James unhooked his pack, a red shot smashed into the thigh of one girl, sweeping her right leg from under her. James realized it had to be Dana, firing from up high. A second later, Bethany booted open the door behind him and shot at the other one. The round missed, but the girl ducked and James used the instant while she was distracted to roll forwards and aim his gun. He took great satisfaction in blasting the girl who'd shot him moments earlier. She fell over backwards, and James pumped her twice in the back from minimum range.

The twist of fortune had taken seconds. Now the twin girls were writhing on the ground with James, Dana, and Bethany pointing guns at them.

"Let's have those guns over here," James said. "No sudden moves."

It took a while, because both girls were hurt. As soon as they'd pushed the guns out of reach, James ran in and grabbed them. He unclipped the magazines before flipping back the operating handles and pocketing the driving springs. Without this small component, the rifles were useless.

"Give us your backpacks," James ordered, menacing the girls with his rifle.

The searing pain in his chest and the fear of getting shot again had left James running on his most basic survival instincts. He didn't give a damn about the feelings of the two girls squirming at his feet.

"You can't shoot us from this close," one girl said desperately as he closed back in to grab their backpacks.

"Sue me," James snarled, jabbing the girl with his gun as he ripped the pack off her shoulder. "Why don't you write a letter to the United Nations?"

James threw one pack backwards towards Bethany and unzipped the other one himself. He threw down the polystyrene egg box and smashed it under the heel of his boot. Bethany did the same. It was a good feeling, destroying one third of team A's eggs less than twenty minutes into the twelve-hour exercise.

"What can we do with them?" Bethany asked as she contemptuously wiped her eggy boot on to her victim's suit. "They know our position and we're not allowed to take hostages; we'll have to move out of here."

As Bethany spoke, James noticed a lump of plastic rolling from beneath one of the cars at the curbside. He instantly knew it was a stun grenade, but didn't get a chance to take cover before its powder-blue flash erupted. He stumbled backwards, half blind, as the bitter taste of smoke hit the back of his mouth.

He recognized Kyle's voice. "How'd you like that little toy, Adams?"

Another stun grenade erupted. This one had been lobbed through the back window of the food stand. Lauren screamed as she stumbled blindly out of the aluminum door with Jake close behind her.

Kyle howled in pain as Dana shot him from up high. She'd picked out a perfect shot through the smoke, hitting Kyle in the scantly protected area where the helmet met the padded overall. James only got a second to gloat before he felt an excruciating pain in his lower back. He caught sight of the blue paint spattered on his sleeves and looked over his shoulder to find all five members of Kerry's team closing on his position in a V formation.

James had already taken three painful shots and he couldn't face getting hit more as Kerry and

Kyle's teams closed from opposing directions. He lost all thoughts of leadership as he scrambled to his feet, cut down a side street, and ran away as fast as he could.

He ran a few hundred meters through the streets, almost to the opposite side of the training compound. He found a house and fired a couple of rounds inside. When nobody fired back, he jumped through the glassless window and dropped to the concrete floor.

There were blue flashes from stun grenades and the constant rat-tat of simulated ammunition as the three-way battle raged on in the distance. The sky was turning amber, meaning it would be dark inside half an hour.

James had taken three hits. The first shot had ricocheted harmlessly off his helmet, there was a dull ache in his stomach from the second, but the shot to his lower back was the killer. An agonizing spasm fired down his leg as he slumped onto the floor. He felt relieved at getting away from the action as he caught his breath, but he quickly realized that as the senior agent, he had to go back and try to reunite his team before darkness fell.

Before standing back up, he broke the rules by turning towards the wall, flipping up his visor, and wiping away the sweat streaking down his face.

When James looked up, he noticed a gray box in the corner. He scuttled across and was delighted to find a dozen ammo clips. Everyone had started with two twenty-eight-round clips for their rifle. James had nearly used a full clip already, and he realized that as the night went on, ammo was going to become a valuable commodity.

James locked a full clip on to his rifle and stacked the remainder into his pack, even though each clip weighed more than a kilogram.

He walked cautiously back towards the window and listened. The battle had splintered into numerous smaller actions, characterized by short bursts of gunfire spread over a wider area. James realized that this greatly increased his chances of coming under fire on his return journey.

He kept low as he exited the building into a narrow alleyway, ducking below the roofline of the parked cars, with a paint-spattered breezeblock wall at his back. He ended up in a main road, keeping a finger on the trigger and breaking into a sprint as he cut across the road.

"Meow."

James stopped in his tracks and crouched down beside a car, unable to work out where the sound had come from.

"Woof," he answered cautiously.

Two heads popped up inside a car parked on a driveway. Because of the orange sunlight reflecting on the visors, it took a second before James recognized Dana and Jake.

"Get over here, dingus," Dana whispered. "There's a bunch of Team A kids hiding out three doors up the road."

James quietly opened the car door. He dragged himself across the multicolored stains over the rear seat, being careful to keep his head below the window height. He noticed Dana was covered in about twenty splats of different colored paint.

"You got nuked," James gasped. "Do any of them hurt?"

"Not too bad, most of the hits were from long range," Dana said bitterly. "I'm gonna have so many bruises, I'll look horrible in the morning. All my eggs got smashed, too."

"Who got hold of you?" James asked.

"Nobody actually got me, they just got mashed up when I was rolling around on the floor being shot at."

"All but one of my eggs are cracked as well," James nodded. "So how come you ended up all the way out here?"

"I tried to fallow after you when you shat your pants and ran away," Dana explained. "Jumped down from a first-floor window and picked up Jake along the way."

"I didn't shit my pants," James said indignantly. "I made a tactical decision to withdraw under heavy fire."

Dana laughed. "That's one way of putting it, I guess."

James decided not to push the point; Dana's description of events was uncomfortably close to the truth.

He looked at Jake and tried to sound encouraging. "So how are you holding up?"

"OK," Jake said brightly. "I shot some people in the battle."

"I think the little guy just found some balls," Dana said, breaking into a rare smile. "I watched him come out of that building you guys were hiding out in. First he kind of froze, but then he took cover and put in some good shots."

James looked admiringly at his little teammate. "Did you get hit?"

Jake rolled over on to his side and proudly showed off the giant splat of lilac paint on his thigh. "It hurts, but I don't care. This must be *fifty* times more exciting than the best computer game ever."

James was delighted by the way Jake had handled stress. Some people freak out in volatile situations, but it looked like CHERUB's selection process had done its usual job of picking out a kid who could handle himself when it really counted.

"Do you still want to quit?" James asked.

"No way," Jake said. "I want to get hold of someone and smash up their eggs."

James laughed. "So, did either of you see the other girls?"

"I think I saw Lauren and Bethany heading off together," Jake said.

"Do you reckon we should go and look for them?" James asked.

Dana pondered for a couple of seconds. "It's too risky. There are fifteen other kids out there, and only two of them are our girls. Lauren and Bethany can look after themselves. If we bump into them that's great, but if we go out searching, we'll most likely get shot up."

"I think you're right," James nodded.

"So what *do* we do?" Jake asked.

James thought for a few seconds. "I've got plenty

of ammo in my pack and three sets of night-vision goggles. This car isn't secure—we're sitting ducks if anyone walks by and spots us. I say we hide out in one of the houses nearby until it gets completely dark. Then I'll hand out the night-vision goggles and we can go out on a little egg hunt."

Dana nodded grudgingly. "I can think of worse ideas."

Reckoning

By midnight it was pitch black. There was no moon, and the only light was a yellow glow from a motorway that ran behind the ten-meter-high walls on one side of the training compound.

Dana, James, and Jake had night-vision goggles fitted on to special clasps built into their helmets. The goggles didn't work in complete darkness; instead they amplified light, turning the world into a strange mixture of blackness, punctuated by intense green outlines. The imaging software inside the goggles took a fraction of a second to process what it saw. This tiny lag between making movements and your eyes registering them made James queasy.

When they clambered from their hideout, they were hoping to ambush the building where Dana and Jake had spotted Team A forty minutes earlier, but they'd moved on. Their only legacy was an empty equipment box and a stinking puddle where a couple of boys had peed in the corner.

"What now?" Jake whispered as a stun grenade erupted somewhere in the distance, turning the view through his goggles into a white sheet.

James was disappointed, but he still had faith in his

night-vision strategy. "We keep hunting," he said.

They began a cautious trek through the compound: moving slowly, keeping low, and speaking only when absolutely necessary. If they got caught in a wide-open space, they could easily get picked off, so they stuck to side streets and alleyways, only venturing into the main avenues when they had to cross them.

James noticed a green outline inside a building as he passed a window, but he didn't say a word until they reached the end of the street and ducked down between two houses.

"Two buildings back," James whispered. "There's at least one person moving inside."

Dana was her usual contemptuous self. "Are you sure it's not a stray cat or something?"

James shook his head. "Too big, definitely human. I'll take it from the front. Dana, you climb over the garden wall and cut round the back. Wait until you hear me make my move and be ready to cut them off if they try to escape. Jake, you wait here. Set your rifle to automatic and be ready to cover us if things get heavy."

"Yes, *sir*," Jake said.

Dana shushed him. "Less noise, you little idiot."

James turned slowly on his heel and crept back to the building where he'd spotted the movement. He leaned in front of the window and cautiously poked his head up above the ledge, moving very slowly because he didn't want the ammunition clips inside his pack to jangle.

His night-vision goggles showed the outlines of

two bodies sitting against a wall. They were a little smaller than James and, although it was hard to tell from his artificially intensified view, he got the impression that they were both female.

Realizing there was a chance it could be Lauren and Bethany, James ducked down and made the signal.

"Meow."

He knew he'd blunted the element of surprise, but James didn't want to end up in a shooting match with his own teammates. The two figures inside scrambled for their weapons as one of them replied hurriedly, "Meow."

As soon as James heard the wrong signal, he jumped up above the window ledge and fired a shot. One girl screamed out, and James ducked again as the other fired blindly into the darkness. When this firing stopped, James popped up and fired two more accurate shots through the window, hitting the other girl both times.

Meanwhile, Dana had entered via the back door of the building. She ran along a short corridor and burst into the room. James would have liked more time to use the advantage of his night vision to psych the girls out, but he had to make his move once Dana was in the room.

"I want your eggs and the driving springs from your rifles," James announced as he jumped through the window.

"Up yours, James," Kerry answered.

James and Dana ducked out of the way as wild shots flew around the room. Then Kerry's gun made a hollow click.

"Oh *dear*," James gloated. "That doesn't sound good."

"I've got more," Kerry said.

"So why are you sitting still, instead of reloading?" James asked.

"Can you see us?" Kerry asked.

"Every move you make," James laughed. "We've got night vision."

Gabrielle sounded furious. "Jammy little . . ."

"Oh, hi Gabrielle," James said. "I didn't realize it was you. I hope that hit's not stinging too badly."

"I bet it's not as bad as when I shot you in the back earlier on," Gabrielle snarled.

"James," Dana said fiercely from the opposite side of the room. "We just made a giant racket. Cut the cute banter and let's get out of here."

Kerry laughed. "Oh, it's Dana. I thought there had to be someone with brains behind this operation."

"Yeah, James," Gabrielle agreed. "I saw how you looked out for your team by running off at ninety miles an hour."

James was irked. "I've got my gun pointing right at you," he said angrily. "Shut your stupid holes, throw us your packs, and hand over your guns."

"Why don't you come over and get them?" Kerry jeered.

James fired a warning shot into the wall a few centimeters above Kerry's head. "Because this clip is stuffed with ammunition. I can see every move you make and I can shoot you at will. Now, I'm gonna count to three, and if your guns and packs haven't landed somewhere near my feet when I finish, you two are gonna feel serious pain. One, two . . ."

Kerry and Gabrielle's pride didn't extend far enough to run the risk of another hit. They surrendered their stuff before James finished counting. He crouched down and grabbed the egg box out of Kerry's pack. It was hard to see in the darkness and tricky to feel through the protective gloves, but so far as James could tell, Kerry's eggs were all intact.

"Six unbroken eggs, for Little Miss Perfect," James giggled as he ground up the eggs under his boot.

"This isn't over," Kerry shouted back defiantly. "You have to let us go and I'm gonna hunt you down."

"I reckon this makes us even," James answered. "Remember last summer at the hostel, when you two blasted me and Bruce with the paintball guns from point-blank range?"

A small voice piped up from outside before Kerry got a chance to respond. "There's four people heading our way from the top of the street," Jake said. "Let's get out of here before World War Three breaks out."

"I've crushed Gabrielle's eggs," Dana said. "Let's roll."

James realized he didn't have time to take the driving spring out of Kerry's gun in pitch darkness and it was too awkward to take it with him, so he swung it by the barrel and smashed it as hard as he could against the wall. As he spun back, Kerry lunged at him. Dana fired a shot, but she'd aimed cautiously to avoid hitting James and ended up missing both of them.

Kerry crashed into James. She was smaller and

lighter than her boyfriend, but her martial arts skills were far in advance and five years of CHERUB training had made her stronger than a thirteen-year-old girl had any right to be. As James smashed into the ground with Kerry on top of him, a stun grenade exploded inside a building a few doors up the road.

Before Kerry pinned James, he found a second to shout at Dana: "Take Jake and get out of here."

James's logic was simple: Eggs were what counted in the final tally. He only had one, while Jake still had six unbroken ones. Rather than get caught up in the melee that seemed set to break out, it was better to run off, even if that left James to tangle with the girls on his own.

As Kerry pinned James's shoulders under her knees and Gabrielle ripped away his gun, Dana escaped out of the front window and ran off with Jake. Kerry thumped James's helmet against the concrete floor, demolishing the night-vision goggles. Shots were being fired in the street outside as the broken goggles over James's visor plunged him into absolute darkness.

"Thought you were pretty clever, didn't you?" Kerry said sweetly. "Remember combat class, James? How many times did I tell you? Never turn away from your target and never let your guard down for a single second."

Gabrielle crunched James's single remaining egg as Kerry pulled his arm tight behind his back.

"Want a broken shoulder, James?"

"Kerry," James gasped. "Please. You got my eggs, you've got to let me go now."

"Why don't you write a letter to the United Nations?" Kerry grinned as she released his arm and smashed the point of her elbow into his lower back.

As James whimpered in pain, Gabrielle sounded happy. "He's got tons of ammo in this backpack."

"Great," Kerry said as she grabbed Gabrielle's gun off the floor and loaded a clip. "Let's head out the back way and try catching up with those other two."

James lay facedown on the bare concrete. Kerry had elbowed him in the same spot where he'd been shot and the pain in his lower back was terrible. As Gabrielle exited, she made James suffer the ultimate indignity: shooting him twice in the thigh with his own gun.

James woke from a weird dream with a string of drool dribbling down the inside of his visor and the taste of smoke in his mouth. The sun was up, though at first he could only see cracks breaking around the edges of the broken night-vision goggles still fitted to his helmet.

He got a sharp reminder of Kerry's elbow in the back the instant he tried to move. He rolled cautiously onto his side and tried to pry the goggles off; but the plastic clip holding them in place had cracked when Kerry knocked them against the floor and now they refused to separate from the helmet. James twisted the goggles, but eventually he had to resort to brute force, showering the room in plastic fragments as they snapped away from the helmet.

Once his eyes adjusted to the daylight, James raised the cuff of his padded suit and looked at his watch. It was quarter to six, meaning he'd been unconscious for about four hours and the exercise still had more than two hours to run. James couldn't remember clearly, but he realized the mixture of pain and exhaustion must have made him pass out; nobody voluntarily nods off in the middle of training when they're tanked up on adrenaline and their heart is banging out a hundred and eighty beats a minute.

With no clue about the safety of his immediate environment, James crawled over the concrete floor towards the nearest wall and sat against it, pausing briefly to study the multitude of colored splats where he'd been shot.

He felt slightly light-headed and desperately thirsty; but his canteen had been in the backpack with the ammo that Kerry had taken. He peered cautiously out of the window, studying the residue of the previous night's battle. It was easy to tell the difference between fresh paint splats and older marks that had been smoothed out by rain.

James thought about searching for the other members of his team, but he'd run the risk of getting shot, and without a gun or ammunition he didn't think he'd be much use anyway.

He decided the best strategy was to stay where he was, counting out the minutes until the exercise ended and hoping that no one would stumble into him. He glanced at his watch again as his mind fixed on the cold drink he hoped to get hold of in a hundred and thirty-two minutes.

Deliverance

The last hours of the exercise contained nothing like the full-blown battles of the evening before. James suspected that most teams had run low on equipment. Ammunition, working rifles, and eggs were in short supply; most important, so was the energy required to fight. Only the sounds of occasional light skirmishes disrupted the morning birdsong.

To pass the time, James messed with Kerry's rifle. Although he'd smashed it against the wall and knocked a lump out of the wooden stock, it only took a light clean and a few adjustments with the attached multi-tool to get the firing mechanism running. The trouble was, he still didn't have any ammunition.

He stretched and massaged the tender area of his back and took a pee in the hallway outside, but after an hour boredom got the better of him and he decided to explore. He started off checking out the rest of the house. He found a couple of discarded ammo clips. Occasionally, people will drop a clip with a few shots left and replace it with a full one if they're heading into action, but all he found were empties.

The back of the building had a small garden, and James crept outdoors with the intention of jumping over the waist-height wall into the next one. But as he raised his leg, he came over light-headed and for a moment thought he was going to be sick. He lay out on the grass and raised his visor a couple of centimeters to breath some fresh air.

James was slightly worried. By CHERUB standards this wasn't a particularly tough training exercise, but he felt weak.

A half hour before eight a.m., he recognized Lauren and Bethany cutting along the alleyway behind the garden wall. They were the first figures he'd seen in more than an hour, so he decided it was safe to expose his position with a "Meow."

"Woof," Lauren replied.

James was happy to see them, despite the humiliation of having no eggs or ammo while the girls' confident air suggested that they were doing OK. As they clambered over the wall, James made a rough count of the splats on their uniforms and realized they'd each taken six or seven hits, about the same as him.

"What's up with you?" Lauren asked. "You're all stooped."

"I was tired before we even started. Then I got a killer shot in the back and Kerry thumped me in the same spot with her elbow. It's agony."

Bethany laughed. "Lovers' tiff."

James ignored the jab. "I lost my canteen," he said. "Have either of you got any water left?"

Lauren nodded as she pulled her pack off her shoulder and handed James a metal canteen with a long plastic straw on top. "We found a standpipe inside one of the houses and topped our bottles up."

James grabbed the canteen, fed the straw up through the base of his helmet, and began to gulp.

"Don't drink it all, greedy guts," Lauren gasped, snatching her canteen back.

"So, have you got any eggs left?" James asked.

Lauren nodded. "I've got two, Bethany's got four. You?"

James shook his head. "Have you seen Dana and Jake?"

"We met up with them at about four a.m.," Lauren said. "They reckoned Kerry and Gabrielle were after them."

"Were they getting on OK?" James asked.

"Dana seemed her usual surly self," Bethany said, shaking her head. "But I actually got the impression that my psychotic little brother had started to enjoy himself."

James nodded. "It might be fun if it was paintball or laser tag; but this simulated ammunition is too damned painful."

"I guess that's the point of the exercise," Lauren said. "We're supposed to be learning how to act when we're tired and under lots of stress, not having some jolly shoot-up."

James nodded. "I just hope we don't get that ten-kilometer run for finishing last. Mind you, I'm wringing under this suit, so I could probably live with the cold shower."

As soon as the siren went off, James, Lauren, and Bethany ripped off their visors and took in giant gasps of fresh air. As they headed towards the square in the middle of the compound where they'd been instructed to meet at the end of the exercise, the three of them unzipped their overalls and pulled their hands through their sleeves, leaving the thickly padded arms dangling down behind their legs.

James was feeling slightly better and forty minutes' chatting with the girls had helped refocus his mind away from his aches and pains, but they'd run out of drinking water.

Bethany scratched beneath the sweaty gray CHERUB T-shirt stuck to her belly as she walked. "God, I'm thirsty," she gasped.

"Tell me about it," James said as he pulled his T-shirt over his head.

"You should be all right," Lauren huffed. "You drank most of mine."

The morning sun felt nice on James's bare back as the T-shirt weighed heavily in his hands like a wet flannel.

"You know what?" he said exuberantly. "I'm so thirsty, I could drink my own sweat."

He held the T-shirt in the air over his head, poked out his tongue, and gave it a squeeze. Bethany recoiled in horror as salty drips rained down on James's face and tongue.

Lauren screamed out and gave her brother a shove. "James, stop that *now*. That's the grossest thing ever."

"Don't you want a drop then?" James giggled as he flung the soggy shirt at his sister.

Lauren dodged and the shirt splatted harmlessly

against the pavement, but she still closed up and gave her brother a brutal kick on the ankle.

"You're disgusting," she raged. "We could go on a field trip to a sewer and you'd still lower the tone."

James laughed as he picked up his T-shirt.

"That bruise on our back is *so* bad, James," Bethany said.

James tried to get a look over his shoulder, but it was impossible without a mirror. "I expect we've all got a few of them," he said.

They rounded a corner into the square and were delighted to see seven kids from various teams standing in front of a foldout table covered in bottles of mineral water. James shoved his way between a couple of smaller kids and grabbed two bottles. He drank half of the first one and was pouring the remainder over his head when he spotted Kerry. She'd stripped off her boots, socks, and overalls. Her long black hair was soaking and she had drips trickling down her face.

They looked awkwardly at one another, unsure how to react after what had passed between them during the night.

Kerry smiled a little. "No hard feelings?"

James smiled back and gave her a quick kiss. "Nah, course not."

"Have you heard about Kyle?" Kerry asked.

"No, what?"

"Took a hit in the neck. They had to take him to the hospital."

"These simulated rounds are bad-ass," James said, shaking his head. "Look at my back."

"Matches mine," Kerry said, lifting up her vest to reveal a giant red welt next to her belly button.

"You've got a couple of bad ones down your legs, as well," James noted.

"So," Lauren interrupted, looking at Kerry, "how many eggs has your team got left?"

Kerry's tone turned serious. She was always competitive and there was the unpleasant prospect of a ten-kilometer punishment run hanging over their heads.

"All my team are back," she said dejectedly. "We've only got five eggs between us."

Lauren snapped her head towards James and grinned. "I've got two, Bethany's got four, and Dana and Jake aren't even back yet."

Kerry allowed herself to smile. "I wouldn't hold out much hope on that score; me and Gabrielle caught up with them."

James couldn't help smiling. "Who cares?" he grinned. "We've still got more eggs than you, Kerry. You'd better hope either Kyle's team or Team B have less than five eggs."

"Some of Kyle's team are over there," Lauren pointed. "Kyle's out, but they've got at least eight eggs."

Kerry looked seriously troubled. "I can run ten kilometers easy, but how am I gonna get my little red-shirt through it?"

"I'm sorry," James said solemnly.

Kerry didn't seem to believe him. "I *bet* you are," she tutted as she swiveled on her bare feet and headed anxiously towards Gabrielle for an emergency conference.

"You can't blame me," James shouted after her, though he knew she would because he'd broken her eggs.

Lauren looked up at James. "I wouldn't worry, you know how moody she gets."

"Yeah," James nodded, breaking into a relieved grin that he made sure Kerry couldn't see. "I probably won't be getting my tongue in her mouth for a few days, but at least we've avoided the ten-K run."

Lauren backed away with a look of disgust. "*Eww,* what an image: your horrible gobby tongue."

A few more kids had arrived at the water table, including Dana and Jake, but it was the arrival of Team B that caught everyone's attention. Whereas the other teams arrived in dribs and paint-spattered drabs, the Bs were all together. Their protective suits were unmarked and they held their helmets under their arms as if they were a NASA crew about to board the space shuttle.

"We were fighting all night long," James gasped. "They're not even sweaty."

Lauren racked her brains. "I can't actually remember seeing *any* of that lot. They must have hidden out while the rest of us massacred each other."

"God they all look so smug," James said. "I bet they haven't lost a single egg."

And they almost hadn't. The instructors, Mr. Large and his assistants Pike and Greaves, arrived in three open-backed Land Rovers, blasting their horns and sending a shower of kids diving across the paved square. Large divided the teams up and began carefully inspecting every egg for the minutest sign of a crack.

Though Kyle himself wasn't there, Team A scored eight. Mr. Large actually broke into a smile after he'd finished inspecting Team B.

"One slight crack means twenty-nine out of thirty eggs. It's not often you brats impress me, but that *is* impressive."

Team B was led by a fifteen-year-old girl called Clara Ward. She was in a couple of James's science classes and he couldn't stand her because she was well behaved, always handed her homework in on time, and always got brilliant marks.

"Thank you *very* much, sir," Clara said as she made James hate her even more by smiling at Mr. Large and saluting him.

James made a gagging noise, then whispered in Lauren's ear, "What a crawler. Cherubs don't salute."

"I know," Lauren whispered back. "What does she think this is, the army?"

"So how did you do it?" Mr. Large asked.

Clara smiled. "Sir, I rode up here on my bike a couple of days ago and checked out the compound. I found two easy-to-defend buildings on the northeast side, next to the lake. They're only accessible via a narrow alleyway. We ran there as soon as the mission started and fortified our positions by moving some of the cars parked outside. The only resistance we encountered was on brief exchange of fire with a couple of members from Team D."

"Good work," Mr. Large said crisply as he moved on to Team C and stopped in front of Kerry.

"Oh deary, deary, dear," Mr. Large said when he saw the five eggs Kerry held out on a single polystyrene box. He took each egg out and carefully inspected it for cracks. "Five eggs," Large said solemnly. "Extremely poor. Even in the unlikely event that another team does worse than you, you can still expect me to write a negative report on your leadership skills."

Kerry looked miserable as Mr. Large strolled onwards with his two assistants in tow. James tried giving his girlfriend a sympathetic smile, but he couldn't catch her eye.

"So, Team D, led by The Addams Family," Mr. Large said, allowing himself a dry laugh at his own little joke.

"Six eggs, sir," James said, holding out the full box.

James had checked the eggs for cracks less than two minutes earlier, but his heart still thumped as Mr. Large ran his eye over them.

"They're all OK," James said edgily.

Mr. Large picked out the first of Lauren's two eggs. "Whose eggs are these?" Large snapped.

Lauren stepped forward with a sense of dread. "Sir," she said weakly.

"It has Lauren Adams written on these eggs," smirked Mr. Large.

"That *is* my name," Lauren said, too knackered to manage a sarcastic tone.

"No it isn't," Large grinned. "Your name is Puke. I'm not counting these eggs, because they haven't got your correct name on them. Four eggs for Team D. You finish *last*."

James, Dana, Bethany, and Lauren were all familiar with the sense of complete doom you get when Mr.

Large nails you for no reason other than the sadistic pleasure it gives him. But Jake hadn't been through basic training and didn't know that answering back only made things worse.

The youngster violently hurled his helmet at the ground. "I'm not doing any run," Jake yelled furiously. "This is a total stitch-up."

Mr. Large swooped forward and grabbed Jake by his damp red T-shirt. He plucked the boy off the ground with one arm and screamed directly into his face. "DO YOU WANT TO PICK A FIGHT WITH ME JAKE *PARKER*?"

Jake looked so scared, James thought the poor kid was either going to faint or piss himself.

"When are you eligible for basic training?" Large snarled.

"May next year, sir."

"Ten months shy of basic training. Not a good time to make an enemy of me then, is it?"

"No, sir," Jake quaked.

"I make the rules here," Mr. Large shouted as he dropped Jake from two meters up. "Don't any of you forget that."

Jake crashed into the ground and tried his hardest not to sniffle as Bethany bent forward to help her little brother find his feet.

"Four valid eggs for Team D," Large repeated. "Team D gets the punishment run."

James looked at Jake and Lauren's miserable faces and struggled to control his anger as Mr. Pike stepped into the fray.

"Come on, Norman," Pike said gently. "You can't

expect these kids to work hard and stay motivated if you pick out the loser before you even start."

James was shocked. He'd worked with Pike on a couple of training exercises. Unlike Mr. Large, he always played fair, but this was the first time James had ever seen one of the junior instructors dare to question Large's authority.

Large turned furiously towards his colleague. "Mr. Pike, when *you* are senior instructor, *you* can count the eggs."

James felt emboldened by Pike's interference. "He's right," he said, hardly able to believe that he was daring to backchat Mr. Large. "I'm not going on any run until I've spoken to the Chairman about this. You can't keep on having a go at Lauren. She's already served her punishment for hitting you."

"I'm giving you a direct order," Large screamed.

"And I'll obey the direct order as long as the Chairman confirms it," James screamed back.

"I'm right with you, James," Dana said, stepping up beside him. "Let's see the Chairman. We can make a formal complaint about Lauren being bullied."

Lauren and Bethany both murmured in agreement and a noise went up from some of the kids in the other teams as well.

"If you go and see the Chairman, you will all fail this exercise," Large shouted.

James shrugged. "So what? It's only an exercise. I've already passed basic training and *you* don't have the authority to suspend us from missions."

"Drop it, Norman," Mr. Pike said. "You're not going to win this one."

Mr. Large turned around and looked at Kerry. "All right," he sighed. "Team C, ten kilometers. Grab your packs."

James turned to Dana and nodded. "Cheers for backing me up."

"I'm going to see the Chairman," Dana said. "I know training's supposed to be tough, but the way he's bullying Lauren is totally out of order."

Lauren looked at Dana and smiled guiltily. "I'm sorry I called you Cheesy earlier."

Soap

It was two o'clock that afternoon when James woke up and decided to go check on Kerry. He listened at her door for a second to make sure she wasn't sleeping, but he could hear her TV.

"Yo." James grinned as he poked his head inside the door. "How was the punishment run?"

Kerry was sitting on her bed in a dressing gown. She paused her DVD recorder and shrugged. "Oh, it was great fun. You can imagine what sort of mood Large was in after you'd all upset him."

"Me and Dana went and spoke to the Chairman about the way he's bullying Lauren. He said he's gonna speak to Mr. Pike and Mr. Large about what happened."

Kerry smiled. "I've heard that Mr. Large has got to watch his step. He's already had a couple of written warnings about his conduct."

"Imagine if he got sacked," James grinned as he reached into his pocket and grabbed a sheet of turquoise paper. "It would be *soooo* beautiful."

Kerry laughed. "Yeah, he'd probably have to take a job as a nightclub doorman, or a security guard."

"I don't care what job he gets," James said, grinning

like an idiot and fanning the piece of paper in front of his face. "Just so long as he's out of my life."

"OK, I get the hint," Kerry sighed. "What's on the piece of paper?"

James flicked the sheet across to Kerry and slumped theatrically across her bed. "I'm a sick little boy," he giggled.

Kerry raised a hand to slap him. "Get your boots of my bed," she said sharply. "How many times do I have to tell you?"

James rolled onto his back and started pulling off his boots as Kerry read the note aloud.

"*James Adams, ten days excused from all physical activity due to dehydration and exhaustion . . .*" How did you pull that little scam?"

"It's not a scam. I went to the medical unit to get the wound on my back cleaned up. The nurse touched me and asked why I was all hot and clammy. I told her how I felt weak during the exercise. She reckons I'm dehydrated and probably still under the weather from that stomach bug last week."

Kerry shook her head. "I still reckon you're faking."

"The nurse also said that lots of snogging would help me recuperate."

"Oh, I'm *sure* she did, James. I'm not going anywhere near you if you're hot and clammy. I don't want your germs."

James's head was flat against the double bed, while Kerry was propped up so she could see the TV. He moved forward a few centimeters and delicately kissed Kerry's wrist.

"You've got cute little hands," James said.

Kerry smiled as she lifted her hand off the bed and stroked James's cheek. "What are you after, Adams?"

"Nothing, I was just thinking. It's a nice day out. Maybe we could make sandwiches and go up to the lake. It's usually packed when it's sunny, but all the other kids are in lessons today so we'd have it to ourselves. Maybe we could splash around, chill out, lie in the sun for a while."

Kerry looked out the window. "It is nice out, but I'm halfway through *EastEnders*."

James scowled at the screen. "You and your dopey soap operas. Violet's varicose veins and Sammy stealing the Christmas club money to pay for his sex change. I don't know how you sit through that rubbish every day."

"Well, I *happen* to like them," Kerry said. "So you can either sit with me quietly until it finishes, or you can bog off."

"Can we go for a picnic after?"

Kerry shook her head. "I've got *Neighbors* to watch after this."

James tutted. "God, Kerry, you're *so* boring sometimes."

"Haven't you got about fifty lots of homework piled up on your desk?" Kerry said bitterly. "Why don't you actually do it for a change, instead of ripping off me or Kyle?"

"Fine, I'll go if you don't want me," James said as he got off the bed. "I just thought a picnic would be fun."

"Let's face it," Kerry said, "you don't want a picnic. You want a quick swim, then you want to spend the rest of the afternoon snogging and trying to get your hands on my boobs."

"Well, you *are* supposed to be my girlfriend. I waited for you for six months while you were in Japan. You come back and you never want to do *anything*. I don't know why you even want a boyfriend."

Kerry jumped off the bed and put on a look of mock astonishment. "Do you know what, James?" she snapped. "That's the most sensible thing you've said all day. Why *do* I want a boyfriend? All you do is moan on and on about school. I'm sick of lending you money and bailing you out with homework that you left until the last minute. I'm sick of not being able to chill out, or go where I want with the girls because you're always around.

"In fact," Kerry spat, "I'm sick of everything about you."

"Are you dumping me?" James asked dumbly.

"Bing." Kerry nodded. "Consider yourself dumped. Now if you'd be so kind as to get your worthless rump out of my room."

"But . . ."

Kerry barged past James and opened her door. "Out."

"Kerry, come on. Don't you think you're overreacting?"

"*Geeeeeeet* out!" she screamed.

James did as he was told because Kerry had one of her *I'm about to shatter your arms and legs* looks about her. He stepped out of the room and a gale rushed through his hair as the door slammed behind his head.

The only other person sharing the long corridor with James was a newly recruited cherub called Andy Lagan. The eleven-year-old blue shirt was at a loose end until the next basic training session started in two months.

James looked at him and shrugged. "You know what, kid? Girls are all bloody loonies."

Andy looked baffled by James's comment. Kerry reopened her door and screamed out, "And you can take your stinking boots with you."

The first boot crashed harmlessly against the wall, but the second hit James square in the back of the head. James turned to have a go back, but the door slammed in his face before he got a chance.

James pounded on the door. "You know what? I'm better off without you . . . moody cow."

James realized Any was grinning. He charged forward and faced the kid off.

"Do you reckon this is funny?"

"No." Andy smirked, trying to keep a straight face.

James grabbed Andy by his shoulders and wiped his grin off by pushing him against the wall.

"You wanna try laughing at me again?" James snarled.

"I'm sorry," the kid groveled as he looked up at his significantly larger adversary. "I just couldn't help laughing when she threw the boot at your head."

Apology or not, James was deeply upset by what Kerry had just done and he couldn't take someone laughing at him. He raised a hand and smacked

Andy across the face, before giving him a powerful shove. The kid bounced off the wall before stumbling backwards into a heap on the floor.

James stood over him with his fists bunched. "Still think this is funny? Laugh some more and see what you get."

Andy gasped tearfully as he crawled back across the carpet. "Leave me alone," he sniffed.

James watched a tear streak down Andy's face. He looked nervously over his shoulder to check that nobody else was around before reaching forward to pick the kid up.

"I'm really sorry," he muttered as his anger deflated. "I don't know what came over me. My girlfriend just dumped me and I went kind of mad. . . ."

Andy screamed out, "Don't come *near* me, you moron."

James's handler, Meryl Spencer, had an office down the hallway and she came out to investigate the noise. James saw Meryl storming towards the scene as Kerry emerged from her room and barged him out of the way.

Kerry crouched down and handed Andy a clean tissue to dab his face. She cast a furious backwards glance.

"For God's sake, James. What is the *matter* with you?"

Unpopular

Meryl spent the best part of an hour shouting at James, while James spent the best part of an hour wondering how one idiotic flash of anger had landed him in such deep trouble. When he finally got out of Meryl's office, he headed down to the canteen for dinner.

He got a creepy feeling that people were talking behind his back while he was in the queue, and none of the gang looked happy when he set his tray down.

James's crowd was gathered around the two pushed-together tables where they always sat: Shak, Connor, Gabrielle, Kerry, and Kyle. The only absentees were Bruce, who was on a mission, and Callum, who was on the toilet. James made a point of sitting as far away from Kerry as possible, in a seat opposite Kyle, who had a foam collar around his neck.

James knew they weren't exactly going to be falling over themselves to congratulate him on thumping an eleven-year-old, but he thought he'd be OK if he apologized and laid the severity of his punishment on thick.

"I'm not allowed to go on holiday to the hostel this summer," he said solemnly. "I'm suspended from missions for a month and I've got to clean up the mission preparation building every night for three months. . . . Oh, and I've got to start anger management sessions with a counselor."

Kyle and the others carried on eating without making a response. James tried again.

"I really messed up. . . . I mean, I know what I did was bad—well, totally unacceptable really—but . . ."

Gabrielle angrily cracked the wall of silence. "James, nobody at this table is interested. Why don't you go and sit somewhere else?"

James wasn't expecting a warm welcome, but Gabrielle's harshness shocked him.

"You know how I fly off the handle sometimes," he said weakly, glancing at the faces around him and hoping for some sign of support.

Kyle spoke firmly. "If you don't move, then we all will. Do you know what Andy's been through these past few months?"

Meryl had been through Andy's life story, but that didn't stop James from getting a reminder.

"His grandma died in a fire," Shak said. "The police found out it was arson and accused Andy of killing her. The poor kid spent six months locked up in secure accommodation, until someone grassed up the kids who really did it."

Kyle nodded. "He tried to kill himself before he came to campus. He passed the introductory tests, but he didn't go into basic training straight away because he's still pretty messed up."

"And *you* beat him up," Connor said accusingly. "You're scum."

"Come on," James said in desperation. "I didn't

beat him up; it was one slap and a push. I'll say sorry and give him a couple of my PlayStation games to make it up. OK?"

Gabrielle and Kyle slowly shook their heads. James realized he wasn't going to talk anyone around.

"Fine," James said as he stood up briskly and grabbed his tray. He tried adding, *I've got other friends,* but he found there was a lump in his throat.

He looked for somewhere to sit. He thought about heading towards Lauren and Bethany, but sitting with a bunch of littler kids wasn't cool and James doubted they'd be very welcoming. He spotted a few other friendly faces—kids he'd been on training with and kids who were in his classes—but they all had their own little groupings and crashing on another crowd wasn't the done thing.

He ended up alone at the back of the canteen. Nobody ever sat there unless the joint was packed out, because you could smell the congealed food that had been scraped into the bins.

After he'd eaten, James crashed out on his bed and sulked. Four hours earlier he'd been planning a picnic with Kerry, he had a ten-day exemption from exercise, and the prospect of five weeks sunning it at CHERUB's summer hostel at the end of the month. Now his whole life was down the toilet: dumped by Kerry, no friends, no holiday, and he could have sworn the mound of homework piled up on his desk was grinning at him.

There was a triple knock at the door: Lauren's knock.

"Yeah," James said unenthusiastically.

He wasn't sure how he felt about seeing Lauren. He kind of wanted to see her, but he didn't want the lecture she was going to give him, however much he knew he deserved it.

"You OK?" Lauren asked as James sat up on his bed. "You look like you've been crying."

"I haven't," he said defensively, but then he shrugged. "Yeah, a bit."

"Kyle said it's OK for me to speak to you, seeing as I'm your sister."

James was narked. "What, you have to ask that idiot's permission to speak to me now?"

Lauren wagged her finger. "Don't knock Kyle. Him and Gabrielle saved your butt."

"You don't know what you're talking about," James tutted. "You should have seen them at dinner. They were the ringleaders."

"Nah-uh," Lauren said, shaking her head. "Andy's being looked after by two *massive* sixteen-year-olds. When they found out what happened they were gonna batter you. Kyle was the one who talked them out of it. He reckoned blanking you would be more effective."

"At least if they'd beaten me up it would be over and done with. . . . It's out of all proportion, Lauren. I threw one punch. In fact, it wasn't even a punch, it was a slap."

"You just don't get it, do you?" Lauren said, grinding her palm against the side of her head in frustration.

"Get what?"

"This *keeps* happening, James. You lose your temper and lash out at people."

"Like when?"

"When you were in Year Five and you beat that kid up and smashed all the art equipment. In Year Six when you twisted that kid's leg around and nearly broke his ankle. You beat up Samantha Jennings the day Mum died. You got in trouble when you were at Nebraska House. You lost your temper and stomped on Kerry's hand in basic training. Come to think of it, you've battered *me* a couple of times as well."

"We were always getting in fights when we were little, Lauren. All kids do that."

Lauren shook her head. "That time you gave me a black eye. We told Mum it was an accident, but it wasn't, was it? You went nuts because I ate a tiny piece of your Easter egg."

"Come on, Lauren. I was ten years old. You're making me sound like some foaming at the mouth psychopath."

"You might not be a psycho, but you *have* got a nasty side. I hope you *do* end up losing all your friends over this, James. I hope you never get back with Kerry. Maybe this will make you see that you can't go around throwing wobblers and beating people up."

James felt punch drunk from Lauren's onslaught. "Thanks a lot," he sniffed. "I needed that."

"Ah diddums." Lauren shrugged. I *thought* you'd finally grown out of this nonsense."

"Kerry dumped me," James sniffed. "There was no reason behind it."

Lauren knew her brother was fishing for sympathy

and totally ignored him. "So what's gonna happen if you don't grow out of this, James? Are you gonna end up battering your wife and kids some day?"

James gasped. "Lauren, don't be *stupid*. I'd never do that."

Lauren mocked James's voice, "*You know I've got a bad temper, I can't help it sometimes.* So, if you can't help it, how can you know?"

"Lauren, I'd never touch my wife and kids. I swear to God."

"Well, here's an oath for you," Lauren said, waggling her finger under her brother's nose. "I'm sick of you acting like a moron. Soon our mum's grave: If this happens one more time, I'm never speaking to you again."

Lauren stood up and headed for the door.

"Lauren," James shouted desperately.

She stopped. "What?"

James shrugged. "I don't know. . . . Stay with me for a bit; watch TV. I don't feel like being on my own."

Lauren shook her head. "There's a birthday party on my floor. I'm gonna go upstairs and try to enjoy myself. If you're stuck here on your own feeling miserable, whose fault is that?"

Lauren turned around and slammed the door after herself.

James collapsed on to his bed. Lauren hadn't so much touched a raw nerve as rubbed over a whole bunch of them with a cheese grater. As he choked back more tears, James realized that every time he lashed out it was him who got hurt most. He had to learn to control his temper.

Promises

CHERUB—Good Behavior Contract

I, James Robert Adams, promise to abide by the following:

(1)   *I agree to respect all my fellow cherubs and CHERUB staff.*

(2)   *I will not behave in an abusive way to anyone, either verbally or physically.*

(3)   *I will go to regular anger management sessions with a counselor.*

(4)   *If I feel angry, I will use the techniques taught by my counselor to control my mood. I will not lash out.*

(5)   *I will write an apology to Andy Lagan.*

(6)   *I will catch up on my backlog of homework. I will not ask to copy work off my classmates and I understand that I will not be allowed to go off campus until I have completely caught up.*

(7)   *I agree to clean the mission preparation building between five and seven p.m. every day except Sunday, either for three months or until I am sent on a mission.*

(8)   I will be banned from missions for one month. This ban will be extended to three months if I have not caught up with my homework within this time.

(9)   I agree that I will not be entitled to a holiday at the CHERUB summer hostel this year because of what I did. .

(10) I agree not to go moaning to my handler Meryl Spencer, asking her to change stuff in this contract after I have signed it.

I understand that this contract will be reviewed after three months. If I have not met ALL ten criteria, I will be subject to severe punishment, which might include being permanently excluded from CHERUB.

Signed: J. R. Adams
Handler's signature: M. Spencer
Witnessed by: L. Z. Adams

Cleaning

For the first eleven years of his life, James had led the same uneventful existence as most other kids: getting up, going to school, coming home to his mum, going on holiday once a year, or twice if he was lucky. Since his mum died, James had led lots of different lives: in a children's home, training at CHERUB, in a commune with a bunch of hippies, as a trainee drug dealer, and even inside an Arizona prison.

But James's favorite was everyday life on campus. He loved his room, he loved the way every mealtime turned into a big gossip session about who'd got punishment laps, who was trying to get off with who, or just busting each other's balls over the football results. Best of all he liked the messing around. You never knew when a water fight was going to erupt, or when the next floor up would declare war with a bunch of flour bombs. The schoolwork and the training were hard, but at its best life on CHERUB campus was the most fun James had ever had.

Now he'd been ostracized, James found it embarrassing hanging around with nobody to talk to, so he spent a lot of time in his room. Once the backlog of homework was cleared, he read motorbike magazines or played his PlayStation. He hated being shut up in the stuffy room, hearing everyone else having fun: chasing, screaming at each other, slamming doors, and an occasional tantrum when something got out of hand. And the worst thing was knowing that it was his own stupid fault.

Cherubs can be sent off on long missions at any time, and when they come back they're expected to catch up with the schoolwork they've missed. Because of this, every cherub is on an individual curriculum and lessons are taught year round, Monday through Saturday. The only exceptions are public holidays and the days between Christmas and New Year. So while all the other cherubs got their five-week turn at the hostel, James went to lessons every single day.

He felt like he'd scored a minor victory if he managed to race through his homework in the hour between the last lesson and setting off to clean up the mission preparation building. He'd managed on this particular Wednesday, so he was in an OK mood as he left his room, but it didn't last.

Bruce stood in the corridor wearing a pair of swimming shorts three sizes too small for him. Shak was looking at Bruce and laughing.

"You've got to go into town and buy new ones before we fly off," Shak giggled. "I don't even know how you got into those things."

Bruce stared down at his skinny legs and nodded. "They fitted me OK last year. But I've spent my clothes allowance. I was wondering if I could borrow your blue ones."

Shak was in the middle of the corridor, blocking James's path to the lift.

"'Scuse us," James said.

Shak tutted as he backed up to the wall and Bruce scowled at James with complete contempt. As he waited for the lift, James considered how a month earlier he would have been in on the joke. He probably would have got the bus into town with them, cruised the shops, and ended up messing around in Burger King.

Things got even more awkward as the lift doors parted, revealing Norman Large standing inside with his head almost touching the plastic ceiling. It was the first time James had seen Large since he'd spoken to the Chairman with Dana, setting off a chain of events that had resulted in Mr. Large being demoted to an ordinary instructor. His former assistant, Mr. Speaks, had replaced him as the head of CHERUB training.

They didn't make eye contact and James tried not to think of how effortlessly the giant man could squish him, as the lift trundled down to the ground floor.

When James arrived at the mission preparation building, he had to lean forward and stare into a lens. A red light scanned his retina for identification and a colored label rolled out of a printer as the door clicked open. He got the same freshly printed sticker with his name and photograph on it every day, so he didn't even bother to look as he stuck it to his T-shirt upside down.

James had his routine sorted. He'd start off by

getting the cleaning cart out of its cupboard. It was a giant contraption with a dustbin built into one end that went up as high as his chin. There was a mop, bucket, and Hoover clipped to the sides, and a rack of shelves, which were stocked with cloths and cleaning sprays. The mission preparation building had a banana-shaped corridor running its entire length, with twenty offices and special equipment rooms off to the sides and the luxurious offices of the two senior mission controllers—Zara Asker and Dennis King—at opposite ends.

James started with King's office because he was always out of the building by five p.m. The routine was the same in every room: Empty the bins, pick up any dirty cups or plates, wipe any surfaces that weren't covered with junk, vacuum the floor, and finish off with a squirt of air freshener. It wasn't exactly backbreaking, but it got boring when you had to do it every night. Plus, you had to be speedy if you wanted to get twenty offices done, clean and restock four bathrooms, vacuum the corridor, and do the washing-up inside two hours. Even working flat out, James could never get through in much less than two and a quarter.

Ninety minutes into the job, James's feet were starting to ache. He'd finished the last of the bathrooms, which was the part of the job he really hated. Getting blanked by his friends and losing his summer holiday was bad, but having to unblock a toilet full of turds and soggy bog roll was easily worst of all.

As James threw his disposable gloves and soggy cloths into the rubbish sack on his cart, he heard a tiny giggle. He knew it was Zara Asker's eighteen-month-old son, Joshua, but that wasn't how you played the game.

"Boo," Joshua squealed as he jumped out from behind the cart.

Joshua theatrically backed up to the wall. "You scared me! You *horrible* little monster."

Joshua giggled as he hugged James's leg. "Joshua monster. *Grrrrrr.*"

"Did you escape from Mummy's office again?"

Joshua beamed as James picked him off the floor. His blond fringe hung over his eyes and he wore striped dungarees with powdery brown marks all over them.

"It looks like you decided to wear that chocolate bar," James said as he carried the toddler up to the door of Zara's office and knocked.

There were a few staff on campus that James liked, but Zara was his favorite. She always worked late, and in the month James had been on cleaning duty, she'd got into the habit of making him a mug of tea part way through his shift. He usually drank it in Zara's office while they had a quick chat.

James stepped through the door and put Joshua down on the carpet. He was disappointed to see that Zara had company.

"I'd better get on," James said, turning back towards the door.

"Actually, James, have you got a minute?" Zara asked.

James turned back and studied the woman facing Zara across her desk. She was in her early thirties, with long dark hair and a fit body.

"Millie, this is James, the one I was talking about. James, this is Millie Kentner, one of your predecessors at CHERUB."

James reached forward to shake her hand, but Joshua snatched James's attention by bashing his boot with a toy car.

"Look," Joshua demanded.

James smiled at him. "Is that a new car?"

Joshua grinned up at James as Zara explained the situation to Millie. "Ewart brings Joshua over here while he gives the baby her bath and gets her off to sleep. He's supposed to be visiting Mummy for half an hour before he goes to bed, but James is his hero."

Millie gave James a toothpaste advert grin. "Is that right, James?"

"I guess." James shrugged as he crouched down and took Joshua's new Lamborghini for a test drive across the carpet.

Zara nodded. "From when Joshua first wakes up, all I hear is James, James, James. When you ask Joshua what he's going to do, he makes all this stuff up. Yesterday he announced that he was going to go fishing with James. He must have seen it on TV, because Ewart's never taken him fishing."

"So, James," Millie smirked, covering her mouth as though she didn't want Zara to hear. "As one cherub to another, how'd you end up on cleaning detail?"

"I got in a fight," James said awkwardly.

Zara smiled. "Well, that's not *exactly* true, is it, James?"

"I dunno, isn't it?"

"Get this." Zara grinned as she pointed at James.

"The silly muppet got himself dumped by his girl-friend. So he storms out and the first person he sees: a little scrap of an eleven-year-old kid."

Millie put her hands over her mouth. "Oh my God." She smiled. "James, how could you? And you're so sweet with Joshua."

James felt awkward and dumb, even though he realized Millie was trying to be nice.

"So, like I said," Zara interrupted, "young James has some very good mission experience, but right now he's down in the dumps. His friends have all given him the boot. He's lost his summer holiday and the only way he'll get out of cleaning duty is if I send him on a mission."

Millie nodded. "I'll take whoever I can get. This is just a favor, really. I can sort out accommodation and I doubt it will take any more than a month."

Zara explained to James. "After retiring as a CHERUB agent, Millie joined the Metropolitan Police. She works as a community officer in east London and she's having a few problems with one of the local villains. It's textbook CHERUB stuff: Move into the neighborhood with another agent, hang out with the villain's kids, try getting involved in his home life and business, et cetera, et cetera. I'll have to type up a proper mission briefing and get ethics committee approval, but I assume you're interested?"

James nodded enthusiastically. "I don't care *what* the mission is if it means I don't have to stick my hand down another toilet."

Zara smiled. "I thought you might say that."

Classified

MILLIE KENTNER

Millie Kentner was born in 1971. She served as a CHERUB agent from 1981-1988, retiring with a black shirt after eleven missions. Her role in the 1985 miners' strike has been described as "One of the most out-standing performances by a CHERUB agent, ever."

Millie left for Sussex University, where she studied forensic science. In 1992 she joined the Metropolitan

Police and her career was fast-tracked, enabling her to obtain the rank of inspector within four years. Following this promotion, Millie transferred from the serious crime squad to a role in charge of a community policing unit, covering the area of east London that includes the Palm Hill neighborhood.

Palm Hill is still notorious for riots that took place there in 1981, but today the area has many affluent residents and crime is below the London average. Millie Kentner's work with the Palm Hill community over the last nine years has been credited for much of this change. In 2002 she turned down the offer of promotion to chief inspector and the opportunity to head a London-wide task force designed to specifically target London's crime black spots. She wanted to continue working in Palm Hill.

THE BROTHERS TARASOV

Leon and Nikola Tarasov were born somewhere in Russia in the early 1950s. Nikola was believed to be one year older than his brother, although their exact ages are uncertain. After serving in the Russian navy, both young men took jobs as fishermen.

In August 1975, their factory trawler suffered a dual engine failure while fishing for cod in the North Sea. Following a distress call, a British lifeboat safely evacuated all forty-two crewmembers with assistance from the Norwegian navy.

Upon landing in Britain, Leon and Nikola were among eight members of the crew who requested asylum. After government officials failed in their attempts to persuade the eight sailors to return home and avoid a diplomatic row with the USSR, the British government reluctantly accepted their asylum requests.

After failing to find work aboard a British fishing vessel, Leon and Nikola gravitated towards the small Russian community centered around Bow in east London. The brothers worked a string of undesirable jobs: driving minicabs, working in hotel kitchens, and portering in hospitals. It is also believed they became increasingly involved in illegal activities. In 1979 Nikola was tried and convicted of stealing more than two thousand pounds in cash from a minicab office where he had worked the previous summer. He was sentenced to three months in prison.

PALM HILL RIOTS

Upon his release, Nikola declared himself homeless and broke, and was allocated a two-bedroom flat in a run-down section of the Palm Hill estate. Leon moved in with him and they continued much as before, earning their keep with a mixture of low-paid work, dodgy dealing, and small-time criminal activity. But their financial status would be changed forever by the Palm Hill riots.

On the night of 13 July 1981, the Palm Hill riots kicked off when police stopped and arrested a youth as he got out of a stolen car. Witnesses claimed that the arresting officers assaulted the youth as he was handcuffed and put into the back of a police car. An angry mob gathered, undoubtedly encouraged by a wave of urban violence that had spread across the country following the Brixton riots three months earlier. Bricks and bottles were thrown, and then the police car was surrounded. The officers were dragged out of their vehicles and beaten by the mob before they got a chance to radio for help.

As darkness fell, youths and police fought running battles in the streets and alleyways around the Palm Hill estate. More than twenty shops were looted, hundreds of windows smashed, cars vandalized, and a block of sixty garages at the back of the estate was completely burned out. It took police more than eight hours to restore order.

GOVERNMENT GRANTS

In the aftermath of the riots, the government hatched a compensation scheme—because riots are not covered by insurance—and pledged to spend money regenerating Palm Hill.

Leon and Nikola Tarasov realized that this was a golden opportunity. The brothers had been dealing in secondhand cars and had lost five of them in the burned-out garage block. The government compensated the brothers generously for the cars; by some estimates they received more than four times what the cars were truly worth.

Unable to believe their luck, Leon and Nikola used the compensation money to buy the lease on a derelict pub and an adjoining plot of land at the edge of the Palm Hill estate. Using a mixture of government grants and subsidized redevelopment loans, they refurbished the pub and turned the land into a secondhand car dealership.

SMALL TIME

Although neither venture was wildly successful, the government money enabled the Tarasov brothers to wear suits and describe themselves as local businessmen to the TV crews who occasionally turned up to report on the aftermath of the riots.

Over the following years, the Tarasovs ran their businesses with a complete lack of respect for the law. They were investigated for unpaid taxes, and on more than one occasion stolen car parts and vehicles were found on their lot. Another raid uncovered a cache of fake vehicle tax discs. Leon and Nikola claimed that the discs had been left behind by a former employee and were found not guilty by a jury after a three-day trial at Bow Crown Court.

Their pub, the King of Russia, quickly became a notorious hangout for petty criminals. It is known around Palm Hill as a place where you can easily buy drugs or stolen goods, drink after hours, or settle in for an illegal all-night poker game.

THE TARASOV DYNASTY

Until recently, the Tarasov brothers led remarkably parallel lives. They both married in 1985 and spawned a son and daughter.

Leon married Sacha Arkady. Sonya was born in 1989 (now sixteen) and Maxim in 1991 (now thirteen and known as Max). Nikola married Paula Randall. Their children are Piotr, born in 1988 (now eighteen and known as Pete) and Liza who was born in 1990 (now aged fourteen).

Paula Tarasov left Nikola and her children in 2000 and remarried shortly afterwards. After a prolonged bout of ill health, Nikola Tarasov died of pneumonia in December 2003. Custody of his children was awarded to Leon, without any contest from the children's mother.

Leon and Sacha currently share two adjoining flats on the Palm Hill estate with their son, daughter, niece, and nephew.

MONEY

Leon Tarasov fell apart in the aftermath of his brother's death.

He drank heavily. The pub and car dealership were both in debt and there were rumors that Leon had run up a large gambling debt with a "serious" underworld figure. Many believed that it was only a matter of time before Leon lost his businesses.

The Palm Hill police were among those relishing the imminent demise of Leon Tarasov. Tarasov had been a thorn in the side of the law, both through his own illegal activities and through the fact that his pub provided a hangout for other criminals. An internal police memo described Leon Tarasov as: *"A man keen to portray himself as a community leader, but in actuality Tarasov's criminality is a cancer that undermines much good work done by others in the neighborhood. Leon is believed to be heavily involved in local car crime and fencing stolen goods. He was suspected of running a protection racket amongst local shopkeepers for a number of years. More recently he has become involved in a violent turf war with a nearby community of travelers."*

But by the end of 2004 Tarasov's luck had changed for the better. He'd caught up with payments on all his loans, purchased a new car, and snapped up the lease on a pub at the north end of the Palm Hill estate. He spent a significant sum refurbishing this second pub, before renaming it the Queen of Russia.

Over the past year, the joke around Palm Hill has been that Tarasov has either won the lottery or robbed a bank. Having established that Tarasov did not win the lottery, the police are anxious to find the real source of Tarasov's newfound wealth.

THE CHERUB MISSION

Leon Tarasov has succeeded in avoiding anything other than a modest court fine in more than thirty years of dubious activity. He keeps his affairs close to his chest and all attempts at using police informants (grasses) and undercover operations have failed.

The thousands of hours wasted on trying to catch Leon Tarasov have made the Palm Hill police increasingly reluctant to put any more effort into nailing him. Millie Kentner has become frustrated with her colleagues' lack of enthusiasm and has asked if her old friends at CHERUB would be able to help out.

Two experienced CHERUB agents will move into a vacant flat on the same landing as the Tarasov family. The younger agent—James Adams, thirteen—will target Max and Liza. The older agent—Dave Moss, seventeen—will target Sonya and Pete.

Dave will pose as Dave Holmes, a young man who has recently been released from foster care. James will pose as his younger brother, who is still in care but who has been allowed to move in with him. Senior Mission Controller Zara Asker will organize the mission, while Millie Kentner will run the operation on a day-to-day basis.

MISSION OBJECTIVES

(1) To infiltrate the Tarasov family unit and try to obtain as much evidence as possible about criminal activity.

(2) To infiltrate Leon Tarasov's business, in particular his car dealership, which is believed to be the hub of his criminal activities.

(3) The main goal is to try and uncover the source of Leon Tarasov's recent financial good fortune.

THE CHERUB ETHICS COMMMITTEE ACCEPTED
THIS MISSION BRIEFING WITHOUT RESER-
VATION.

This mission has been classified LOW
RISK. Experienced agents will be allowed
to operate without close supervision
from a mission controller.

Home

James and Dave drove to Palm Hill in a battered ford Mondeo. It was a Saturday morning, the rear seats were folded down, and the back of the car was packed up to the roof with stuff. The air conditioning was busted, so they fought the heat by hurtling along the motorway with the windows down and a jet of air turning their hairstyles crazy.

This was James's second mission with Dave. The seventeen-year-old sat at the wheel, with longish blond hair, big blue eyes, and a handsome face that seemed a year or two younger than the muscular body attached to it. James was heavier set, with a flatter nose, but it didn't take any stretch of the imagination to believe that the two lads were brothers.

Dave was into old-school rock, and the journey passed with a mix of Led Zeppelin, Black Sabbath, and The Who. James preferred more recent stuff, but by the time the CD was on its third spin, he was playing air guitar in the passenger seat.

It was early afternoon when they arrived at Palm Hill, pulling into a courtyard filled with a mix of shabby family saloons and more exotic fare, including BMWs and Audis belonging to trendy young professionals who had begun purchasing flats on the better parts of the estate. The three-story housing blocks surrounding the courtyard on all sides had recently been refurbished: brickwork cleaned, windows repainted, and secure doors installed at the bottom of every stairwell.

As James stepped out of the car and walked off the stiffness from a three-hour car journey, he glanced through the gap between two blocks and spotted the crates of empties stacked at the rear of the King of Russia pub.

James and Dave grabbed a bag each from the back of the car and headed towards the stairs. As they walked up, James felt the mix of excitement and anxiety that you get at the start of every mission, but this time he was also glad to get away from campus. He didn't want to be around when Lauren, Kerry, and everyone else got back from the hostel with their golden tans and anecdotes about all the fun they'd had.

The flat was twenty meters along the first-floor balcony, four doors away from the two homes occupied by the Tarasovs. It had the musty smell of a place that hadn't been aired in months. You could only guess at the original color of the carpets, and the previous owner's taste in patterned wallpaper and plastic chandelier light fittings was pretty horrific.

"Not much furniture," James said as he stuck his head into a living room containing a single sofa and a coffee table with a cracked glass top.

Dave nodded. "You read the briefing. Kids released from care get a three-hundred-quid grant for furniture. We can drive out to Ikea in the week and get beanbags and stuff, but nothing flash."

James carried on inspecting. The kitchen and bath-room weren't too horrible, but the main bedroom con-tained only a metal clothes rail and a brand new bed. It had flamingo pink carpet and flock wallpaper.

"Gross," James said.

Dave barged in behind him. "The other bed-room's white, you want that one?"

James shrugged. "OK."

"Cool." Dave grinned as he bounced on the double bed. "I'm gonna have a different chick in this every night."

James grinned back and shook his head. "You reckon, do you?"

James's room was smaller, with a few girlie touches and a single bed. It made him a little sad because it reminded him of the room he'd had when his mum was alive. As he sat back on the mattress— which was still sealed in plastic with the price ticket on it—he could imagine banging on the wall to tell Lauren and her mates to shut up during one of their sleepovers, or his mum's snores vibrating through the wall.

James was boiling by the time he'd made ten trips carrying things up the stairs, so he took a shower and changed into clean shorts and one of his Arsenal shirts. They'd brought a few cans of Coke and some junk food from campus, but the boys needed milk and other fresh stuff. They'd spotted a Sainsbury's down the road when they arrived, so James headed off while Dave washed.

He stocked up on the basics, like bread, milk, and breakfast cereal, before heading towards the ready-meal cabinet. He grabbed microwave Chinese, some pasta dishes, and a couple of curries for Dave. As he headed back into the courtyard around the flats he got his first sighting of a Tarasov: thirteen-year-old Max and a couple of his pals whizzing past on bikes.

James got up to the locked door at the bottom of the stairs and realized he'd forgotten to put his keys into his clean shorts when he'd changed. He hit the intercom button for their flat and waited. After half a minute he pressed the button again and shouted tersely into he speaker.

"Dave, let me up."

After another thirty seconds, James started getting seriously impatient. He glanced at his watch, and after deciding that Dave couldn't possibly still be in the shower, he jabbed the buzzer half a dozen times and yelled:

"Dave, you moron, buzz me in. Are you deaf or what?"

A girl's voice came at James from the first-floor landing directly above his head. "Are you stuck?"

James stepped backwards so that he could get a good look at her. He guessed the girl was a year older than he was.

"My brother won't let me up. He's either gone deaf or he's trying to wind me up."

The girl smiled. "I'll open up for you."

James watched her come down the staircase through the safety glass in the door. First a set of flip-flops and purple-painted toenails on the top step. Tanned legs and a little denim skirt emerged as she moved farther down. She gave James a big smile through the glass and flicked back her long hair as she released the catch on the inside of the door.

"Cheers," James grinned back.

"I saw you and that other guy carrying your stuff in. My name's Hannah. I'm next door but one."

"I'm James," he said as he followed the girl up the stairs with a Sainsbury's carrier bag in each hand. "That other guy was my brother, Dave."

"I only saw the two of you. Where's your parents?"

"Six feet under," James said as he rounded the top of the staircase and stepped out of the half-light on to the balcony.

"Oh . . . I'm sorry."

James realized he'd imparted the information too casually and shocked Hannah. "I was four years old," he shrugged. "I can barely remember them."

"How come the two of you are allowed to live on your own?"

"We were in foster homes, but Dave's just turned seventeen, so he gets a flat. I'm allowed to live with him on a trial basis, but we've got a social worker who's gonna be checking up on me a few times a week."

Hannah giggled. "So you can't go *too* wild."

"Nah, I'm afraid not," James said as he stopped outside the door of his flat and rang the bell. He could hear music thumping inside.

"So, it was good to meet you, James. I expect I'll see you around."

James smiled. "Are you doing anything? You want to pop inside and say hello to my brother?"

"Why not?" Hannah shrugged.

A blast of "Baba O'Riley" by The Who hit them as Dave opened the front door, dressed in nothing but a pair of cargo shorts.

"Where's your key?" Dave asked.

"Up my butt," James said irritably. "What do you think? I forgot it. Maybe if you weren't trying to deafen the entire neighborhood you would have heard me buzzing the intercom."

Dave raced into the living room and turned the music down so they could hear each other speak. He reached out to shake Hannah's hand and she went all gooey.

"Good to meet you, Dave."

James had managed three proper girlfriends and got off with a few other girls at parties and stuff. He didn't think he was doing too badly for thirteen years of age, but Dave still made him jealous. When girls met Dave they turned bright red and giggled at all his jokes. He'd had a string of beautiful girlfriends, and according to most people you talked to on campus, he'd treated every one of them like dirt.

"How'd you get that scar on your chest?" Hannah asked, stopping her index finger a few centimeters shy of Dave's blemish, as though his body was a beautiful ornament that she dared not touch.

"I got a blood clot on my chest wall a few months back," Dave explained. "They had to put a tube in and suck it out."

Hannah recoiled. "Yuk."

"Ruined my chances of a career in modeling," Dave joked.

"I better put this shopping in the fridge before it goes off," James said.

"Good idea," Dave nodded. "Why don't you make us all a cup of tea while you're at it?"

If Hannah hadn't been there, Dave would have got a mouthful for being cheeky, but James headed into the kitchen and filled the kettle. As he stacked the food away, he looked over the fridge door and spotted Hannah in the doorway.

"I can't really stay," Hannah said. "I've got some homework I want to finish off before tonight."

"What are you up to?" James grinned. "Hot date?"

Hannah shook her head. "There's a big reservoir over the back of the estate. Loads of the local kids go up there when the weather's nice. It's just hanging out really, but you can come if you want. We'll grab some booze and I'll introduce you to a few faces."

James nodded. "Yeah, for sure. So, I don't need to dress up or nothing?"

"Well you could lose the Arsenal shirt," Hannah said, putting two fingers into her mouth and gagging. "It could seriously damage my reputation if I'm seen hanging out with a gooner."

Pulling

The boys were eating microwaved lasagna in front of a TV with a crummy indoor aerial when Dave spotted Sonya Tarasov walking past the window. He tripped over James's feet as he dived out of the room, down the hallway, and out of the front door. He jogged up behind Sonya and tapped her on the shoulder.

"Hey, Melanie," Dave said enthusiastically.

Sonya turned around. She was mousy and slightly overweight, with a circular face.

"I'm not Melanie," Sonya said irritably.

Dave put his hands over his face and acted embarrassed. "I'm so sorry," he gasped. "I didn't mean to startle you. It's just . . . you're the absolute spitting image of a girl I used to go out with."

James crept out into the hallway with his lasagna and listened while he ate. As soon as Sonya realized she hadn't just been accosted by some weirdo and caught a glance of Dave's handsome mug, she broke into a big smile.

"That's OK," Sonya giggled. "I've done the same thing myself."

"I should have known it was too good to be true,"

Dave said. "You know, I've just arrived and I don't know *anyone*."

"You just moved here?"

Dave nodded, pointing his thumb back towards the front door. "Me and my little brother moved into number sixteen."

Sonya smiled, but couldn't think of anything to say.

"So, does much go down around here on a Saturday night?"

Sonya pointed through the gap between the buildings. "There's the King of Russia over there, but that's usually an older crowd. If you walk past there and go across to the opposite end of the estate, you'll come to the Queen of Russia. That's more my kind of crowd, and there's a live band most Saturdays. I actually work behind the bar sometimes when it gets packed out."

"Cool," Dave nodded. "If I pop in later, maybe you'll let me buy you a drink?"

Sonya bit the end of her thumb and grinned. "Sure, maybe I'll even buy you one back."

"I'm Dave, by the way," he said, reaching out to shake hands.

"Sonya," she replied.

Dave took her hand and grasped it gently. "It was good meeting you, Sonya. I'd better get back. I'm making dinner for my little brother."

Dave strolled into the flat and closed the front door with an exuberant backwards kick.

James's jaw hung open. "I can't believe you did that," he gasped.

"What?" Dave asked innocently.

"You *totally* got off with her. You'd never even met her before."

"It's not so hard," Dave said. "I used to be scared when I was your age, but birds aren't swamp creatures from the planet Zog, you know. Just go up and start a conversation with them. You either get somewhere or you don't."

"Still," James said, shaking his head in disbelief. "Just walking up to a stranger and getting off with them is *so* slick."

"Of course," Dave grinned smugly as he picked his lasagna off the coffee table, "it does help if women find you totally irresistible."

He swallowed a mouthful of food and did a gigantic belch.

"Did you have to make me sound like a five-year-old?" James asked as he settled back on the sofa beside Dave.

Dave looked mystified. "You what?"

"I'm making dinner for my little brother," James quoted. "I wouldn't mind, but I'm the one who took it out of the cardboard and pierced the film."

Hannah had a couple of girlfriends with her when she rang for James. He recognized Liza Tarasov's podgy features from police surveillance photographs Millie Kentner had shown him. The other girl was called Jane.

"Jane used to live in your flat," Hannah explained as James pulled shut the front door and set off along the balcony with the girls. "She moved down to a ground-floor flat on another block, 'cos her nan can't handle the stairs anymore."

It was a ten-minute uphill stroll to the reservoir. The area around the man-made lake was a mixture of lawns and shrubs. Joggers and dog walkers used the paths and little kids played football or Frisbee on the grass while their parents kept watch. But the three girls led James away from civilization into an over-grown area beside a quiet road. The only charming feature amidst the empty beer cans and car tires was a fast-flowing brook that fed into the reservoir, but even that was partially damned with rusted kitchen appliances.

James had read up on the history of Palm Hill. He knew a three-million-pound youth and community center had been built after the riots, along with teen-friendly zones on the estate where kids could hang out without their racket disturbing residents. But over the course of his missions, James had noticed that kids his age tended to reject any place they were meant to go, in favor of some unsavory spot where they could get up to all the stuff their parents had nightmares about.

There were about thirty kids aged between twelve and fifteen, mostly sitting in fours and fives. The atmosphere was mellow. A few of the younger lads made a racket as they whizzed around on bikes, but most kids sat in the long grass gossiping as the sun dipped behind the houses beyond the field.

James's mission priority was to chum up with Liza and Max Tarasov, but Hannah was a major distraction. She'd made a big deal out of telling James that she didn't have a boyfriend, and they were having a really good conversation about everything from Premiership football to ways of getting out of homework.

Liza disappeared with a group of girls. That left James and Hannah sharing a can of Heineken she'd bummed off an older boy who blatantly fancied her, and Jane was feeling left out. Eventually, Jane got fed up and said she had to go home early to check on her nan.

A few kids stopped by to speak with Hannah and introduce themselves to James. When Max Tarasov reached over to give James a high five, it was eight p.m. and he knew he couldn't afford to miss a chance to pal up with his main target, even though it might endanger his chances of snogging with Hannah.

"You're my balcony buddy, James," Max said. "It's good to have another Arsenal fan in the neighborhood."

James grinned down at his shirt. "Seems like we're an endangered species in this part of town."

"You *know* it," Max grinned. "West Ham and Chelsea scum is all you get."

James was chuffed. CHERUB had set the situation up so that he had the best possible chance of getting on with Max, but sharing a football team made everything easier.

"Me and a couple of other dudes are heading down to the off-license to get more beer in," Max said. "You wanna tag along?"

"I've got cash," James said, "but I don't exactly look eighteen."

"We know a place. The owner would sell nerve

gas to a six-year-old if he thought there was a couple of quid in it."

James grinned. "Does he have that in stock too?"

"You can always ask."

James got up. He glanced down at Hannah and caught resentment in her eyes. "I'm only going off to get some beers. You don't mind, do you?"

"Why would I mind?" Hannah shrugged.

But she was all thin-lipped and stiff-shouldered. James reckoned she minded quite a lot.

"I'll get you a prezzie from the offie," James said, trying desperately to reconcile the requirements of his mission with the fit girl sitting in the grass. "Chocolate bar, crisps, whatever you want."

This won Hannah around. "Get us a Coke, a half-liter one, not a can, and a small bottle of vodka to mix with it."

James realized that was going to cost him the best part of a tenner, but it was food money from Zara lining his pockets, so he let it slide.

Two slightly older boys led the way downhill to the off-license. James and Max walked a few paces behind.

"You're a customer, James," Max said. "Getting off with Hannah first night out."

James tried to sound as cool as Dave had a couple of hours earlier. "It's confidence, man," he shrugged. "Birds aren't aliens from the planet Zog. You've just gotta talk to them."

"Yeah . . . ," Max slurred. James realized his new friend had downed way more than the single can of lager he'd shared with Hannah.

"But Hannah's been weird since that whole thing with her cousin last year," Max continued.

"What was that?" James asked.

"Hannah's cousin, Will. He was eighteen. Total hash-head, burnout, hippie, freak. He fell off the roof at the back of our block. Everyone reckons he was so stoned he didn't know where he was."

James hadn't seen anything about this in his mission briefing, but there would have been no reason to because it had nothing to do with the Tarasovs.

"Was Hannah close to him?" James asked.

"Not especially." Max shrugged. "But Hannah and Jane were standing five meters away from where he landed."

"No *way*," James gasped.

"Yes way." Max grinned. "Front-row seats to watch your own cousin turn himself into spaghetti Bolognese. Seeing something like that has *got* to mess up your head."

Max

It was a twelve-minute walk to the off-license, but the owner was as good as advertised, letting James buy Hannah's vodka and a six-pack of beer without missing a beat. He didn't even have to ask the two older guys, who were both fifteen, to go up to the till.

It was nearly dark when they got out, so they took a slightly longer route back to the field, using the road instead of the unlit paths around the reservoir. James twirled the bag containing the cans of beer as he walked. Max didn't say much, but James preferred that to the type of kid who never stops yapping.

They had to clamber over a shoulder-height wall to get back into the field. There seemed to be fewer kids about and the atmosphere felt tight.

"Bloody hell," Max said bitterly. "What are *they* doing up here?"

James spotted the new arrivals: four beefy lads aged sixteen or seventeen. They wore jeans and boots and the two girls who were with them looked rough.

"Are they from round here?" James asked.

Max nodded. "They're from the Grosvenor Estate, over on the other side of the reservoir. You don't usually see 'em up here."

James spotted Hannah standing about fifty meters away. She'd rejoined Liza and a couple of other girls and they all stood in a huddle. James split from the older lads and jogged towards them, with Max in tow.

"Hey," James said. "Everything OK?"

Hannah looked edgy. "We were just waiting for you two to get back before we split. You know what that lot are like. They're bound to start something."

"Shall we go to the youth center?" Liza asked.

A skinny girl called Georgia tutted. "That place is so lame. Ten-year-olds yelling their heads off and chasing around with ping-pong bats. Let's just hang out in the neighborhood."

"Yeah," Max nodded. "Grosvenor kids won't come near our neighborhood."

"How come?" James asked.

Max giggled. "'Cos they'd get battered."

"Where do *you* want to go, James?" Hannah asked.

"I dunno," James shrugged. "Whatever you guys do, I guess. I don't know what goes on around here."

"Diddly squat's what goes on here," Liza snorted. "Saturday night's so rubbish. I can't wait till I'm old enough to go out clubbing and stuff."

"And get off with some nice fit bloke," Georgia giggled.

"Trust *you*," Hannah said as all three girls broke into fits of giggles. "At least I've got James, he's lovely."

James slipped his arm around Hannah's back, glad that she wasn't holding a grudge from earlier.

"Sounds like you're all having fun," a deep voice said.

James turned to find that two of the thugs from the other neighborhood had come up behind them. The taller one had a wispy teenage beard. Both had the broad shoulders and muscular arms of the kind of people who are better not messed with.

"You know what? I'm parched," the bearded one rasped, rubbing his hand over his hairy throat to emphasise his point. "I couldn't help noticing that you've got some cans on you and I thought you might like to share."

"Just a couple of tins," his mate added.

Max scowled at them. "Why don't you buy your own, instead of poncing?"

The bearded kid looked at his mate and shook his head. "Was that very nice, calling us ponces?"

"I'm wounded." His mate grinned as he pointed at Max. "You know who this one is? His dad's that fat blob who owns the King of Russia."

"A whole pub full of booze and he won't spare us a couple of tins. Come on, hand 'em across."

Max backed up as the shorter thug lunged at his carrier bag.

"Leave off," Max juddered. The fear in his voice was obvious.

"Aren't you a brave boy?" the beard giggled.

Hannah tugged at James's arm and whispered in his ear. "They're massive. It's not worth getting done over for a few cans of beer."

After wrecking his life with the last punch he'd thrown, James felt inclined to swallow his pride. He reached into the bag and snapped two cans away from the plastic binding strip.

"Take 'em," James said sourly. "On me."

"How about the whole sixer?" The big dude grinned ungratefully. "I've worked up a thirst and I really didn't like your chum calling me a ponce."

"Or maybe you'll be wanting a slap," the shorter one added as he stepped forward so that his chest almost touched James's nose.

"Give it up, James," Hannah said desperately as she backed away.

But the sudden change in terms gave James a nasty feeling that the two lads now required more than beer. Max had offended them and James suspected the thugs wanted to humiliate them in front of the girls.

If he offered more beer, they'd probably ask for something else, like his money. And once he gave that up, they'd probably still give him a slap for his trouble. James reckoned he was going to have to stand his ground sooner or later, and it might as well be sooner.

"You know what?" James said, trying to sound cool. "I tried the peace offering, but now you're getting zip."

The thug in James's face stepped back to take a punch, but as soon as he kicked off, James grabbed his T-shirt with both hands, tugged him forward, and nutted him. The thug stumbled backwards, then crumpled up in the grass clutching a bloody nose.

The one with the bear dived in and tried grabbing James around the waist. James intercepted the arm and wrung his adversary's elbow into an excruciating lock.

James had no idea if the other two boys from the Grosvenor Estate were about to join in. He couldn't risk a four against one situation, which meant he had to take at least one opponent out of the equation. He yanked the thug's arm straight, then thrust a palm into the back of his elbow, tearing the tendons and splintering the bone.

James had practiced the move hundreds of times, but the difference between deliberately missing in training and the crunch of real flesh and bone was sickening.

As the bearded teenager screamed in agony, James felt weird: a mixture of nausea and awe at the extraordinary power he'd attained through hundreds of hours of combat training. He'd shot and killed a man ten months earlier, but anyone could have done that. The sensation of effortlessly breaking a human limb with his bare hands actually felt more horrifying, even though the consequences were nothing like as serious.

The other two thugs were closing on James, with their girls egging them on. James didn't want to fight them and decided that megaconfidence was the best strategy for keeping them at bay.

He pointed at the guy clutching his nose on the grass. "Anyone want some of that?" James sneered. "Come near me and you'll get it."

All the other kids in the field were looking at James, struggling to see what was happening in the moonlight. James was massively relieved when the yobs stopped a few meters shy. One of the girls crouched over the dude with the busted arm.

"You'd better call an ambulance," James said, with a hint of sympathy creeping into his defiant voice.

The mention of adult presence turned the mood of the twenty-strong crowd from tense to panicked. *What if the cops show up with the ambulance? What if the thugs go back to get their mates?* Every chain of thought hurtled to the same conclusion: *Got to get out of here.*

As his audience began to scatter, James felt Hannah tugging at his arm.

"Come on, James," she begged.

Max, James, and the three girls set off, chasing the shadows of other kids jogging downhill towards the exit gates on the Palm Hill side of the reservoir. Hannah gave James a tissue to wipe his face, while Max had suddenly found his tongue and taken the chair of the James appreciation society.

"Where'd you learn to do that, James? It was awesome, like . . . like *The Terminator* or something. That crunch when his arm smashed sounded a bit . . . oh, *man!* You know when you get a chicken out of the oven and rip off the leg?"

James didn't like being reminded and he was frustrated at how slowly his new pals were moving. The mixture of CHERUB training and frequent punishment laps meant James was fit enough to run five kilometers without getting seriously out of breath. His companions were gasping after a tenth of that distance.

"Where'd you learn it, James?" Max repeated, wide-eyed and grinning in awe.

"One of my foster parents was a karate instructor," he lied.

"Can you show me some moves?"

"It takes months," James said irritably as he looked back over his shoulder to find that the girls had fallen even farther behind.

The first siren didn't worry anyone; they assumed it was an ambulance. But the symphony that broke out half a minute later wasn't good. There should only be on ambulance, which meant the other four or five sirens belonged to police cars.

James spotted torchlight when a group of kids running a couple of hundred meters ahead of him reached the exit gate. "Cops," Liza said anxiously.

James felt a shot of fear. He considered hiding out in the trees or doubling back and going over a wall, but he didn't know the neighborhood and reckoned they could bluff their way through.

"Stop running," he said. "Act normal."

Max looked anxiously at James. "We'd better dump the booze."

James sighed as he lobbed the carrier bag containing twelve quid's worth of vodka and lager into a bush.

He looked back at the girls. "Is there another place where kids hang out in here?"

Georgia nodded. "There's a playground."

"That's good," James said. "If the cops ask, we were in the playground."

Hannah closed in on James. "Let me look at your face."

James stopped walking for a second. Hannah licked a tissue and used it to wipe the last few traces of blood off his forehead. He felt edgy as they approached the cops, but the previous bunch of kids had been waved through after less than a minute of questioning.

"Hello," a female officer said politely, stepping out in front of the kids and switching on her torch. "Do you mind if I ask you a few questions?"

"Has something happened?" Hannah asked innocently as they all stopped walking.

The second officer, an Asian man, stepped out and lit up his torch. Max recognized him immediately. "Hello, Sergeant Patel."

"Hey, Max," the officer said, nodding halfheartedly. "Keeping out of trouble I hope. Not broken any more windows?"

"Nah." Max grinned guiltily.

"Where have you kids been?" the female officer asked.

Georgia and Liza spoke in unison. "Over the playground."

"Not up top, by the brook?"

The girls both shook their heads.

"We've had reports that some lads from the Grosvenor Estate got ambushed and beaten up. One of them's ended up with a broken arm. You could get yourselves in serious trouble by lying to me, so I'm going to give you another chance. Are you sure you weren't really up by the brook?"

James was relieved when all the girls shook their heads. "No, miss."

"Like I say, there's been a serious incident. So I'm going to have to ask all of you for your names and addresses and we might be in touch later."

Hannah was at the end of the line and she faithfully read her name and address to the policewoman. James was next.

"James Robert Holmes. Flat sixteen, block six, Palm Hill."

The policewoman smiled. "And your postcode?"

James fumbled. "E, something?"

The policewoman clearly thought she'd caught James out.

"Don't you know your own postcode? How long have you lived here?"

"We just moved in this morning."

"Did you indeed," the policewoman said suspiciously.

"It's true," Max said. "He's four doors down from me. I can vouch for him."

But she didn't sound convinced. "What's your home phone number?"

"We're not hooked up yet," James said.

"Well, what about your parents? Do they have mobiles so that I can ring up and speak to one of them?"

"My parents are both dead," James explained. "My older brother looks after me, but he'll be out."

"So you moved in today to live with your *brother*, who just *happens* to be out," the policewoman said incredulously. "How old is this brother?"

"He's seventeen, technically I'm still in foster care, but I'm allowed to live with Dave. . . ."

The policewoman clearly thought James's story was bull. She moved her torch beam upwards and shone it in James's face. It took a second for a look of revelation to blossom.

"What's that under your chin?"

"Where?" James asked.

James touched his chin with his index finger and felt the tip drag through something that could only be a drop of blood.

"And how did that get there?"

James realized he was in trouble, but Hannah nailed down the coffin.

"Miss, it's not James's fault," she yelled. "It wasn't an ambush. They started on *us*."

"Yeah," Georgia added. "They were miles bigger than him."

"OK, one at a time," the policewoman shouted, hardly able to contain her grin. She looked over her shoulder at the other officer. "Michael, get James here in handcuffs and call another car. We'll have to take all of this lot in for questioning."

"He's a bit on the small side," Patel observed.

James was angry at getting himself caught. He should have remembered something as obvious as his postcode. And now he thought about it, Hannah had said hers thirty seconds earlier and it was probably identical.

"Get over here," Patel said wearily as he pulled a set of handcuffs off his belt. "And you'd better not start mouthing me. I'm not in the mood."

James stepped forward and held out his wrists. Patel snapped on the cuffs and read James his rights in a monotone as they walked to a police car parked on the double yellow lines outside the gate.

"You do not have to answer any questions, but anything you do say will be taken down and used in evidence. . . ."

James had been arrested before and knew the words off by heart, but this particular reading had a surprise ending. As he ducked down to get in the back of the car, Patel grabbed James's head and thumped it hard against the edge of the car roof.

James was seeing stars as he collapsed across the rear seat.

"We'll sort you out," Patel snarled as he slammed the car door. "You've got no idea how sick I get of nicking dumb little brats like you."

Cops

James woke up on a bare vinyl mattress and shuffled across to the cell toilet in his socked feet. While he peed, his fingers explored the small cut on the side of his head where Sergeant Patel had assaulted him.

After zipping up, James stepped over to the door of the graffiti-etched cell and rang the buzzer. It took a minute for the custody officer to open the flap.

"Can you flush my toilet?" James asked.

The beanpole officer, with stained teeth and scruffy red hair, was in a jovial mood. "Are you up for some breakfast, sonny?"

James felt queasy and wasn't sure if eating would help or hinder the situation. "What have you got?"

"It's a full English. with bacon or sausage, eggs any style, and granary toast with a selection of fresh fruit preserves and whipped butter."

James was well off-form at this time of the morning. It took him longer than it should have to realize he was having his leg pulled.

"I am a bit hungry, I suppose."

"Well, it comes wrapped in cellophane and I'm told it's highly nutritious. Do you want it or not?"

James shrugged. "I guess."

The cop came back and slotted a gray plastic tray through the flap, followed by a plastic mug filled with milky tea.

"Do you know what's going on?" James asked. "I've been stuck down here all night."

"You're underage, so we can't question you, release you, or do anything else until your parent or guardian turns up," the custody officer explained.

James had named Zara as his social worker and given the police a local phone number that would automatically reroute to the twenty-four-hour situation room on campus. Having ascertained that James wasn't in any danger, it looked like nobody on campus was in any great rush to get out of bed in the early hours of Sunday morning and drive to his rescue.

James ate the cereal and nibbled at the rubbery waffle-type thingy with cubes of pink and orange fruit in the middle. He couldn't help wondering what Lauren would say when she found out he'd got into another fight. He'd planned to stay out of trouble, but that's not always easy when you're on a mission.

There was the tantalizing sound of a key in the cell door as he drained his mug.

"Looks like you're headin' home," the custody sergeant said as the door swung open.

He flung a box containing James's belongings onto the bed.

"Aren't they gonna question me or nothing?" James asked as he slid his feet into his trainers and began shoving his keys, mobile, and stuff back into his pockets.

"I believe they questioned quite a few of your

pals," the sergeant explained. "But that lot like settling their own scores. The two lads in the hospital refused to give the police any statement, which leaves you in the clear."

"Thank God for that," James said.

"Don't get *too* full of yourself," the cop warned as he led James out of the cell towards the reception area. "I wouldn't want to be in your shoes if they catch up with you."

John Jones had landed the task of driving down from CHERUB campus at five on a Sunday morning. John was a dome-headed ex-police, ex-MI5 agent, who'd joined CHERUB as a mission controller less than a year earlier. He'd worked with James on his two biggest missions.

John showed the custody sergeant a fake ID that said "London Borough of Tower Hamlets, Social Services."

"How come *you're* here?" James asked as they walked out of the police station into a drizzly Sunday morning.

"Zara's got two kids," John explained. "She sees little enough of them without having to make fake IDs and drive to London in the middle of the night. Besides, she's a senior mission controller and this job is strictly small-time."

"Are you taking over as mission controller now?" James asked as they started walking towards the car.

John nodded. "For my sins."

"Sorry I got you out of bed in the middle of the night."

"I expect I'll live," John replied. "I've been working undercover since before you were born, James.

It's not the first night's sleep I've missed and I'd have a few quid on it not being the last."

John had driven down in one of the CHERUB pool cars, a black Vauxhall Omega. James spotted Millie Kentner hunched over in the back as he got in the front passenger seat.

"Morning," James said.

Millie looked at John. "Can we shift out of here pronto, before someone from inside the station recognises me?"

The police station was only a few minutes' drive from Palm Hill. John pulled up in a side street, and the three of them had a conversation while the rain pelted the roof of the car.

"What happened, James?" Millie asked tersely.

James looked back over his shoulder, surprised at her tone. "Two nutters tried to start on us. I did what I could to keep them happy, but they wanted trouble and they got it."

Millie tutted. "I have enough problems with the lunatics around here without you trying to set off World War Three between Palm Hill and the Grosvenor Estate."

"I didn't start *anything*," James said irritably. "You were a cherub, you know how it works. You don't get to make friends with villains by sitting indoors and being a good little boy."

"Point taken," Millie nodded. "But *please* try to remember that you're here to help me get rid of Tarasov and make Palm Hill a *better* place to live."

James huffed. "And who was that Asian guy who arrested me?"

"Michael Patel," Millie said. "What about him?"

"He's a psycho, that's what," James answered. "He smacked my head against the car as I was getting in. My head's killing me."

Millie looked incredulous. "That must have been accidental."

"Look at it," James said, peeling away the hair around his bruise.

John was concerned. "That's quite a knock. Maybe you should get it checked out."

"I've survived worse," James said.

"Well, if you're sure," John said, before turning to look at Millie. "Does Patel have any history of assaulting suspects?"

"He certainly does *not*," Millie gasped. "Mike is my deputy in the community unit. He's our only Asian officer. There's a huge Asian community around here and the inroads he's made amongst them since he came here four years ago have been absolutely fantastic."

James couldn't believe what he was hearing. "I don't care what he's done for the Asian community," he shouted. "What about the git trying to bust my head open?"

"James, I know Michael Patel. It *was* an accident."

James shook his head furiously. "Millie, you might have been a cherub twenty years ago, but you're all cop now: sticking up for your own kind. Why would I lie to you, you stupid cow?"

"*Whoah*," Millie said, shocked. "You'd better watch that mouth, young man."

"James," John interrupted stiffly. "Don't speak to her like that."

"Typical," James said. "Another cop, takes her side as well."

"I'm not taking sides," John shouted, with an uncharacteristic ferocity that made Millie and James shrivel into their seats. "This mission will go absolutely nowhere if we can't work together.

"James, I know it can be difficult, but try to bear in mind what Millie said and steer clear of trouble. Millie, when you work with CHERUB, you have to respect what the young agents tell you. Otherwise there's no point using them."

"Mike is probably the best officer on my community policing unit," she answered tersely.

"Then I'm sure you won't mind having a little dig into his personnel file and seeing if any similar allegations have been made in the past."

Millie raised up her hands. "Fine, if that's what it takes to settle this. But I know my officers. I'm the godmother of Michael's daughter, for crying out loud."

John smiled. "Maybe he was having a bad night. Police work can be extremely stressful."

"So what now?" James asked, feeling better now he knew John was at least partly on his side.

"Do you know the way home from here?" John asked.

"More or less," James nodded.

"OK, then I suggest you walk it. Everything carries on as planned—trying to work your way in with the Tarasovs. I'll drive Millie home, then I'll head back to campus."

Millie looked at James as he climbed out of the

car. She smiled like she was anxious to make up, but he wasn't having it.

"I'll call you boys on your mobiles this evening," Millie said. "We can have a mini briefing to see how you and Dave are getting on."

"Superb," James said sourly as he slammed the car door and set off into the drizzle.

"Dave, you home?" James shouted as he stepped into the hallway. He could hear a radio in the kitchen. "That Millie's a right—"

James was set to go off on a rant about Millie not believing him, but as he rounded the corner into the kitchen he was confronted by Sonya Tarasov. She had wet hair and wore Dave's white toweling robe.

"You must be James," Sonya grinned.

"Um . . . yeah," James said awkwardly. "Where's Dave?"

"In the shower. He'll be out in a minute. Would you like tea or coffee?"

James sat down at the table while Sonya made him a cup of tea. "So, you spent the night," James said as Sonya planted a mug in front of him.

"Uh-huh," Sonya said, smiling coyly. "I hear you got busted with my little brother, Max."

James nodded. "A whole bunch of kids got taken in for questioning."

Dave rounded the corner, buttoning up his jeans.

"Morning, jailbird," Dave grinned as he grabbed Sonya and made a big show of kissing her on the neck.

James was embarrassed by the display of affection and Dave knew it.

"What's the matter, bro?" Dave asked as he broke away from Sonya and clicked on the kettle. "So we spent the night together? We're both over sixteen, there's nothing illegal about it."

James stared into his mug and wrung his hands uncomfortably. Partly James was jealous because he was a virgin, but mostly it just felt really weird being in a room with two people who'd spent the night having sex. It reminded him of the feeling you get when you pull a hair off your tongue and realize it's not one of your own.

"I'm gonna clean up," James said, pushing his chair back as he stood up. "I stink like that police cell."

The doorbell rang as James stepped out into the hallway. He recognized Max Tarasov through the frosted glass.

"Hey," James said. "How'd you and Liza get on with the cops?"

"They took all of us in one at a time and asked about what happened and that. We all said it was totally the other lot who started it."

"That lunatic Patel smacked my head against the car roof."

Max nodded. "He's a nutter, that bloke. I've seen him on TV being interviewed and he's Mr. Smooth, but I've heard *so* many stories about him."

"Like what?" James asked.

Max shrugged. "Oh, you know, giving kids slaps. Nothing massive, but he's got a reputation for being a bit handy."

"So'd you get in trouble with your dad?" James asked.

"It wasn't that bad," Max said. "He was pissed off having to leave the pub to come and collect us, but he's had a few run-ins with the Grosvenor kids and he hates their guts."

"How come?"

"There used to be this bunch of lads from over there who kept coming down the High Street and raising hell. They busted the pub windows a few times and my dad reckons some of them broke into the car lot and nicked his cash box. Anyways, I came round 'cos some of us lads usually have a kick-about on Sunday morning. It looks like the weather's settling down. Are you up for it?"

"Right now?" James asked. "Only, I was gonna have a shower. It makes my skin crawl thinking about all the drunks and dossers who slept in that police cell before I did."

"No worries. You know where the pitches are. Just meet us down there when you're ready."

James nodded. "But I'm warning you, I'm not exactly God's gift to football."

"I'll make sure you're on the other team then," Max grinned. "See you in a mo."

James pushed closed the front door. As he passed by the kitchen, he noticed Sonya clambering out of the cupboard under the sink.

"What the hell are you two up to?" James laughed.

"I thought you might ask Max inside," Sonya explained. "I had to hide."

"Dave told me everything was legal and above board," James grinned.

"That's just the law," Sonya explained. "My dad is an entirely different matter."

"Max wouldn't grass you up though, would he?"

Sonya shrugged. "Probably not, but I wouldn't put blackmail or extortion past the little swine."

Lunch

James didn't acquit himself too badly on the football pitch and even curled in a fluky goal from the halfway line. When the six lads got knackered, three of them headed off to the shop to buy drinks, leaving James and Max and a black kid called Charlie. They sat on the remnants of a vandalized wooden bench and had the conversation thirteen-year-old boys always have: football, fit girls, and funny stuff that had happened to them, or to other kids.

Charlie was the kind of guy whose story had to top everyone else's, and James suspected he was making stuff up, or at least exaggerating. Not that he minded. Anything that kept the conversation away from his fictional background was good. Even the most detailed back story requires you to fill in some details on the fly, and the more you invent, the easier it is to forget something you've said and contradict yourself later on.

When it got to lunchtime, Max invited James and Charlie for Sunday lunch.

"Won't your old lady mind?" James asked.

"My mum's a nutter," Max explained. "She *loves* cooking."

The layout of the Tarasovs' flat was identical to where James and Dave lived, except there was a narrow staircase off the hallway that led to extra rooms on the next floor up.

Max led the chain of boys into the kitchen. "I've got two extra for lunch, OK, Mum?"

James could hardly believe the amount of stuff crammed into the steaming hot kitchen. There were shelves lined with pickle jars and catering-sized tins. Pots and pans hung from a rack over the dining table and sacks of vegetables were piled beneath. Sacha Tarasov had pale skin, rounded features, and a Garfield apron knotted around an ample waist.

"I think your brother is upstairs with Leon," Sacha said, giving James a friendly grin. She fixed her eyes on Max and used the more severe voice that parents reserve for their own offspring. "Get these boys something to drink, then fetch me down a frozen stew. And shoes off in the house."

Max poured three glasses of Coke, which the boys carried upstairs after ditching their trainers in the hallway. The patterned wallpaper, zigzag carpets, and exuberant paintings of wild animals on the staircase seemed to be locked in a battle to see who was the gaudiest. There were piles of folded laundry and boxed electrical goods stacked against the walls.

Although everything was tacky, James appreciated the overall effect. It was the kind of home that's full of people, smells, and noise—where everything is a little shabby and you immediately feel comfortable.

"Here's why I say my mum's a nutter." Max

grinned as he led James and Charlie into a box room at the top of the staircase.

It was Leon Tarasov's study. There was a desk mounded in paperwork and a faux-antique swivel chair, but it also contained the largest chest freezer James had seen outside of a frozen-food store. Max raised the lid, revealing half lambs, pork loins, and a mass of homemade meals in plastic tubs. Each tub was labeled by hand in Russian script, and James was pleasantly surprised to find that the limited understanding of the language he'd picked up at CHERUB enabled him to read most of them.

"You could eat for a year out of this lot," Charlie gasped. "All we've got in the freezer round my house are chicken nuggets and ice cream."

"At least you've got a freezer," James said.

"I tell you what, James," Max said. "If you and your brother ever get hungry, just ask my mum. She loves giving food away, as long as you wash up the dish before you bring it back."

Max crunched the solid lumps of food around until he found a circular Pyrex dish filled with frozen beef stew.

"You two might as well go through to the living room," Max said. "I'll take this down to my mum."

The Tarasovs all slept in the flat next door, so they'd knocked two of the upstairs bedrooms together to make a giant living room. James's socks got swallowed in shaggy turquoise carpet as he stepped in.

Dave was in one corner, sitting on the arm of a sofa alongside eighteen-year-old Pete. Sonya sat on the opposite side of the room pretending not to know

Dave, while Liza curled up on a rug in front of the TV. Liza looked happy to see Charlie, who sat cross-legged on the floor next to her like a regular member of the family.

"You must be James," Leon Tarasov said, reaching out his hairy hand. His accent was east London, with barely a hint of his Russian heritage.

Leon was a huge fat man, with a bald head and a line in chunky gold jewelry. James had to step around the side of Leon's fully reclined armchair and reach over his giant belly to shake hands.

Leon burrowed into his shirt pocket and stripped out a twenty-pound note. "Here."

"What's that for?" James grinned.

"Bounty," Leon said. "A tenner for every Grosvenor Estate yobbo you lay out. If I had my way, I'd go over there with some baseball bats and sort out the bastard lot of 'em."

"*Jesus,* Dad," Sonya said angrily. "You're a total fascist."

Leon shot an evil glance back at his daughter. "Shouldn't you be out in a dinghy, saving whales with all the other hippies?"

He pressed a button on his armchair, making his giant body whir electronically into an upright position.

"Pete and Leon have been absolute stars, James," Dave said enthusiastically. "I couldn't get my car started this morning, so Pete came down to take a look at it. Leon says he knows a scrap dealer who can get me a good deal on a compressor for the air-con and a couple of other bits I need to get the car sorted."

"I thought we were broke," James said. "I mean, we need the money we've got left for food and furniture."

"Don't worry about it," Leon said. "I've known this dealer for years. He'll charge me pennies. So I'll get the parts and you can use my lot to fix up the car. In return, Dave's gonna run me some errands. Between the car lot and the two pubs, I can always use a dogsbody for a few hours here and there. You can work off your tab at a fiver an hour."

Dave nodded. "I really appreciate that, Mr. Tarasov. And I'll work hard, I swear."

"How do you manage to insure that car?" Leon asked. "Seventeen-year-old driving around in a two-liter Mondeo. That must have set you back a few bob."

Dave acted uneasy. "I got insurance quotes, but it was over a grand. There's no way I could ever pay that much."

Leon shook his head. "You want to be careful. When some middle-class kid gets pulled up, he gets a fine. Magistrate sees some peasant like you or me driving without insurance, they'll throw the book at you. Especially if you've got previous."

"Have you got previous, Dave?" Pete asked.

"I've been in a few scrapes," Dave said, acting ashamed.

CHERUB had carefully tuned every detail of James and Dave's background stories to maximize their chances of getting close to Leon Tarasov. The broken-down car enabled Dave to approach him for advice on getting it repaired, while the combination of criminal records and shortage of money made

James and Dave the kind of youngsters that experienced crooks like Tarasov enjoyed taking advantage of.

"I got nicked driving a stolen car a couple of years back," Dave explained. "I thought I was gonna get sent down, but they put me in this special program where you learn to fix cars and stuff."

James had to smother a grin as he caught the glimmer of opportunity in Leon's eye. It was spooky how a well-planned CHERUB operation could manipulate someone.

"You know, David," Leon said, interlocking his sausage-shaped fingers and grinning. "My late brother and I arrived in this country thirty years back. All we owned were rubber boots and overalls spattered in fish guts. So when I see kids like you and James, my heart goes out. I know what it feels like and I'm gonna see what I can do to help you out."

Dave and James both smiled. "Thanks, Mr. Tarasov," Dave said. "We appreciate it."

James was back home, watching TV with his feet on the coffee table. Five hours after lunch he still felt bloated from Sacha's cooking; it was no wonder the Tarasovs were all on the porky side. Dave came in holding a microwave curry with Bombay potatoes.

"How can you eat after that lunch we had?"

Dave demonstrated the technique as he sat down next to James. "Stick in fork, remove from dish, insert in mouth. Want a chunk?"

Dave held a fork-load of curried chicken under James's nose. He batted Dave's arm away.

"*Don't*," he said angrily. "If your stinking curry makes me spew up, I'll be turning my head in your direction."

"You've got nobody to blame but yourself," Dave said. "You ate that massive bowl of stew, then pork chops, roasties, piles of veg, and three chunks of cake. You ate as much as Leon and he must weigh a hundred and twenty kilos."

James contemplated Sacha's frosted carrot cake. He couldn't reconcile how amazing it had been when he'd eaten it, with how ill it now made him feel just thinking about it.

"Do you still feel sick?" Dave grinned as he swallowed a mouthful of Bombay potato. "What would you least like to eat right now? Runny eggs? How about nice sloppy trifle? Or a beef burger, all raw in the middle so you feel the blood trickle out when you bite into it?"

"Dave, you're not funny," James tutted. "Can't you shut up and let me watch this?"

Dave cracked up. "What, you're seriously watching *Songs of Praise?* I never had you down as the religious type."

James shrugged. "I was watching this show about hippos. I wanted to change channel when it ended, but I think the remote went down between the cushions and I'm too stuffed to move."

This made Dave laugh harder and James couldn't help seeing the funny side of his own predicament.

"Stop taking the piss," he grinned, rubbing his belly. "I'm in agony here."

"Tell you what," Dave said, turning serious for a

moment. "I think there's indigestion medicine in that green first-aid box Zara gave us. I put it on the shelf in the bathroom."

"Oh, cool," James said, pulling himself up off the sofa. "A swig of that should do the trick."

Bright

The medicine helped and James felt OK by half-ten, when he went to bed. He slept through until the doorbell rang at eight a.m., Monday morning. He dashed out into the hallway and found Dave opening the door to Leon Tarasov.

"Hi, Mr. Tarasov," Dave said, dressed in his boxers and sounding surprised.

"I'm not your teacher, Dave. Call me Leon."

"I thought I was coming to see you at the car lot," Dave said.

"I've got a little proposition," Leon said. "Easy work. Mind if I come in?"

Dave gave the impression of not being awake. "Um, I guess . . . sure, sure."

Dave led Leon through to the living room. Leon's giant gut lumbering down the hallway had an outlandish quality that reminded James of a geography lesson where he'd watched a video of a supertanker passing through the Panama canal. Leon collapsed on to the tiny sofa as James stepped through the doorway behind Dave.

"You two have both been in trouble with the law," Leon began. "So you should understand the old saying: loose lips sink ships."

Dave nodded. "I'm no grass."

"It's not so much grassing with you young lads, it's all this," Leon said, making his hands talk to each other. "Mouth. Word gets around, you understand?"

"Loose lips sink ships," Dave smiled as James nodded.

"I know the only money you boys have coming in is social security. I was thinking in bed last night and I realized I could put something your way that'll really kick start your finances. Maybe even to the tune of a couple of grand over the next month or so. You interested?"

James and Dave made a point of grinning at one another, like you'd expect from a couple of dirt-poor kids who'd just had four figures dangled under their noses.

"Course we're interested," Dave beamed.

"Good," Leon said. "The scheme obviously isn't legit, but it *is* solid. I know dudes who work for some of the biggest domestic cleaning agencies going. The clients are mostly well-off folks who can't be bothered with the hassle of employing a cleaning lady. Instead, they ring up Big Kleen, The Brite House, Supa-Maid, or whoever. Missus mop turns up and cleans when they're out at work, and the closest they ever get to scraping the mold out of their own shower basin is when they pay their credit card bill.

"Now here's the beautiful part: At this time of the year, most of these rich turds take a nice long holiday and cancel the cleaning service. That leaves my contacts holding sets of their house keys and burglar alarm codes for two or three weeks, while their expensive motors sit in the garage."

"Let me guess." Dave grinned. "The cars aren't waiting for them when they get home."

"Bingo." Leon smiled, making a popping sound with his tongue. "We're only interested in nearly new cars that can be shipped to eastern Europe, or stripped down for parts. Once I get the house keys and alarm codes, I send in a scout who has all the time in the world to search the house and find the car keys. The following day, someone else breaks in and sets off the burglar alarm. It hardly matters, because my scout will have found the car keys and left them in the driver's door. You'll be away before the cops get a sniff."

"Why can't we use the house keys when we rob the joint?" James asked.

Dave gave James a look of contempt. "Because then it's *obviously* an inside job."

"Oh," James said, realizing he was being slow. "Gotcha."

"Don't the police ever suspect the cleaning agency?" Dave asked.

"It could happen," Leon said. "If you robbed ten cars in a short space of time and they all had links to one company, the police might tag on, but we spread it around—different areas, different companies— and keep the number of thefts sensible.

"So anyway, with summer holiday season coming up, I could use an extra set of hands to do some of the actual breaking in and driving away."

"How much is in it for us?" Dave asked.

"Two-fifty a pop," Leon said.

"Each?" James asked.

"One man can handle the job," Leon said. "You can both go if you want, but I'm not paying any extra."

Dave knew this was a big step into Leon's criminal world, but it might seem suspicious if he accepted without seeming apprehensive.

"The thing is, Leon, I've got previous. If I get nicked in another stolen car, I'm looking at two years' juvenile detention."

"Look." Leon shrugged. "No hard feelings if this isn't for you. I'm just making you guys an offer. Five or six jobs over the next month will earn you enough to get that car running and put this grotty flat into some sort of shape."

"Two-fifty's not a lot," Dave said. "I mean, you're talking about stealing twenty or thirty grand's worth of car."

"I got expenses," Leon said. "The scout, the cleaning agency. And the man who's gonna ship the cars overseas doesn't exactly get his numbers out of Glass's secondhand price guide. I'm doing well if I can get five grand for a Mercedes that just came out of the showroom at thirty."

"I appreciate the offer, Leon," Dave said. "But risking two years of my life must be worth nearer to four hundred."

"The summer rush is on and I've got more cars than thieves right now." Leon smiled. "So I'll stretch to three hundred, but that's your lot."

"Three-two-five," Dave said.

Leon rocked his head uncertainly before his hand crept out towards Dave's.

"One other thing," Leon added as they shook on the deal. "I've kept the cops off my back all these years by being careful. So now this is set up, we don't ever talk about it again, OK? My people will call you. The money will come through your letterbox. If you ask me something about this, I'm not gonna be happy and all you'll get for your trouble is a blank look."

"What if there's a hitch, like if I don't get paid or something?" Dave asked.

"You'll have a number to call," Leon said as he began hauling himself off the sofa. He turned to look at James. "I don't mix my family up in the naughty stuff. So if you're hanging out with Max or Liza, you keep this under your hat. OK?"

"No worries," James nodded, slumping on the sofa as the incredible bulk headed for the front door.

James sprawled out and allowed himself to grin at the rapid progress of the mission, then shot half a meter in the air as a finger touched his shoulder.

"Is my dad gone?" Sonya Tarasov whispered.

"Jesus," James gasped as he spun around to look at the sixteen-year-old sitting on the carpet behind the sofa. "You scared the arse off me. Were you behind there the whole time?"

He broke into a grin as the shock wore off and he realized Sonya was naked.

Sonya wrapped her arms around her chest. "Stop staring, you little pervert," she said furiously.

"I've seen better," James giggled.

"James, behave," Dave said stiffly as he walked

into the room. He tossed his robe at Sonya. "I brought your dad in here because I thought you were still in the kitchen."

"And crawl under that sink again?" Sonya said fiercely. "My back still hurts from yesterday."

"What were you two doing in the kitchen with no clothes on?" James grimaced. "I swear to God, I'm never eating off *that* table again."

Sonya quickly slid into the robe and knotted the cord around her waist as she straddled the sofa.

"Dave I'm begging you, please don't start doing my dad's dirty work."

Dave shrugged as he pulled on his T-shirt. "He's offering me a leg up, Sonya. Look at this dump we're living in. I need money to do it up and that'll take five hundred years from what I'd earn working in some supermarket or fast-food joint."

"But what if you get caught? You'll go down for sure and probably take James with you, or he'll have to go back into foster care."

"Then I won't get caught," Dave said.

He moved in to calm Sonya down with a kiss, but she wouldn't buy it.

"My dad shouldn't be dragging you into this," Sonya stormed. "He doesn't even need to do it anymore. He's got two pubs that are doing nicely and the car dealing on top. He's using you, Dave. If he really wanted to help, he could offer you a straight job, or find someone else that could."

"Sonya, I've known you for *two* days," Dave said. "I really like you, but you can't run my life."

"Fine, ignore me." Sonya shrugged. "But I'll warn

you now: My dad only looks after number one and I won't be visiting you behind bars."

"Look, Sonya," Dave said. "I know you're trying to look out for me, but I *need* this money."

"My dad's like Teflon: Nothing ever sticks to him. You know last year? He made an absolute killing, the biggest score of his whole life. My poor mum worried herself sick that the police would turn up the heat, but Dad never even got his collar felt."

"What did he do?" James enquired innocently.

"He never tell us, but everyone reckons he got a cut of some massive robbery," Sonya said. Her face changed to a look of shock as she noticed the clock on the wall. "Oh *hell*. It's half-eight and I'm not even dressed. I'm gonna be so late for school."

Sums

While Dave went to the scrap yard with Pete Tarasov, James bummed around the flat. There was no point enrolling in one of the local schools, because it was only two days until the beginning of summer holidays.

There was nothing James could do for the mission while Max, Liza, and all the other local kids were at school. Unfortunately, Zara had picked up on this and asked a couple of James's teachers to set him work.

After Dave went out, James started playing FIFA 2005 on his PlayStation. He had saved a game, with Arsenal five points clear at the top of the Premiership, and he extended it to eight by stuffing Chelsea. James knew he ought to start his schoolwork, but the goals kept going in and it was midday by the time he'd swept aside Liverpool, Charlton, and Aston Villa. He finally lost his touch in a disappointing game against Tottenham, with the computer awarding itself a penalty in extra time for a 2–2 draw.

"Penalty my arse," James screamed as he kicked the coffee table, lobbed the controller, and furiously switched off his console. "Stupid poxy game . . . programmed by a Spurs fan, or some other kind of moron."

When he'd calmed down, James realized he was hungry. He spread Nutella on toast and garnished each slice with squirty cream. It was nearly one p.m. by the time he hit the books.

James lay on his bed and wondered how with all the great battles, civilizations, and catastrophes from history to choose from, his teacher had decided to set a 1,500-word report, with a minimum of three illustrations, on the achingly uninteresting subject of water sanitation during the Victorian era. James loathed anything that involved writing long essays, especially as Mr. Brennan had a habit of complaining about his left-handed scrawl and making him rewrite entire essays from scratch.

James found himself drawn towards the one subject he was good at. Most kids don't even start GCSE maths until they're fourteen, but James had passed with an A grade the previous November and was well into his studies for Advanced level. He settled on his bed with a clipboard and a fat textbook on his lap, confidently penciling his way through the test at the end of *Unit 14F: The trapezium rule for approximate integration*.

Being brilliant at maths wasn't the kind of thing that set the girls swooning. But while James played it down, he was secretly proud. It was good having one subject where he got all As and his teacher smiled when they passed in the corridor, instead of dragging him aside and making demands for late homework like the others.

James had started *Unit 14G* and was really into it when the doorbell rang. He walked out of his room and was surprised to see a policewoman's uniform through the frosted glass.

"Hello," Millie smiled as James opened the door. "So you *are* here. I tried your mobile."

James reached towards the tracksuit top hooked up by the door and grabbed his phone from the pocket. "I bet it's gone flat. I'm the world's crappiest person at remembering to charge up my mobile."

Millie invited herself in. "I thought it would be OK to drop by, just this once," she said as she closed the door. "If any of the locals ask why I was here, just say I was following up on your arrest."

James thought Millie looked good, even in sensible shoes and with her body armor squashing everything out of shape. She unzipped a small backpack as she sat on the sofa and pulled out a paper bag.

"I got us some nice sandwiches and cakes," Millie explained. "Have you eaten?"

"Only some toast," James said, opening up the bag and studying the selection of goodies. "OK if I take the smoked salmon sandwich? The other one's got mayo on and I can't stomach it."

Millie broke into an awkward smile. "Have whatever you want. I'll mostly be eating humble pie."

"Eh?"

"Humble pie," Millie repeated as she reached into her backpack and pulled out a few sheets of photocopied paper. Each sheet was a copy of a form: "289B—Official Notification to an Officer of a

Misconduct Investigation," with Michael Patel's name written in the top corner.

"If someone makes a complaint about a police officer, a copy of this form gets sent to the officer and another one goes on to their permanent file. Every frontline officer picks up a few complaints. I've been investigated twice myself; both times it was someone I'd nicked trying to get revenge for making a false allegation."

James counted the sheets of paper. "There are eight complaints here."

Millie nodded. "That's more than average, but none of them were upheld and ethnic minority officers tend to collect more than whites."

James nodded. "Racists?"

"Exactly, James. But the thing is, look at the two forms at the back that I've marked with the highlighter pen. Read box seven."

James separated the forms. "Box seven—Primary accusations," he read aloud. "Assault of a minor while in charge of the custody suite at Holloway police station." He looked at the complaint on the other form. "That a fifteen-year-old girl was assaulted by the officer while being put into a vehicle. Victim later suffered a concussion and cut to the head that required three stitches."

"Neither accusation was upheld because there was no strong evidence, making it a case of Michael's word against the accuser. Both complaints are more than five years old, but still . . . ," Millie said.

James took a bite out of his sandwich. "That second one sounds exactly like what he did to me."

"I know," Millie said weakly. "When I saw it, my jaw dropped. I just felt *completely* rotten. I all but called you a liar in front of your mission controller, James. I'm really, really, sorry."

"Everyone makes mistakes," James shrugged. "Ask that eleven-year-old I thumped."

"And your other comment, about me sticking up for Mike because he's a cop," Millie continued. "You have no idea how true that is. Nobody likes the police. Crooks don't like us for obvious reasons, and the only time we ever deal with normal people is in high-stress situations—like when they crash their cars, or they've been burgled and they can't understand why we haven't dispatched the entire serious crime squad to recover their stolen TV. Everyone's always having a go at us, and you get into a state of mind where you stick up for your colleagues, because they're the only people who'll ever stick up for you."

"By the time I've stuffed this sandwich and the chocolate cake, I probably won't even remember."

"That's sweet of you to say, James," Millie grinned. "I haven't told John yet and I'm not exactly looking forward to admitting that I've made a fool of myself. I'll let you keep those forms to show Dave when he gets home, but make sure you don't leave them lying around for anyone else to see."

"Do you want a cup of tea?" James asked.

Millie glanced at her watch as she hurriedly bit an unladylike chunk out of her sandwich. "Better not, I've got a meeting at the station in half an hour. But there is one other thing I brought to show you."

Millie pulled another sheet out of the bag. "Dave

called met his morning and told me what Sonya said about her dad getting the money from a robbery. This is a list of the major unsolved robberies that took place between March and July of last year. There are eight-six altogether, but we estimate Leon needed to make over two hundred thousand pounds to pay off his debts and buy the second pub. That rules out all but four cases."

"So, is Leon a likely suspect in any of them?"

Millie shook her head. "We don't think so. In three of the four big robberies the serious crime squad has a good idea who the suspects are, but don't yet have enough evidence to make arrests. The final robbery was of a security truck taking three million in old banknotes to the Bank of England to be destroyed. But it was very high-tech and almost certainly an inside job."

"That sounds a bit beyond Leon Tarasov," James said.

"Certainly does," Millie nodded. "There's been lots of talk about a robbery amongst the local villains, but if you want my hunch, it's all a smokescreen put out by Leon. There's only one way I can see a lowlife like Tarasov making an easy two hundred grand."

James finished Millie's sentence. "Drug dealing."

"You just read my mind, James."

When he went back to work, James realized it would be best to make at least a start on his Victorian sanitation essay. He began by skimming through the relevant chapter of his textbook, then he poised his pen at the top of his exercise pad and wrote his full name and the essay title, which accounted for eleven words.

James started off his first paragraph:

> *During Victorian times there was loads of sewage running everywhere in the streets of London. People were getting sick with diseases we ~~donut~~ do not hardly have anymore like malaria, plague, bowleg, and typhoid which were rampant. As time went by it got better because the Victorians built sewers and made the water ~~more~~ cleaner.*

James counted sixty-five words, including his name and the ones he'd crossed through. He scribbled out plague and changed it to *the black death* because that made two extra words. With one thousand four hundred and thirty-three words to go, James got that awful feeling that he'd already written everything he knew about Victorian sanitation.

He realized that his best option was to steal something off the Internet, and he was going under his bed to grab his laptop when the doorbell rang.

It was Hannah, dressed in white tights, long gray skirt, a pale green blouse, and striped tie.

"Let me in *fast*," Hannah squealed, barging past James and shutting the door.

"What's the panic in aid of?" James asked.

Hannah didn't answer. "You don't have a girlfriend do you, James?"

James shook his head. "What's going—"

Before he finished, Hannah put her arms around James, went up on tiptoes, and started snogging him.

It lasted half a minute before she pulled away.

"What's the matter? What's with the weird uniform?"

Hannah spoke hurriedly. "I hate wearing this. I got suspended from my old school after Will died and my parents made me go private. What's your mobile number?"

Hannah wrote the numbers on her wrist as James recited them.

"I couldn't stop thinking about you in class today, James. The way you defended us on Saturday was amazing. But my dad went nuts after he collected me from the police station and I'm *so* grounded. He hates me hanging out with the kids around here and I don't think I'll be able to wriggle out of it for at least a week. But I'll try calling later for a chat, OK?"

James smiled. "Yeah, sure."

Hannah gave James another kiss. "If my dad catches us, you can always break his arms."

She picked her backpack off the floor, twirled around in her pleated skirt, and headed along the balcony towards her flat.

James went for an after-school kick-about with Max and Charlie and got invited to the Tarasovs' for dinner. After his previous experience of a four-course Russian meal, James turned down all Sacha's attempts to make him eat extra helpings.

When he got home, Dave and Sonya were watching TV in the living room, though mercifully they had their clothes on for once. James went to his room and noticed there was a text on his phone:

DO YOU SUFFER FROM VERTIGO? HANNAH :)

James thought it was a weird message and replied with: NO Y?

Hannah was confined to her bedroom with her phone right beside her, so she replied instantly. DO U WANT 2 PLAY A GAME?

James was intrigued: YES

It took Hannah a while to type the next message. GO 2 2ND FLR TURN LFT. WALK 2 END OF BALCONY. TXT WEN U GET THERE.

James had no clue what Hannah was up to, but he wanted to play along. He grabbed his door keys and phone and headed out the front door and up the concrete steps to the top floor.

ME HERE, James typed as he headed along to the concrete wall at the end of the balcony. His phone rang a few seconds later.

"Hannah?" James grinned. "What's this about?"

"Can you see the emergency exit door?"

"Yeah."

"Go through the door."

"Hannah, what the *hell* is all this about?"

She giggled. "Go through the door and you might find out."

James held the phone to his ear and stepped through a graffiti-sprayed door into a concrete stairwell.

"Christ," James gasped. "It reeks of piss in here."

"Go up the ladder and through the hatch."

James looked at the aluminum ladder bolted to the wall and the hatch in the ceiling above it.

"Hannah, there's a dirty great padlock on it."

"Climb up and push hard," Hannah said. "I've

got to go, I'm nearly out of calling credit."

James heard the call go dead. He pocketed his phone and clambered up the ladder. He couldn't see a way past the padlock, but he pushed as instructed and a crack of sunlight opened up. James realized the screws had been removed from the hinges opposite the lock. He shoved the flap all the way open, then pulled his body up through the opening and out onto the flat roof of the block. The sun was right in his eyes, but he recognized Hannah's silhouette coming over the asphalt towards him.

"Jailbreak," Hannah grinned as she wrapped her arms around James. "There's another hatch in my flat. It's outside my room and my old man's downstairs watching TV."

She'd changed out of school uniform into a T-shirt and leggings.

"You look great," James said, suddenly conscious that his hair was everywhere and he smelled sweaty from playing football.

"Thanks," Hannah said. "Did you ever hear about Will?"

James felt a little awkward. "Max mentioned it. He was your cousin or something, wasn't he?"

"The silly fool," Hannah said sadly. "Come here, I'll show you."

Hannah took James's hand and led him to the edge of the roof. She stood with the toes of her Nikes poking over the edge.

"Careful," James said, stopping a shoe-length farther back. "It's a good view over central London; we must be quite high up here."

Hannah gave a half smile. "Well, it is called Palm *Hill*."

James felt stupid. "Yeah, I suppose it is."

"But you've got to look down," Hannah said. "And you've got to be right on the edge to get a buzz out of it."

James shuffled half a step forwards and looked down the face of the building. Compared to the highest part of the assault course on campus, it didn't seem that scary. At least, it didn't until James noticed the helplessly mangled banister down at ground level.

"This is the exact spot," James said.

"They haven't even had the decency to repair the railing," Hannah said, backing away from the edge and looking sad. "Every time I walk past there, I can see Will with his back broken and the blood pouring out of his ear."

"Were you two good friends?"

"I used to like playing with him when I was little," Hannah said. "But not so much later on. Will was a geek; into computers and stuff. He didn't have any mates, but he was funny and really, really clever. Towards the end he started getting wasted all the time. I think he was depressed."

James wasn't sure what to say. "Did he kill himself?"

"He might have done," Hannah shrugged. "But he didn't leave a note or anything. Most people reckon he just got so wasted that he forgot where he was and fell off."

"Poor guy," James said solemnly, taking a final glance down the face of the building before stepping away from the edge.

Hannah rested her head on James's shoulder and giggled nervously. "You must think I'm a right nutter asking you up here. I spent all day thinking up a way to meet you while I was grounded and . . . well, this must be your worst date ever."

James put his arm around Hannah's back. "Nah, it's cool," he smiled reassuringly. "The view up here is great. I bet all the lights in the city look beautiful when it gets dark."

James kissed Hannah briefly on the lips, but she still looked sad and James realized it wasn't the right moment for a snog. He ended up sitting on the warm asphalt with his back resting against a metal vent and Hannah's head in his lap. They talked about all kinds of stuff as the sun dropped.

James really liked Hannah. She had a laid-back air and a cruel sense of humor. He wished they'd met under different circumstances. Then he could have told her about Lauren and his mum and who he really was, instead of having to stick to his stupid back story.

Cayenne

Dave was at the dining table reading the *Daily Star*. James strolled in and waggled a mass of crumpled exercise paper under his nose.

"Ta-da," James announced. "Not a bad morning's work. One thousand, five hundred, and eleven words on Victorian sanitation. Three color diagrams and all in my best handwriting."

Dave looked up and grinned. "You really pushed the boat out with the extra eleven words, eh? What's with the big stain?"

"I knocked a can of Coke over it, but luckily the ink didn't run."

"Maybe you should rewrite that page, James. You know how fussy Mr. Brennan is. Turning in Coke stains is just begging for him to make you do a total rewrite."

James realized Dave was right, but the prospect of doing more work knocked the edge of his good mood. "Damn. . . . Oh well, I'll redo it tomorrow, it's only copying out one page. So how come you didn't get any schoolwork?"

"I'm waiting for my A-level results," Dave explained. "My handler says I still look young enough to stay on at CHERUB for another year before I start university, but I reckon I might go off traveling instead. I fancy seeing Thailand and Australia and stuff."

James grinned. "Cool."

Dave turned the page of his newspaper and gasped, "Sweet! Imagine waking up next to a set of those."

James scooted around the table to look at the picture of a topless model sitting on a soccer ball. "Legs are too skinny." He grinned. "Although I still wouldn't say no."

Dave glanced at his watch. "Oh, it's quarter to twelve. Raul wants the car delivered before eight this evening. . . ."

"Who's Raul?" James interrupted.

"Just some guy who works with Leon. He rang me through with the job. I don't want to get caught up in the rush-hour traffic, so I say we head off somewhere decent and get lunch. Then we've got to ride the tube up to Pinner."

"Is that a long way?"

Dave nodded. "Northwest London, way out on the Metropolitan line. We'll have to change trains at Baker Street and the house is a quarter of an hour from the station. Then we've got to deliver the car to some lockup near Bow Road."

"Have you told Millie all this?"

"Course," Dave said. "Once there's no risk of it compromising our mission, she'll tip off the vehicle crime unit."

"They might even be able to bust Leon that way."

"Yeah, James, *if* they find evidence strong enough

to prove a link between Leon and the stolen cars in court. But that's a very big if. You've seen how well he covers his back."

The house was farther from the tube station than the boys expected. They both had baseball hats pulled down over their faces and Dave slipped on a pair of mirrored sunglasses as they turned into Montgomery Grove. It was a posh street, lined with detached houses.

They passed a couple of kids on bikes; Dave turned to James as soon as they were out of earshot. "The burglar alarm will go off thirty seconds after we enter. So no messing about, OK?"

James tutted. "Well *d-uh*."

"The car is in the garage and the scout left the keys in the driver's door. We'll take one number plate each."

"What type of car is it?" James asked.

"Porsche Cayenne Turbo."

"Oh *cool*," James gasped. "The four-by-four one. Can I drive? I'm more into motorbikes than cars, but Cayennes to a hundred an seventy miles an hour, even though they're absolutely massive."

"Good idea," Dave said. "A thirteen-year-old driving a sixty-grand car through London in broad daylight. That's not gonna attract any attention."

James grinned. "I still think we should have done this last night."

"It's swings and roundabouts," Dave explained. "Darkness is an advantage for the actual break-in, but there's a lot less cars around at night, so it's harder to blend in with the traffic during the getaway."

James stopped walking and called back to Dave. "Number thirty-six, Dave. This is it."

The boys pulled on washing-up gloves as they walked up the driveway.

"Nervous?" Dave asked.

James smiled. "Only a bit."

"Remember, James, we're not risking our lives over Leon bloody Tarasov. If it gets heavy, we surrender."

"OK," James nodded as he walked on to the front doorstep and rang the bell.

Dave crept through to the back garden and pulled a crowbar out of his backpack. Once James had given it half a minute to make certain nobody was in, he followed Dave around the side of the house and gave him the nod.

Dave plunged the crowbar into the frame of a glass door in the conservatory. It took a couple of strong pulls on the metal lever to break the lock, followed by a shoulder charge and a kick to break the chain on the inside.

Dave held his shoulder and clenched his teeth with pain as he charged through the steamy conservatory and into the house with James on his tail. James felt a surge of anxiety as he caught the sound of a burglar alarm control panel bleeping; counting down the half-minute until the main siren erupted.

They cut through a luxuriously furnished living room, with a giant photo of a married couple and their two sons hanging over the fireplace. Dave opened a narrow door that led into a double garage. There was a black BMW parked beside the giant Porsche.

"Quality," James grinned.

Dave handed James a number plate. "Fix that on."

Raul had given Dave a set of stick-on plates. The number corresponded to another Cayenne Turbo finished in the same color, so if the police spotted the vehicle and ran a computer check, they'd come up clean.

The main alarm went off as James and Dave crouched at opposite ends of the car. James had to take one of his gloves off to get his nail under the sticky backing on the plate, but his nervous state meant he was all fingers and thumbs. His heart went into overload when he realized that Dave had stuck on the rear plate and was already climbing into the driver's seat.

"What are you pissing around at?" Dave shouted over the wailing alarm.

James finally lifted up the sticky backing and peeled it away. Dave had started the engine by the time he'd fixed it on. James sprinted around the car and jumped into the passenger seat. Dave was in a complete state.

"I can't find the plipper," Dave shouted.

"What?" James gasped.

"The button on the dashboard, or the little doo-dah box thingummy that works the garage door," Dave explained frantically.

James joined Dave in the hunt. He popped open the glove box and a torrent of maps and sunglass cases spilled into his lap.

"Oh *shit*."

"Get out and push the switch," Dave shouted,

pointing at a green button mounted on the wall.

James got as far as opening the passenger door, but as he stepped out he spotted the plipper dangling off the steering column.

"It's on the key fob, you tosser," James shouted.

Dave manically grabbed the fob and pressed the button. The double garage doors began rumbling towards the ceiling at an agonizingly slow pace. When the door was halfway up, an elderly woman dressed in a straw hat and gardening gloves ducked under and furiously opened up the door beside James.

"Get out of that car, young man," she demanded. "We don't tolerate ruffians like you around here."

She grabbed a handful of James's T-shirt. Dave had begun rolling the car forwards, but he had to hit the brake. James had a free right arm and enough strength to punch his adversary into the following week, but he couldn't bring himself to thump an old lady.

"Get rid of her," Dave shouted.

James gave the woman a shove, but she had her nails sunk into his T-shirt and the neck ripped apart as she tumbled backwards. He swiveled on his leather seat and used his legs to shove the woman out of the way before reaching across to slam his door. The garage was now fully open.

"Drive," James shouted.

"Are her legs out of the way?" Dave asked.

"Yeah."

James locked his door as Dave rolled cautiously away.

"I don't want to run her over," Dave said. "Are you sure her feet aren't under the car?"

"I told you she's clear. Get a bloody move on."

The big Porsche roared as Dave pulled it out of the garage. He spotted the old lady's husband doddering up the driveway. He wore a blazer with gold buttons and came armed with a garden fork.

"You little *buggers*," he shouted.

For one nasty moment, James thought the old man was going to dive on to the bonnet. Instead, he launched the fork at the car like a javelin. James instinctively ducked down as the metal prongs bounced against the windscreen.

As the fork clattered harmlessly into the gravel, Dave slammed on the brakes to avoid swiping a kid who was racing his bike along the street. A whole family was rushing down the driveway of the house opposite to see what had set off the alarm.

Dave checked the road and pulled out at speed. He hit sixty before braking sharply and taking a right into a busy main road.

"Them two old codgers must have a death wish," Dave shouted furiously. "If we'd been real robbers, we could have had knives, guns, or anything."

"Bonkers," James said, staring at his ripped T-shirt and shaking his head. "Stark, raving bonkers."

Dave blasted his horn, swerved around a car stopped at a crossing, ran a red light, and then piled on the accelerator as they flew past the underground station, touching seventy miles an hour.

"It'll be a miracle if we get out of here without

the cops nailing us," Dave said. "And I don't care how much Leon offers, or what it means for the mission, I'm not gonna be stealing any more cars."

"Too right," James said, anxiously looking back over his shoulder for any sign of chasing cops. "It's not worth it."

Computer

Dave's rusting Ford rolled onto Leon's used car lot just after nine a.m. The plastic signs hanging over the Portacabin declared that Tarasov Prestige Motors specialized in "the finest secondhand Jaguar and Mercedes automobiles," but the reality was a ragged mixture of retired company cars and small hatchbacks.

Not many people buy cars on a Wednesday morning, so Pete Tarasov didn't mind helping Dave fit the new compressor for the air-conditioning and some other bits that they'd picked up at the scrap yard the previous day. Both lads were underneath the jacked-up Mondeo when Leon lumbered out of the cabin holding two mugs.

"Hot tea standing on the bonnet," Leon shouted.

Dave crawled out from under the car and got a weird ground-level perspective on Leon's massive gut.

"Raul tells me yesterday was your one and only." Leon grinned.

Dave wasn't sure if he was supposed to talk in front of Pete.

"It's OK. He knows the score."

"A little granny trouble, so I'm told," Pete

smirked as he picked up his mug with greasy fingers and took a swig.

"I'm sorry, Leon," Dave said. "I've been in foster homes and institutions my whole life. I want to make this work for me and James. I don't want to run the risk of getting banged up."

"I understand," Leon nodded. "No hard feelings. It sounds like you caught a rough one and not everyone has the stomach for nicking cars."

"You know, Uncle Leon, I was thinking," Pete said.

Leon grinned. "Why is it every time you use your brain my wallet gets nervous?"

Pete smiled. "Seriously, Uncle Leon, I'm off to university in a couple of months. Dave's gonna be my perfect replacement here on the lot. He knows his way around a car. He can fix up any little niggles when the new stock comes in from the auctions. Keep 'em clean, maybe even start doing a bit of selling when it gets busy on Saturdays."

Leon shrugged. "I can think of worse ideas, but what about school?"

"I'm thinking of applying for college, but only part-time," Dave said.

"I can show Dave the ropes over the next month or so while I'm still here," Pete said.

"I'll put you on a month's trial. Six quid an hour to start and we'll work out your hours as things go along."

"Cheers, Leon," Dave grinned. "I can't believe how great you guys have been to me and James."

Dave turned and thanked Pete as Leon lumbered back to the Portacabin.

"Don't mention it," Pete grinned. "Just make sure you're not lying under one of the cars when my uncle finds out what you've been up to with his daughter."

James recovered from the disappointing draw with Tottenham, taking a couple of easy scalps in his FIFA 2005 Premiership campaign. He ended up ten points clear with five games left to play, meaning the title was almost in the bag. He paused the game when Hannah rang his mobile.

"Aren't you in school?" James asked.

"I'm too cool for school," Hannah giggled. "I'm on the bus home. It's the last day of term. I got up to the school gates and I thought, *I can't handle this.*"

"Last day of term's usually a riot," James grinned. "Running around the corridors and booting the classroom doors open. One school I was in, we had seven fire alarms in a day."

"Not at my school. I think the high point of the festivities was going to be a clarinet recital. So, do you fancy hanging out, or what?"

"Cool." James grinned. "I'm only sitting on my butt playing computer games."

"My parents will both be out at work, and your place isn't exactly, erm . . ."

"You can say it," James laughed. "I know I live in a complete dump. It'll be much better round your gaff if you're sure it's safe."

When Hannah hung up, James took off the pause and finished his match. It was only a few minutes after that when Hannah tapped her ring on the living room window. She led James to her flat, which had an upstairs, like the Tarasovs'. The interior was over the top, like somebody watched too many home makeover shows on TV, but Hannah's room was cool. She had a collection of lava lamps, a white sheepskin rug, and a life-sized Austin Powers cutout pinned on her door.

"Retro," James grinned as he inspected an old record player with its loudspeaker built into the front.

"I like finding old things in markets and that," Hannah explained. "Shops are so boring, everyone ends up with exactly the same stuff."

James knelt down and inspected a two-meter line of singles. "Where'd you get all these?"

"My dad was gonna throw a load of them out. I got some others in secondhand shops and on Ebay. So pick a tune then, let's see what kind of taste you've got."

Most of the records were in plain sleeves, so you had to slide them out and read the song titles through the hole in the middle. While James flipped through, trying to find something he recognized, Hannah swapped her school skirt and blouse for a T-shirt and cargo shorts. He wasn't bold enough to stare, but he liked what he glimpsed out of the corner of his eye.

"OK," James said, pulling a single out of its sleeve and lifting up the top of the record player. He realized he'd never put a vinyl record on before.

"It's automatic," Hannah explained.

She laid the disk on the platter and pushed the button that made the arm swing out and drop down on to the vinyl. After a few crackles and pops, the theme tune from *The Monkees* broke out.

"Oh, cool," Hannah giggled. "Good choice."

"I used to watch *The Monkees* on satellite when I was little." James grinned.

Hannah stood barefoot on her rug, jiggling to the song. "Yeah, me too." She nodded.

They sat on Hannah's bed for more than an hour, listening to old tunes and talking about stuff. Hannah acted cheerful, but James sensed sadness beneath the surface. She was a fish out of water at her posh school, she had major hassles with her dad, and her best friend now spent nearly all of her spare time looking after her nan.

They had their first proper snog, but Hannah abruptly decided that she was hungry when James tried to sneak a hand down the back of her shorts for a feel of her bum.

James trailed her into the kitchen, straightening up his crumpled clothes with a look of disappointment that was probably visible from outer space.

"Why the sour face?" Hannah asked as she laid fish fingers under a hot grill.

"Oh," James said listlessly, sitting with his elbows on the dining table and his cheeks resting in his palms. "Nothing."

Hannah turned and gave James a smile that made him realize he was falling for her. The CHERUB training manual has a whole chapter on the dangers of forming close attachments to people you meet on undercover missions, but this was still the thing about being a cherub that James had the most difficulty with. When this mission ended, the attractive fourteen-year-old girl who was making his lunch and grinning at him would be confined to a memory and he'd be back on campus facing life as a social outcast.

"Don't think about it," James mumbled.

"You what?" Hannah said.

James snapped out of deep thought and realised he'd said something he'd only meant to think. "I'm tired," James said sharply, by way of explanation. "Me and Dave were up until three a.m. on the PlayStation."

"It must be *so* cool living without parents. Mine are such dicks."

James nodded. "I guess, but we've got sod-all money. And the social worker's supposed to come in twice a week to see how I'm doing."

"You know, I was thinking about your flat. You should get some paint to brighten the place up."

"We got a furniture grant from the council. Dave's gonna drive us up to Ikea when he gets the car fixed."

"*Ikea*," Hannah tutted. "That place is the worst of the lot."

"Well, some of their stuff is dirt-cheap. And your parents might be dicks, but they've kept you in nice clothes and fancy stuff for your room that me and Dave couldn't afford."

"I know," Hannah said as she pulled out the grill and tried turning the fish fingers quickly, without burning her fingers. "I love my parents, James, of *course*. It's just, after what happened to Will they're so strict. They're scared about me hanging with the local kids and getting involved with drugs and that."

"Do Will's parents still live round here?"

Hannah shook her head. "My aunt and uncle couldn't take it. They sold up and moved down to the coast."

Hannah paused, then her face lit up. "Actually," she said, waggling her finger and grinning like mad.

"What?" James asked.

"You just gave me an idea, James. When Auntie Shelley went, she didn't want anything of Will's. She threw out all of his stuff and I thought it was sad. So I went up there and rescued some of it. My dad's got one of the lockups over the back. There's bits of furniture, like Will's desk and chair. I mean, it's all sitting there gathering dust."

Stuff

The damp smell made James's nose tingle as Hannah opened the padlocked door of her father's lockup. She flicked on a bare bulb. The space was a couple of meters wide, maybe four deep, and it needed a good tidy. There were boxes of books piled up to the ceiling, half-empty paint tins, old rolls of wallpaper, and a hover-mower resting on a tatty armchair.

"You don't even have a garden." James grinned.

Will's stuff was all in one corner: boxes of school books, an office chair, a wooden desk covered in aged Action Man and Power Rangers stickers, a bedside table, angle poise lamp, and even a dilapidated computer.

"What do you reckon?" Hannah asked as James stepped over a couple of folding chairs to get a closer look.

"Yeah," James nodded. "I could definitely use a chair and desk in my room, for homework and stuff."

"You might as well have his computer as well. They go out of date really quickly and it's just sitting there."

James had a spiffy laptop with wireless Internet back at the flat, but he realized his alter ego, James

Holmes, would probably jump at the chance of a free computer.

"It's cool." James nodded. "But what about your folks? Are they gonna mind you giving this stuff away?"

"My dad didn't want me keeping any of Will's stuff in the first place. He said it was morbid."

James gave Hannah a peck on the cheek. "This really means a lot to me." He smiled as he pulled his mobile out of his pocket. "I'll ring Dave. He's only round at the car lot and he can help us carry."

Although James and Dave were only going to be in the neighborhood for a few weeks trying to get the inside line on Leon Tarasov, they had to create the impression that they were starting a new life and setting up home in Palm Hill. After Dave helped move Will's stuff up to the flat, the boys set off for Ikea to spend some of the 325 pounds that an associate of Leon's had shoved through the letterbox while they'd been out.

The Mondeo was running smoothly and the freshly repaired air-conditioning was doing its job. Unfortunately, they ran into a black spot on the M25 and ended up crawling through three lanes of traffic at walking pace.

"So what about Millie's idea that it's something to do with drugs?" James asked.

Dave shrugged as he rolled the car a couple of lengths forward then dabbed the brake. "It's the obvious choice if you can't link Leon to a robbery. He's got no history in the drug business, but he's an opportunist. You saw how quickly his mind worked, slotting us into his little car-theft scam. If Leon saw a chance of making big money through drugs, I think he'd take it."

"Mind you, that list was only robberies in the Metropolitan Police area. For all we know, it could have been anywhere."

The traffic was making Dave moody. "Whatever," he said irritably. "I mean, you can speculate all day long over where Leon got his money from. The only way we'll get a real answer is by plugging away at this mission. Me with Sonya, Pete, and Leon; you with Max and Liza."

"I know," James nodded as he watched a wasp crawling up the outside of his window. "I'll try getting into their house more now that Max is off school. Do you think we should plant some listening devices?"

Dave shook his head. "If you're on a big mission, you can lay bugs everywhere and we'll have backup teams listening in. But we're small-time here. All we've got is me, you, Millie, and a bit of oversight from John Jones. It's not worth running the risk of placing a bug unless we know when and where something juicy is going down. We'll just end up with hundreds of hours of recordings that nobody's ever gonna listen to."

James nodded.

"To be honest, James, I don't reckon you'll get much from your end of this mission. Leon runs his business out of the Portcabin and keeps Sacha and the younger kids well out of it. With me working part-time on the lot, I'm gonna get to hear what's going down. I'm friendly with Pete and I'll eventually get an opportunity to rummage through everything in the Portacabin when Leon goes off to a car auction or something."

"You could be right," James said sadly.

Dave blasted his horn as a car cut in from the next lane, forcing him to jump on the brake. "Oh, that's gonna get you home *so* much earlier."

The driver of the car in front poked his hand out the window and flicked Dave off.

"Up yours too," Dave snarled before calming down a little and resuming his conversation with James. "You've been pretty lucky on your missions so far, kiddo. You earned most of the glory on that drugs mission and when we were locked up in Arizona, but I reckon it's gonna be the David Moss show this time."

James thought about it for a second and realized that he didn't really mind.

"Who cares?" he grinned. "I won't be earning any black T-shirt for this sideshow. So you can have the glory. As long as the weather stays nice and I get to spend a few weeks chilling with Hannah. . . ."

"Kids these days," Dave tutted as he shook his head and struggled to keep a straight face. "Fancy putting a bit of skirt before the mission."

James started to laugh. "Oh yeah, Dave, you'd *never* do that."

The boys arrived back at five in the afternoon. They'd bought cheap blinds to go up all the windows, bedside lamps, some shelving for the living room, and a couple of rugs to cover over the grubbiest areas of carpet in the bedrooms.

Hannah was grounded, but Max and Pete Tarasov both turned up. Pete brought some tools and a stepladder. He helped Dave put up the blinds, while James and Max screwed the pine shelving together. When the younger boys finished, they moved into James's room and wired up Will's old computer on the battered desk. The machine ran fine, but there weren't any games or other cool stuff on the hard drive, so they headed down to the football pitches to join the nightly kick-about.

The end of school had put Palm Hill's teenage population into a jubilant mood. James enjoyed himself too. At CHERUB, everyone was in good shape and his lack of footballing talent was evident; but amongst ordinary kids, his strength and high level of fitness made him look average.

The game meandered through an orange sunset into the bluish glow from the streetlamps, but they ran out of players just before eleven, when Charlie went off with Liza Tarasov and a couple of slightly younger kids got hauled in by tetchy mums. James picked his shirt off a wooden bench and used it to wipe the sweat dripping out of his hair.

"You wanna come over to my place some time tomorrow?" Max asked as they walked upstairs to their flats. "I've got four controllers on my Xbox. We can call up a couple of other guys and have a FIFA tournament or something?"

"Yeah, that sounds cool." James nodded, grabbing his keys out of his pocket as they stepped onto the balcony. "We'll sort it tomorrow. You've got my mobile number."

James couldn't decide whether to take a shower as he pushed open the front door. On one hand he was boiling hot, but on the other his legs were wasted and he just wanted to crash out in bed.

"Dave, you awake?" James asked as he leaned into the living room.

He didn't get an answer, so he wandered through to the kitchen, stuck his head under the cold tap, and began gulping down water. When he was satisfied, he wiped his mouth on the shirt and dumped it on the dining table before cutting across the hallway to his room.

As James opened the door, he caught a strong whiff of burning. His heart raced as he scrambled out into the hallway and yelled.

Smoke

"*Fire!*" James screamed.

Dave was sprawled across the double bed, with his bum on display and his duvet tangled around his legs.

"Come on," James shouted frantically, slapping Dave on the leg. "Dave, wake *up*."

Dave rolled onto his back and opened his eyes. "What's the matter?"

"I think there's a fire in my room!"

Dave shot up and flicked on the new Ikea lamp beside his bed.

"Are you sure?" he asked as he rolled out of bed and pulled his shorts up his legs.

"I'll call the fire brigade," James said, reaching for his phone.

"Did you see flames?" Dave asked. "Maybe the smell blew in from somewhere out the back. Let me check it out first."

James lowered his phone, as Dave jogged up to his bedroom and rested his palm flat against the door.

"It doesn't feel hot, James. Did it feel hot when you opened the door?"

James shook his head. "No, just really smelly."

Dave opened the door a few centimeters. Both

193

boys caught the burning smell, accompanied by a whirring noise. Once Dave was satisfied there were no flames, he reached in and flipped on the light. The room was ungulfed in a gray haze. Dave stepped across to the window and flung it open. James followed him in and realized the smell was coming from the back of the computer.

"I must have left it switched on," James said, reaching under the desk and yanking the plug out of the wall.

Both boys leaned over the tower case standing on the desktop as the whirring fan slowed and a plume of dirty air began seeping out via the CD-ROM drive at the front.

Dave tried to turn the computer around, to get a look in the back and locate the source of the smell, but the metal case was too hot to the touch. He grabbed a dirty tracksuit top off the floor and used it as a mitten.

"Jesus," Dave gasped as he squinted into the back of the computer. "This fan is all clogged up with dust. Didn't you clean it out before you plugged it in? Didn't they teach you that computers run hot when you learned about computer hacking?"

"I didn't think . . . ," James said weakly.

"Man," Dave said as he wafted his hand under his nose. "It's totally clogged up with grease and dust in here."

James was furious. "My bed and all my clothes and everything are gonna stink," he sulked. "I'll have to wash the whole lot tomorrow."

Dave peeled a greasy worm of dust from between

the fan blades at the back of the computer and flicked it at James.

"If this had been left much longer, it could easily have gone up in flames."

Dave's tone changed abruptly from shocked to curious. "What the . . . ? I've never seen *that* before."

"What?" James asked as he crouched down beside Dave to take a look.

"There's something behind the fan. See, like a plastic bag."

"Oh, yeah," James nodded. "I'll get my multi-tool."

James grabbed the foldout tool from a sports bag under his bed and Dave used it to undo the four screws that held the computer case together. The metal was still warm, so Dave draped the tracksuit top over before lifting it away. The bag Dave had spotted was taped to the inside of the case and the clear plastic felt tacky, like it had been close to melting. He ripped the bag away and unraveled it. There was a mass of green strands, like tea leaves, in the bottom.

"Marijuana." Dave grinned as he gave the contents a sniff. "I think we've uncovered Will's stash."

"Makes sense," James nodded. "Hannah said Will was stoned off his head half the time."

"And if his parents snooped, they might have turned out his drawers and looked under the mattress, but you can bet they wouldn't have opened up his computer."

James stared at the computer's innards and spotted something else. He slid it out and removed a cheap-looking birthday card with a picture of a footballer on it.

James read the inscription out loud. "Dear William, have a fabulous eighteenth birthday, Nana and Pop."

But the envelope contained more. James's eyebrows shot upwards as he pulled out a thin wad of fifty-pound notes and a CD-ROM with "PATPaT" written on the label.

"And the plot *thickens,*" Dave said dramatically. "How much is that?"

"You count," James said, throwing the money at Dave. "I want to know what's on this disk."

James slid his laptop out from under the bed. He put it on the desk and flipped up the lid.

"Two thousand, two hundred smackeroos," Dave said while the laptop booted up. "Not a bad haul for an unemployed eighteen-year-old."

James blew the dust off the CD-ROM before putting it into the drive on the side of his laptop. It spun for a few seconds before an error message popped up:

> This disk is not Microsoft Windows compatible.
> Do you wish to exit Windows and run this program
> in MS-DOS mode?
> YES/CANCEL

James had done an entire lesson about MS-DOS when he'd learned computer hacking, but he could hardly remember it.

"Dave, help us out here, will you?"

Dave looked at the screen. "Click yes," he said. "MS-DOS stands for 'Microsoft Disk Operating System.' It's what everyone used before Windows came out."

James was confronted by a black screen with a single marking on it:

C>:

"I should know all this," James groaned. "What's that thingy I do to get a list of all the files on the disk?"

"Pass it over," Dave said, grabbing the laptop. "You need to type 'DIR,' which is short for 'directory.'"

Dave typed it and a list of about three hundred files scrolled up the screen and whizzed off the top. He scrolled through before pointing out one called "cpx.exe."

"Can you remember what '.exe' means?" Dave asked. "It's the same as in Windows."

"It's short for executable, which is another word for a program," James said.

"Exactly." Dave nodded. "And the batch of files next to it with '.cpx' at the end of their names are saved files that work within that application."

Dave picked one of the .cpx files at random and typed its name. The screen flickered to a crude depiction of a roulette wheel and the laptop played a couple of bars of "Viva Las Vegas" before a screen of text popped up:

Welcome to CPX—Casino Module for Nimbus
Accounting System
Copyright Gamblogic Corp 1987
Please enter your operator password >_

Dave correctly guessed that the password was PATPaT. A list of options opened up on the screen.

(1) Inputs
(2) Staff
(3) Payroll
(4) Cash Account
(5) Nominal Ledger
(6) More Options

Dave was mystified. "This must have come out of some old computer, but why would Will have it?"

"God knows," James shrugged. "Maybe it's just data he found on a secondhand PC. Hannah mentioned that Will was a serious computer geek. He took computers apart and made a bit of money upgrading them, and setting them up for people and stuff."

"But that doesn't explain why he burned the data on to a CD and hit it inside another computer," Dave said. "There's got to be more to it than that."

"Open up the files. See if you can work out what casino it belonged to," James suggested.

Dave selected option one and a screen popped up with a list of data fields.

"Golden Sun Casino, Octopus House, London SE2," James read aloud, then he gasped, "Holy turd on a stick!"

"What?" Dave asked.

"Millie's list, the one I showed you with all the robberies on. Have you still got it?"

"I tossed it after you showed me. We can't leave stuff like that around with Max, Pete, and Sonya coming in and out every five minutes."

"OK, forget that," James said. "Switch that disk off for a minute and go to the Internet. Do a news search for 'Golden Sun Casino' and see what you get."

It took James's laptop a couple of minutes to shut down, reboot, and connect to the Internet. But a quick Google News search confirmed his suspicions:

<u>Golden Sun Casino Robbery Nets Over £90,000</u>
BBC London News—03 Jun 2004
LONDON—A security guard was seriously injured
following an armed raid on the Golden Sun Casino.
The raid took place over . . .
(<u>8 Related Stories</u>)

Dave grinned at James. "Well remembered. The only snag is, Leon would have needed way more than ninety grand to buy that pub, especially if he had to share the loot with partners."

"But look at the date on that web article: June 2004 ties up perfectly," James said. "It's obviously not the whole story. But you can't tell me it's a coincidence that a kid who lives on this block has information about a casino that was robbed at exactly the time Leon came into the big money."

Dave nodded. "I think Millie's on duty tonight. I'll leave a message about this on her answerphone. You contact the twenty-four-hour desk on campus.

E-mail them the data on that disk and get them to send it to MI5 for a detailed analysis. Carbon-copy the message to John Jones, so he knows what's going on as soon as he get to work in the morning."

Glamour

By the time James had converted the information on the CD into a format that could be read by Windows and attached to an e-mail, it was gone one a.m. He dragged his duvet and mattress through to the living room to escape the lingering smell of burnt dust.

Dave had already set off for his first morning's work on the car lot when James got woken by a text message from campus:

AM ON THE CASE. WELL DONE ;)
SPEAK LATER. JOHN

James snapped his phone shut and snuggled up. He fancied a lie-in after the late night, but he realized he had to get off his butt and go to the laundrette, unless he was prepared to walk around smelling like a bonfire for the rest of the week.

It was a quiet morning on the lot. Pete had gone fishing with a couple of mates from college. Dave waxed cars and Leon watched daytime TV in the cabin until the first customer turned up. She wanted to test drive a Vauxhall Astra with a "Car Of The Week" sticker in the front window.

"Back in a flash," Leon yelled as he clambered into the car with his customer. "Any problems, go next door and speak to George in the pub. If any more customers turn up, be polite. I'll be back in under half an hour, and tell 'em I'll make it worth their while for waiting."

Once Leon drove off, Dave strolled into the office. He bent under Leon's desk and plugged a flash memory drive into the USB socket on the front of Leon's computer. The machine was already on and had no security whatever, not even a basic password. Dave simply clicked on the My Computer folder and dragged the icon for the hard drive across to the window that had popped up when he'd plugged in the miniature drive. It took five slightly nervous minutes to copy everything over.

Dave was back to waxing, with the contents of his boss's computer tucked into his shorts, when Leon returned. He squeezed his barrel-shaped body out of the Astra and led his customer into the cabin to sort out the fine points of the deal, emerging ten minutes later and shaking her hand enthusiastically before she drove off the lot.

"If every customer was as dumb as her, I'd be driving round in a Rolls Royce," Leon grinned as he sauntered up to Dave with a finger in his ear. "She could have got that same car at a supermarket for six hundred less than what she paid me. Not a bad rack on her either."

Dave nodded. "Yeah, but a few too many miles on the clock for my taste."

"Let's lock the gates for half an hour and we'll get a fry-up. My treat."

The Palm Hill Grill was on the corner a few hundred meters from the lot. The staff and regulars all knew Leon. A couple of elderly men sucked roll-ups at the table next to Dave and Leon. The other diners were spattered in paint or brick dust.

"Bacon, beans, two fried eggs, bubble, fried slice, and a mug of tea," Dave said when the waitress came over to the table. She was small and curvy, with pouty lips and a spray of zits across her forehead.

"Look but don't touch, Dave," Leon grinned. "My Pete's been after little Lorna for two years."

Everyone in the café roared with laughter, except Lorna, who flushed bright pink. Dave realized that this was a good moment to find out if anything had ever gone on between Leon and Will.

"So'd you hear about my brother's new computer?" Dave asked.

Leon shook his head as he drank a mouthful of tea.

"He got off with Hannah Clarke. She took pity and gave it to him, along with some bits of furniture."

"Lovely young girl, that Hannah," Leon nodded. "Quite friendly with my Liza, though she's being sent to some posh school now."

"It belonged to Hannah's cousin, Will. James left it plugged in and the poxy thing was clogged up with dust. It overheated and damn near burned us out. I blasted his room with air freshener, but it still reeks in there."

One of the old men at the next table overheard. "Isn't Will Clarke the young fellow who came off the roof?" he asked, with a heavy Irish accent.

"Yeah." Dave nodded.

The man shook his head slowly. "A real pity, that was."

"Tragedy," Leon said. "Really bright kid. He was only about thirteen when I got my first computer on the lot, but everyone told me Will was the bee's knees. I had him over for a couple of afternoons and he set everything up for me and showed me a few tricks. When Max wanted a computer in his room, I got hold of a dodgy one off a bloke in the pub. Will came over and fixed it up—you know, put the Windows disk on it and the latest games. It would have cost *hundreds* to have bought the real stuff."

Dave was satisfied. He couldn't push further without seeming suspicious, though he'd fish for more later.

The Irishman looked at Dave with the bloodshot eyeballs of a man with a serious taste for drink. "Why do you think that boy killed himself?"

"How should I know?" Dave shrugged. "I just moved here, so I never even met the guy."

"But you're a young person," the Irishman explained. "So I thought you'd know how these things go."

"Drugs killed him," Leon interrupted with the authority of a man who weighed over a hundred kilos. "Whether he fell, or whether he topped himself, it was the drugs messing with Will's mind that made all the problems."

Both the old men nodded sincerely. "It's true. It's terrible what these young fellows pump into themselves."

The cook was weaving between the tables holding Leon and Dave's breakfasts. "There you go, boys. Enjoy."

"Cheers, Joe," Leon said as he grabbed the salt and showered it over a set breakfast, with extra sausage, extra fried egg, and four slices of toast. "I'm absolutely famished."

The cook looked at Dave. "Course, you know the real reason why Leon doesn't like kids doing drugs?"

Dave shook his head. "Why?"

"'Cos he wants all of yous in his pub, drinking his beer and smoking his cigarettes."

Dave smirked, but the two old geezers at the next table started wailing like it was the funniest thing ever. One of them pounded the table so hard that the brown-sauce bottle tipped over and rolled on to the floor.

"That's a good one. He wants them in his pub . . . *ha-haah!*"

The other old man exploded into a machine-gun laugh, right in Dave's ear. "Leon's beer and cigs," he snorted. "Good one, Joe."

James lugged his stuff to the laundrette and spent twelve quid washing the smell of smoke out of clothes and bedding. He got into a tedious conversation with the manager.

She rambled on about her son, who was in the army. She told James it would be a good career for a handsome boy like him. James didn't mind answering the first couple of questions, but when it started to seem like the woman wanted to know his entire life story, he got ratty. He leaned forwards and lowered his voice.

"You know, I can't really talk to you," James grinned. "You see, I'm a secret agent. I work for an undercover organization called CHERUB and if I told you any more, I'd have to kill you."

"You don't have to be bloody sarcastic," the woman said sourly, crossing her arms as she stormed off in a huff. "I was only making a bit of conversation to pass the time."

James felt like an asshole. He'd only made the comment out of boredom, but the woman looked really upset. Then the door jammed on one of the dryers and he had to go and ask her for help. The manager did her job switching off the power to reset the machine, but the look on her face as she refunded James's coins could have cracked a boulder.

Two and a half hours after entering, James emerged on to Palm Hill High Street holding four giant carrier bags of dry washing. He threw them in the back of Dave's car, which was parked on a double yellow.

"What's the matter with you?" Dave asked as James slumped miserably into the passenger seat beside him.

"I'd sooner have spent the morning in school," James huffed. "*That's* how bad it was."

Dave didn't look sympathetic. "Yeah? Well, I just spent a morning washing and Hoovering out cars. This woman brought in a part exchange. Her kid must have spat about fifty lumps of gum into the ashtrays and I had to chip it all out."

"Gross," James gasped, screwing up his face. "I guess that *is* worse than doing the laundry."

Dave smiled. "I signed up for parachute jumps, exotic islands, and getting chased down mountains by masked men on snowmobiles."

"Yeah," James giggled. "And what do we get? Chewed-up gum and laundry duty."

"Anyway, the Chairman was heading down to Whitehall for some meeting and John hitched a lift in the chopper. So we're meeting up at Millie's house for a conference. It's ten miles out, over Romford way. Get the map book from under the seat. I know how to get there, but I'm not sure about the local streets when we arrive."

Millie lived in a semidetached house, with a Toyota RAV4 finished in a girlie metallic purple in her driveway. She opened her front door as they pulled up and the boys walked down a hallway and through to the kitchen. John Jones sat at a knotted pine table, with two plates of sliced cake set out in the center.

James and Dave both used the toilet before settling down and grabbing chunks of Battenberg while Millie made the tea.

"I bumped into your sister early this morning," John said, looking at James as he bit the marzipan off the edge of his cake. "She's just got back from the summer hostel."

James nodded. "Did she say anything?"

"Not much," John said. "She's looking very tanned and she asked how you were. I told her you'd give her a call when you got the chance."

"Cool," James nodded. "I'll ring her after she's finished lessons."

Millie put the boys' mugs on the table and sat herself down. James read his mug before his first mouthful: "Metropolitan Police Squash Club" written beneath two crossed rackets.

"OK," John said, gently rapping his hand on the table to get everyone looking his way. "First of all, good work last night, lads. I know there was a hefty chunk of luck involved in your discovery, but you deserved a break after doing such a bang-up job getting yourself involved with the natives.

"I passed the casino data on to MI5. They had some difficulty with the accounting software, but I got their initial report through twenty minutes ago. I've also asked to be sent all of the documentation on the Golden Sun Casino robbery. It should be coming over from Abbey Wood serious crime squad within the next couple of hours. Now, I've only had a few hours to get cracking, but I'll run you through everything we've discovered so far.

"First off, there's the discrepancy between the amount of money Leon made and the amount that was stolen from the casino. I spoke to the inspector in serious crime at Abbey Wood. The Golden Sun Casino only has a license for fifteen table games and thirty slot machines. However, the police believe that a lot of illegal high-stakes baccarat gets played in two suites on the upper floors that aren't licensed for gaming.

"The amount stolen from the casino was probably much greater than the ninety grand that got reported to the police, but the casino owners couldn't report having a larger amount of cash on the premises without running the risk of losing their gaming license. I can also confirm that it was an inside job. The thieves knew the code for the burglar alarm and the combination of two safes.

"Secondly, the data James e-mailed to campus contained a full membership list for the Golden Sun. Leon and Sacha Tarasov were both members. Leon's account showed that he owed the casino over six thousand pounds when the records were stolen on May sixteenth last year. He was briefly investigated in connection with the robbery."

"How come the cops didn't make any link to Leon?" James asked.

John shrugged. "The Golden Sun had over a thousand members, seventy or eighty staff, and a few hundred others who've worked there in the past. It would have taken a team of a dozen officers more than a month to track down and investigate every single suspect. The police just don't have that sort of manpower. Abbey Wood serious crime squad has four or five officers and they probably deal with two or three incidents per week. They might have pulled up Leon's criminal record at some point, but it's featherweight. There's nothing there that makes him look like a suspect in a major robbery."

James smiled. "On TV you always see a whole roomful of officers investigating one crime."

Millie nodded. "That's right, James. But in real life—unless you're talking about something like murder or child abduction—you're more likely to find one or two officers investigating dozens of cases. At Palm Hill we're twelve officers short and we don't even have enough vehicles to go around. You have to book them out weeks in advance."

John resumed his briefing. "Thirdly, MI5 are still analysing the data, but they believe the two passwords written on the CD belonged to employees called Eric Crisp—a part-time security guard—and Patricia Patel, who is a croupier."

Millie looked like she'd been hit by a rock. "*John,* are you winding me up?"

John straightened up in his chair and looked mildly offended. "What's that supposed to mean?"

"Patricia Patel is married to Michael Patel, the officer who thumped James on Saturday night. Pat Pat is Michael's nickname for her. I'd never even heard of the Golden Sun until this morning, but I knew she worked nights as a casino dealer. I babysat their daughter a couple of times last year when Patricia's mum was sick.

"I also had an officer called Eric Crisp on my squad. He moved out to Battersea when he got promoted to sergeant a couple of years back. He was best man at Michael's wedding. Then he picked up a nasty back injury and got kicked off the force."

Everyone around the table exchanged shocked glances.

"Oh-*kayyy,*" John said, drawing a sharp breath. "I was *about* to say that the next task for this investigation was going to be finding out who Patricia Patel and Eric Crisp were and establishing their links with Leon Tarasov, but it looks like Millie just filled in most of those gaps."

"What about Will?" James asked. "Where does he fit in with the robbery?"

"That software was out of the ark," Dave said. "It was obviously copied and stolen because it contained information that the robbers needed, on staffing, or security, or whatever. My guess would be that Patricia Patel or Eric Crisp copied the information across, which is easy. But they *didn't* have the expertise to get the software running on a modern computer, so they called in Will and he sorted them out."

"It's interesting that Will kept the data hidden inside the computer though," Millie added, still sounding shell-shocked. "You'd have to be scared of someone or something to hide the information, rather than just delete it."

"Maybe Leon, or whoever, didn't tell Will what they wanted the data for," James suggested. "According to Hannah, Will was a complete nerd, so he would have shat himself if he saw news about the robbery and realized he was an accessory to a major crime."

Dave nodded. "Especially if he was smoking a lot of dope. That stuff makes you *so* paranoid—or so I've been told. . . ."

"The thing is," James added, "when I spoke to Hannah she was all like: 'Will was just a harmless geek, he either killed himself or got so stoned that he fell off the roof.' But if he got mixed up in a giant robbery and Tarasov was scared that he might go to the police, couldn't he have got someone to go up on the roof and give him a little shove?"

John nodded. "James is absolutely right, of course. We *must* now face the possibility that Will was murdered by someone linked to the casino robbery."

"Mind you," Dave said, "if he was smoking loads of dope and stressing out over the cops nabbing him for the robbery, that might have been what drove him to suicide."

"Another valid theory." John nodded. "I'll get hold of the coroner's report and police records relating to Will's death. We'll have to broaden the focus of this operation and try to learn everything we can about Michael and Patricia Patel, Eric Crisp, and Will Clarke."

"We don't have an awful lot of resources though," Millie said. "We've been stretched thin just looking out for Tarasov."

John nodded. "I know, but now we're looking at bent coppers and a potential murder investigation, rather than a local villain with too much money on his hands, I'm sure Zara will spare the resources to crank things up a notch."

James spotted a tear welling up in Millie's eye. "Hey, are you OK?" he asked, reaching across the table and touching her wrist. He thought she was about to cry, but she rubbed the moisture away and exploded with anger.

"No, I'm *not* OK," Millie yelled, scraping her nails across the tabletop. "I've been out hundreds of times with Mike and Eric covering my back. I was their superior. . . . I wrote their appraisals. *Glowing* appraisals. I lent Mike money when he was having a struggle after the baby was born. I pushed Crisp into taking his sergeant's exam. Those two must have been having a right good laugh behind my back the whole time."

John tried to calm Millie down. "Hey, there are a lot of bent cops around, you know? I was on the force and I've served alongside a few myself."

"They've made me look *such* a fool." Millie glowered. "It's no wonder nothing ever sticks to bloody Tarasov if he's got half the cops in Palm Hill in his pocket."

John dared to smile a little. "Two cops is hardly half the force."

Millie shook her head. "Two that we know about, but there could easily be others. You know how it works, John. A big scandal breaking out amongst officers in my squad means my career is down the pan. They won't sack me, but I'll be transferred well out of harm's way—somewhere like the traffic department or the archives."

James watched in horror as Millie froze briefly, then slumped forwards and burst into tears.

"I don't deserve this," she sobbed. "The force has been my whole life since I left university. I've worked too hard . . . too *bloody* hard."

William

Michael Patel's close friendship with Eric Crisp, Leon being a casino member and paying off his debts shortly after it was robbed, Patricia Patel's password written on the CD found inside Will's computer—everything pointed toward these five people being involved in robbing the Golden Sun Casino. But to make a case stand up in court, you need more than coincidences and tangled fragments of information. The pieces had to be turned into a story that made sense and was backed by solid evidence.

Everyone had a job to do. John headed back to campus to get hold of the records relating to Will's death and ask Zara for extra resources. Dave had to carry on sticking close to Pete and Leon. Millie had to hide her hurt feelings and work normally alongside Michael Patel, while subtly trying to find evidence of his misconduct.

Although James felt bad for Millie, he was in a good mood as he drove back to Palm Hill with Dave. Not only was he optimistic about the mission succeeding, but John had asked him to switch his focus away from Max and Liza to concentrate on finding out more about Will. This meant hanging out with

Hannah, which suited him fine. By the time James arrived back at the flat, he'd already set up a midnight meeting.

James got his butt kicked in the FIFA tournament that evening. They played two a side: James and Max as Arsenal, versus Liza and Charlie as Chelsea. Liza wasn't into computer games. She kept getting the pass and shoot buttons mixed up and was only playing because she liked hanging out with Charlie, but Charlie more than made up for his teammate. He weighted every pass beautifully, had a fantastic line in curved shots from outside the penalty area, and most of the luck was running his way as well.

Max chucked a massive strop when Arsenal went three down for the second game in succession, claiming that Charlie was using a cheat code to score goals. After bouncing his controller off the wall, Max stormed out of his own bedroom.

"He's *such* a spoiled brat," Liza said, shaking her head jadedly. "Max expects his own way 'cos he's Uncle Leon's favorite."

"Do you want to play two against one?" James asked.

Liza edged up to Charlie and smiled at him.

"Maybe we'll clear off to Liza's room." Charlie grinned as he gave Liza a quick kiss.

James nodded. "Don't do anything I wouldn't do."

"I wouldn't dare," Charlie giggled. "Leon might sit on me."

Liza gently swiped Charlie across the head and told him not to be rude as they stumbled out of the room, grinning at each other. James wasn't too happy at being left alone with Max. He wasn't a bad guy, but he was quite boring and sometimes acted more like he was ten, instead of nearly fourteen.

Max looked embarrassed when he came back, holding two cans of Coke and a giant bag of spicy tortilla chips. He wanted to carry on playing FIFA, but James didn't want him to start showing off again if he started losing, so they ended up watching *Jackass* DVDs, while James showed him a couple of basic self-defense moves.

When it got to midnight, Max gaves James a lift and he hauled himself through a wooden hatch above the Tarasovs' landing, into a crawl space between the ceiling and the flat roof. He had to clamber over some fiberglass loft insulation, before breaking open a second hatch and sliding outdoors onto the roof itself. Hannah was already out there and she gave him a hand up.

"Wow . . . ," James said, awed as he did a three-sixty.

He looked at the stars and the skyscrapers at Canary Wharf lit up in the distance, then at Hannah, who wore a denim microskirt and a tight yellow top. They closed up and exchanged a big open-mouthed kiss.

"I just had the biggest row with my dad," Hannah said as she stepped backwards. "My head-mistress rang up and told him that I bunked off yesterday. Now he says I'm grounded for the whole summer holiday."

"Bummer," James said.

"I told Dad to shove it. He can't stop me going out in the week, because he and Mum go to work every day. So he goes, 'I'll put a padlock on your room if I have to.' So I told him I was gonna run away and get myself pregnant to piss him off."

James started to laugh. He loved Hannah's warped sense of humor. "I bet that went down well."

"He's *such* an idiot, James. It's because of what happened to Will. He wants to keep me in a box like a china doll. But Will was a sad case. He got stoned all the time because he was lonely and *didn't* have any friends, not because his friends were a bad influence. I told Dad that if he keeps on like this, I'll end up depressed and lonely, just like Will."

"Your dad sounds like a turd. What about your mum, what does she say?"

Hannah shrugged. "Mum's OK, but she's a wimp. When I talk to her she agrees with me, but when Dad's there, she won't stand up to him. I know you've got no money or that, James, but you're *so* lucky not having parents around."

"It's not such a big deal," James grinned, teasing Hannah. "It's just *total* freedom to do whatever I want, that's all."

"Anyway, from now on I don't care *what* my dad says. I'm going out enjoying myself. I've already arranged for me and Jane to go swimming tomorrow."

"Oh, cool," James said. "Max reckons the leisure center's got really cool waterslides. Can I come?"

"Actually, it's kind of a girls' outing. Liza's coming and we already told her she's not allowed to bring Charlie."

James looked at his watch. "So what time have you got to go back indoors?"

"We can spend the whole night up here for all I care," Hannah said.

She'd already spread out a blanket and a couple of cushions, which was a lot nicer than sitting on the prickly asphalt. They snogged a little bit, but mostly just talked. Hannah was the fifth girl James had got off with since his first ever kiss sixteen months earlier. Out of the five, Hannah was easily the one he had most in common with: She was blond and good-looking, she had a temper, she hated school, and she was always in trouble.

After an hour of talking about all kinds of stuff, James realized he had to do his duty and steered the conversation back towards Will and the robbery. Dave had already confirmed that Will knew Leon, so he thought he'd see what Hannah had to say about Michael Patel.

"So, you heard about the computer blowing up?" James said.

Hannah kissed him on the neck. "Yeah, I'm really sorry about that. I should have warned you how dusty it is in that lockup."

"It's not your fault. If I'd had half a brain, I would have worked that out for myself. When I was putting Will's things in my room, it felt so weird. It belonged to someone only a few years older than us and he's *dead*. You know what I mean?"

"I cried so much," Hannah said, nodding slowly. "For about a week after Will died, I couldn't get it out of my head, no matter how much I tried to think about something else. Even now I wake up with this funny feeling sometimes. Like, I'm all stiff and sweaty and I'm kind of thinking to myself, *Was that a dream or did it really happen?*"

"Do you think he was in trouble?" James suggested. "A dark secret, like a girlfriend with a bun in the oven or something?"

Hannah grinned. "Will with a girl? No, no, *no*."

"What, was he gay?"

"He wasn't gay—at least not so far as I know. But Will never had a girlfriend in his whole life."

"When was the last time you saw him?" James asked.

"Why are you so interested?" Hannah asked back.

James realized he'd been rattling off too many questions, like a policeman or something.

"I dunno," he said, trying to sound as if he couldn't care less. "I guess I'm morbid or something. We don't have to talk about this if it makes you sad."

Hannah seemed satisfied with the explanation and edged into a little smile.

"I don't mind," she said. "It's more than a year ago, I'm mostly over it now. The last time I saw Will, I bumped into him on the balcony two days before he died. He looked wasted. Come to think of it, he always looked wasted; but he was in a good mood. He'd just made a couple of grand and he was talking about taking a break and going off to Thailand for a long holiday."

James recalled seeing a Lonely Planet guide to Thailand amongst Will's books in the lockup.

"So, how do you reckon he made that sort of money, selling dope?"

Hannah looked offended. "James, Will smoked a bit of dope but he wasn't a drug dealer. He had a good reputation for mending computers and setting them up for people and stuff. He'd just done some job for Leon Tarasov."

"Right," James said, making a mental note of this fact as he sneakily picked off the tiny scab in his hair to make it bleed.

"Oww," he said noisily.

Hannah sat up on the blanket, looking concerned. "What's up?"

"I accidentally scratched my head. I'm bleeding where that pig belted me against the car roof."

Hannah looked at James's bloody fingertip. "You poor little lamb," she said, grinning dopily.

"That Patel's a nutter," James said. "Max reckons he's smacked a few other kids around, as well."

"I've heard that," Hannah nodded. "But he was really nice to me when Will died. He was just around the corner when it happened. He went over and grabbed Will to see if he was alive, then he came running over to me and Jane. I was hysterical. He put his arms around me and rubbed my back to calm me down. . . . Actually, you know what, James? It's a beautiful warm evening and we're supposed to be having a nice time."

"Sorry," James said. "What *do* you want to talk about?"

"Nothing," Hannah said, moving her head towards James so that they could start smooching again.

James woke up at seven, busting for a pee with a sunrise breaking out over his head and a dead arm where Hannah's head was resting on it. He tried moving her gently on to one of the cushions without waking her up, but her eyes flickered open.

"Oh," Hannah moaned slowly as she stretched into a yawn. "My back's *really* stiff."

As James stood up and walked the cramp out of his legs, he noticed loads of cricks and twinges to go with his dead arm.

"Who'd have thought a hard asphalt roof wasn't a good place to sleep?" He grinned. "Do you think your dad's noticed that you've gone?"

Hannah shrugged. "If he did, he'll shout at me; if he didn't, he'll shout at me about something else. So what difference does it make?"

"I need the toilet. You can come down to my flat for breakfast if you want. Mind you, I don't think there's much in the fridge except milk for cereal . . . and I think we're out of cereal."

"Might turn that one down then." Hannah grinned as she wrapped the blanket around the two cushions, gathered it up by the corners, and slung the bundle over her shoulder.

"So I'll see you then," James said.

"What do you think will happen when I tell my dad that we spent all night having sex on the roof?"

"Eh?" James gasped. "I *wish*. All we did is snog and fall asleep."

"Yeah," Hannah giggled. "But I want to see if I can make Dad's head explode."

James started to crack up. "You're *insane*, Hannah. Whatever you tell him, don't bring my name into it. I don't want him bursting in on me and trying to chop me up with a machete or something."

"I wouldn't worry on that score. My dad's got little cocktail-stick legs and a big potbelly. After the way you demolished those two thugs on Saturday night, I'll be betting my pocket money on you if a fight breaks out."

"That's if our dad ever reinstates your pocket money," James grinned as he gave Hannah a goodbye kiss. "I'll give you a call later," he yelled as he rushed off to use the toilet. "Have fun at the pool."

Breaking

Dave had been out food shopping the night before. He was at the table eating scrambled eggs on toast when James got in.

"Hey, stud," Dave grinned. "How'd the night of passion go?"

James grabbed the milk from the fridge and started drinking out of the carton. "Not bad," he said. "Got a quality feel up her shirt."

"Nice one," Dave grinned.

"So, is Sonya around?"

Dave shrugged. "Typical woman. At first she's all over me, now she keeps texting me and asking if I really care about her."

"Which of course you don't," James said as he swiped a triangle of Dave's toast.

"Hey, you've got all morning to make your own breakfast," Dave said bitterly. "I've got to go off to work in a minute."

James spotted a brown paper file on the kitchen worktop and stepped over to it. "What's this?"

"Oh, yeah," Dave said. "It's a copy of the police paperwork relating to Will Clarke's death. John's assistant Chloe delivered it last night, not long after you left. You'd better read it through, but I'd wait till after breakfast if you've got a weak stomach."

James flipped the file open and was confronted by a photograph of Will's mangled body.

"Oh . . . ," James gasped. "That is *so* nasty."

Dave nodded. "Your girlfriend must have felt one hell of a jolt."

On second glance, James had a brainwave. "Hang on," he said, holding the photo close to his face and carefully studying Will's injuries.

"What?"

"Last night, Hannah told me that Michael Patel was on the scene within a minute of Will going ker-splat."

"We know," Dave nodded. "You'll see it in the file when you read it."

"Right," James said. "But Hannah *also* said that Michael walked up to the body and touched it. She thought Patel was checking to see if Will was still alive, but look at that picture. His body's practically decapitated. You didn't need to start poking Will about to work out that he's a goner."

Dave looked surprised. "Hannah *definitely* told you Michael touched the body?"

"Hundred percent, Dave. And what do they teach us in basic training? Never touch anything at a crime scene because it could contaminate the evidence and ruin the chances of a successful prosecution. So why would an experienced police officer wade into a possible murder scene like that?"

Dave put in a few seconds' thought before replying. "OK, so we can place Michael on the scene shortly after Will died and he was behaving oddly. For argument's sake, let's suppose that Michael *did* push Will off the rooftop and try to suss out how it could have happened."

"OK," James said. "For starters, you don't just bump into someone on a rooftop. Michael and Will must have arranged to meet up there. Presumably it was to do with the casino robbery, but I can hardly see Michael *planning* to kill someone by pushing them off a rooftop in broad daylight."

"Too right," Dave nodded. "It's not even high up. Will might even have survived if he hadn't hit the stair rail before the ground. Some sort of row must have broken out and Michael ended up pushing Will off. Michael would have climbed down the ladder and moved away as quickly as possible. He would have been worried that there was a witness—someone down on the ground, or someone looking out of a window in one of the other blocks."

"I know," James gasped as an idea fitted together in his head. "Patel must have been trying to cover up the forensic evidence."

Dave looked confused. "How do you figure that?"

"After fighting with Will, Michael must have had traces of Will's blood, clothes fibers, and DNA all over his uniform, right?"

Dave nodded.

"But he'd be able to explain all that forensic evidence away if people saw him touching Will's dead body on the ground."

Dave broke into a smile. "*Riiiiiight,* James, I get

what you're saying. If Patel got put on trial for murder, he'd be able to claim that he got Will's DNA on him when he touched the body to make sure that he was dead. With the forensic evidence discredited, the case would boil down to Patel's word, against the word of an eyewitness standing at least fifty meters away.

"In the end, Michael needn't have worried because nobody saw anything and everyone assumed Will fell off, or topped himself. But at the time, Patel must have been terrified that there was going to be a full-scale murder investigation, with him covered in forensic evidence and fitting the description of the main suspect."

"Exactly," James nodded. "What reason could there be for an experienced cop to contaminate a crime scene, except to cover his own butt?"

Dave shrugged. "There's none that springs to mind."

"So is this just a theory?" James asked. "Or do you really think Michael Patel killed Will Clarke?"

"There's too many variables to be sure of anything," Dave said as he glanced at his watch and stood up abruptly. "But it does fit all the facts.

"Anyway, James, it's only my second day on the job, so I'd better not turn up late. Go in your room, read the file to see if you can pick anything else up, then give John a bell. Tell him what you learned off Hannah and run our theory about why Patel touched the body past him."

James nodded. "OK."

Dave added his empty mug and plate to the

mountain of dirty dishes in the sink. "At the end of the day, it probably doesn't matter if the theory's right or wrong. I doubt we'll ever be able to prove anything: It all happened more than a year ago, there were no eyewitnesses, and Will's body has been cremated."

"So why bother carrying on?" James asked sourly.

"The robbery," Dave said as he headed for the door. "That's why we came here in the first place and if we can get more evidence linking Michael and Leon to the robbery, they'll both be going down for a long stretch."

"I guess," James said, opening the fridge door and grabbing a couple of eggs. "But it's bogus if they end up getting away with murder."

John was pulling onto a roundabout when his mobile started ringing. He had Lauren and Kerry in the back.

"Answer that, will you?" John said. "I've gotta concentrate here."

Lauren grabbed John's wireless headset off the console between the front seats and hooked it over her ear. "Hi, James, how are you?"

James was pleasantly surprised to hear his sister's voice. "Hey, Lauren, how was the hostel?"

"Mental." Lauren grinned. "We had the best laugh *ever,* better even than last year. Me and Bethany nearly got sent home for nicking some boys' clothes while they were skinny-dipping in the lake. Kyle got the neck brace off, then busted his ankle on some bet that he could jump his skateboard over two cars. Jake and a couple of his mates demolished a Jet Ski by driving it into rocks. There was *total* craziness, every single day."

"Sounds nutty," James said, resenting the fact that he'd missed out. "So is John on another call? What are you doing in his office?"

"You diverted through to his mobile. I'm in his car with Kerry. John asked for extra resources, so we're on the same mission as you now."

James was shocked. "Really, doing what?"

"Breaking and entering," Lauren said. "The house belongs to some guy called Michael Patel."

"Right," James nodded. "I know who he is."

"You should see us, James. Me and Kerry are dressed up like bad girls. I've got these grubby white Reeboks, a tracksuit, big earrings, and a ton of makeup. We look rough! And we're doing your favorite."

"Oh," James gasped. "They're letting you vandalize the place?"

Lauren grabbed her mission briefing out of her tracksuit top and read James an excerpt. "'Agents must make copies of financial documents, computer data, and other personal papers belonging to Michael and Patricia Patel. In order to minimize suspicion, the agents must give the impression of being petty child burglars by damaging property and stealing small items.'"

"You're so jammy," James said. "Do you know how long it's been since I got to trash anything?"

"Kerry's sitting next to me, do you want a quick

word with her? . . . Oh, wait, she's shaking her head. It looks like she's still blanking you."

James had been enjoying the conversation, but didn't appreciate being reminded that he was still a leper on campus.

"John's pulled on to the motorway now and he's nodding. I'll pass the headset across."

James heard a few bumps and rustles before John's voice rang out, "Good morning, young man. What have you got to tell me?"

It was an hour later when John pulled the Vauxhall up at the end of Michael Patel's street.

He looked back at the two girls. "Good luck. I checked with Millie, and Michael is definitely on duty this morning. Patricia ought to be at a mother and toddler group, but ring the doorbell to be on the safe side. If things go pear-shaped and you end up getting nicked, just keep your traps firmly shut and I'll get you out as fast as I can."

"No worries, John," Kerry said as she joined Lauren on the pavement and slammed the car door.

It was a bright morning. Kerry and Lauren exchanged a grin as they set off down the road. The Patels' 1930s-built house was a dump. There were no cars on the crazy-paved driveway and a ring of the doorbell confirmed that nobody was home.

Kerry pulled a crowbar out of her backpack and thrust it through the narrow glass panel beside the front door. It made a hell of a racket and the girls looked around edgily, making sure they hadn't attracted any attention from the neighbors.

They slid thick gardening gloves over their plastic disposables, then carefully pulled away all the glass shards jutting from the window frame so that Lauren didn't get cut as she clambered through.

"It's smaller than it looked in that surveillance picture," Lauren said edgily.

"It'll be OK," Kerry smiled. "You're not that big."

Lauren put her arms and shoulders through the window frame. Kerry picked Lauren up by her ankles and fed her through, only letting go when her hands were touching the carpet inside the house.

Lauren stood up, but nearly fell back down again as she stepped on a wind-up car and twisted her ankle. The hallway walls were covered in scratches and grubby handprints, and the smell of stale cigarette smoke lingered in the air. Lauren tried letting Kerry in through the front door, but it was deadlocked.

She crouched down and shouted through the letterbox. "I won't bother picking it. It's easier if I let you in around the side."

Lauren walked through to the living room. She undid a catch and pulled open the central sash of the bay window.

"Cheers," Kerry said as she straddled through. "Millie said the computer was upstairs in the back bedroom when she babysat. You copy everything off that and I'll start hunting for paperwork."

"Aye aye, captain," Lauren said as she ran off up the stairs.

The computer was covered in crayon and there was sticky orange stuff all over the keyboard, which Lauren hoped was juice. It struck her that the Patels were slobs; definitely not the kind of people who organized household accounts or other valuable data on their computer.

Downstairs, Kerry had found a mountain of unfilled paperwork in a living room cupboard. She had a high-speed document scanner in her backpack, but she realized it would take hours to copy every piece of paper, particularly as loads of them were still in their delivery envelopes accompanied by leaflets offering low-interest loans and discount car insurance.

Lauren looked through the program menu and found nothing but a bunch of games for preschool kids. It took her under a minute to put everything from the computer on to a flash memory drive, then she ripped the power leads out of the back before shoving the monitor off the side of the desk. After that she yanked out the keyboard and used it to batter books and ornaments off two shelves before swinging it above her head and demolishing a paper lampshade.

She checked the drawers built into the computer desk for documents, then moved into the bathroom. She grabbed the shower gel, shampoo, and toothpaste in turn and squirted them across the floor and up the walls. Then she found a lipstick and wrote on the bathroom mirror "HOPE U ENJOY CLEARING UP MY MESS" with a smiley face underneath it.

There was a jewelry box in the main bedroom. Lauren stuffed her tracksuit pockets with Patricia's collection of brooches and rings before opening up her wardrobe and ripping all the clothes off their hangers. She found a couple of credit cards and about a hundred pounds cash in the cabinet on Michael's side of the bed. After a further rummage, she uncovered a little bag of white powder that was probably cocaine.

"Aren't you a naughty boy." Lauren grinned as she ripped the small drawer off its runners and hurtled its contents across the room.

Next, she opened up Michael's wardrobe, which contained half a dozen sets of police uniform in dry cleaner bags. She shot everything out of the sock and underwear cubbies before she spotted a small safe bolted to the wall with three pairs of polished shoes standing on top of it. Lauren hadn't studied safe cracking and didn't have the tools with her even if she had, but she knew CHERUB might want to send someone back for another look.

She cleared a space around the chunky metal box, then slid out her digital camera and took two photographs. The first was of the front of the safe. The second was a close-up of the sticker on top that had the name of the manufacturer and the serial number on it.

After a brief rummage through a chest of drawers, Lauren moved to the final room on the upper floor: the bedroom where the Patel's daughter, Charlotte, slept. She tipped out a few boxes of toys and games, but she didn't have the heart to smash up the property of a three-year-old, and headed back downstairs to find Kerry. She was kneeling on the living room floor surrounded by piles of paperwork.

"I don't know how long we've got," Kerry gasped as she ran the portable document scanner over a credit card statement before hurriedly folding it and stuffing it back in an envelope. "But we won't get all this junk copied, even if the Patels stay out till midnight."

Lauren knelt down beside Kerry.

"Help me sift through," Kerry said. "We want credit card statements, bank statements, phone bills, large invoices. Ignore the rubbish, like gym memberships and stuff."

For the next hour, the girls were like robots, repeating the same task until their backs and shoulders hurt. Lauren sifted through documents. Anything that looked interesting got put into a pile for Kerry to copy with the handheld scanner. The other 80 percent got stuffed back into the cupboard. The sorted pile was twice the size of the unsorted when John Jones called from his car at the top of the road. Kerry grabbed her mobile.

"I don't know what you ladies are still playing at, but Mrs. P. has turned into the top of the road."

"Roger that, John, we're out of here."

Kerry snapped her phone shut, jumped up, and began stuffing the document scanner into her pack. Lauren kicked the papers around the room, upended the coffee table, and stole a couple of DVDs. They were about to step out through the bay window when they spotted Patricia pulling up the driveway in a silver BMW.

"Tits," Kerry said. "We'll have to go out the back."

The girls sprinted through to the kitchen. Kerry pulled down on the backdoor handle, but the door onto the garden was deadlocked, just like the one at the front. Lauren reached across a kitchen cabinet and swung open a window as Patricia Patel screamed at her daughter:

"Charlotte, no, *sharp*. Please don't touch that, baby, it's broken glass."

Lauren glided across the kitchen cabinet, passed through the open window, and dropped onto the Patel's shabby back lawn. Kerry followed a couple of seconds later. The garden was surrounded by overgrown bushes and a high wooden fence, which meant the only easy way out was around the side of the house.

As the girls moved, they could hear Patricia sobbing into a mobile phone. ". . . I don't know, honey. I daren't go inside, they might still be in there. I can see paper all over the living room and I think I heard some noise. . . . OK, I'll call the police. But you're coming right home, aren't you, Michael?"

They poked their heads around the front of the house. The sight of Patricia crying and the bewildered toddler staring up at her mother made both girls feel rotten. Patricia hung up on her husband and dialed 911 as Kerry leaned against the side of the house and whispered to Lauren.

"I don't think she'll chase us. She can't abandon the kid."

Lauren nodded. "OK, let's run for it."

The two tracksuit-clad girls sprinted out from the side of the house, passing within a couple of meters of Patricia's grasp.

"Oh my God, they're right here!" Patricia yelled into the phone as Lauren and Kerry turned left and began sprinting towards the top of the road. "Can you send a car quickly? They're two girls with long black hair, and they're running towards the top of Tremaine Road right now."

John was parked around the corner in the next street with the back door of the car open. The girls clambered inside.

"That poor little girl," Kerry said sadly as John pulled away from the curb. "I know we had to do it and I know it makes it realistic if we trash the place, but her mum was crying and she looked really worried."

"You can't make an omelet without breaking eggs," Lauren said, repeating a phrase that often came up during CHERUB training; though she now felt guilty about the amount of fun she'd had trashing the bathroom.

"So what did you get?" John asked. "You were in there for long enough."

"Financial stuff mostly," Kerry said. "About four hundred pages' worth. It took ages because nothing was filed. Half of it was still stuffed inside envelopes."

"And the computer?"

Lauren nodded. "I copied all the data, but I don't think you're gong to find anything useful, unless you get a sudden urge to play Jimmy Bear Learns His ABCs."

Conclusions

John was now working the Tarasov mission full-time. He had no intention of driving between London and campus every day, so he'd booked a two-bedroom suite at a hotel overlooking the river Thames.

Lauren and Kerry were on attachment, which meant they were assigned to the mission but would go back to campus when they weren't needed. John picked up swipe cards at the hotel reception, stepped into a glass-sided lift, and went up to the seventeenth floor with the two tracksuited girls.

A vanload of paperwork and equipment had beaten them to the scene and Chloe Blake—an ex-cherub who'd recently taken a job as an assistant mission controller—was busy stacking papers into filing trolleys and setting up the laptop computers and the satellite link to campus. Kerry and Lauren unpacked a few personal items in a room with two double beds, then took showers and changed into hotel robes before ordering a Thai curry from room service.

The girls were lying back on their beds watching MTV when John came after them.

"Come on, ladies," he said firmly. "You're here on a mission, not to loaf about. Kerry, I want you to print off all the documents you scanned and try making sense out of them. Lauren, e-mail the Patels' computer data to campus."

"Yes, boss," Kerry puffed.

"Don't give me that look," John said stiffly. "This isn't a hotel, you know."

Lauren started to giggle. "Actually, this *is* a hotel."

John was usually mild-mannered, but he didn't appreciate Lauren's cheek. He went into the living room, grabbed a picture of Will Clarke's body from one of the files, and held it up in front of the girls. Neither of them had seen the picture before and they both winced.

"I'm trying to catch the people who did *this*," John said. "I was hoping you two would want to see them go to prison as badly as I do."

"Sorry, John," Kerry said defensively, standing up quickly and grabbing a pair of jeans from her wardrobe.

Lauren looked sheepishly down at the carpet. "Yeah, sorry. We'll get right on it."

John called everybody together for a nine p.m. conference. James and Dave parked up underneath the hotel. They got into the lift at the parking level and bumped into Lauren and Kerry when it stopped two floors farther up. Both girls wore robes, pool shoes, and had streaks of water running out of their hair.

"Nice cushy mission for some," Dave grinned. "Swimming in the hotel pool while me and James have to live in a slum."

"James likes slums." Lauren grinned. "They're

his natural habitat. And I'll have you know that me and Kerry spent four of the last five hours doing our brains in trying to make sense out of the Patels' financial records. John told us we could take a break and go for a quick swim before the meeting."

James could smell the chlorine on Kerry's skin as the lift moved upwards. He hadn't given her a lot of thought since he'd met Hannah, but she'd really grown up since they were thrust upon each other as basic training partners nearly two years earlier. James thought she looked more attractive than ever as he imagined leaning forward and kissing her damp cheek.

"Seventeenth floor," Dave said, stepping into a drab corridor and heading for the suite.

John and his assistant Chloe were in the room, as well as a bearded lawyer called Mr. Schott. He was one of CHERUB's legal advisors and also a member of the ethics committee that had to approve every CHERUB mission. Millie turned up last. Dressed in police uniform, she entered as Lauren and Kerry emerged from their bedroom in shorts and T-shirts.

The four cherubs and four adults arranged themselves into a circle in the living room, using a hotchpotch of sofas, dining chairs, a footstool, and a long coffee table.

"OK," John said. "Glad you could all make it. We've had a flood of information coming at us from different sources since James and Dave made their initial breakthrough with the computer a couple of days back. Chloe and I have spent the last few hours trying to make sense of it, with some valuable assistance from the girls. Now everyone is here, I'll give you a quick rundown on the situation. Feel free to butt in with questions, or if I miss anything out.

"First of all, we've established that Leon and Michael Patel were both members of the Golden Sun and owed the casino significant amounts of money. We already knew that Leon had debts. According to the paperwork the girls copied at the Patels' house this morning, it appears that Michael and Patricia were a few months behind with their mortgage repayments and owed more than thirty thousand pounds on credit cards and two car loans. In other words, both men were desperate for money.

"According to the police file on the robbery, on May sixteenth last year, a member of staff at the Golden Sun Casino went into the computer room and stole a backup tape containing all the casino's data. We don't know who stole it, but when a copy was later passed to Will Clarke, it was accompanied by passwords belonging to Eric Crisp and Patricia Patel.

"Three weeks later, on June seventh at about five p.m., casino manager Ray Li called out an engineer to report that the CCTV system inside the casino had gone wrong. The engineers didn't turn up until after the robbery. They found that several wire connectors had been twisted and broken off, making sabotage the only likely cause.

"Eleven hours after that, Eric Crisp was the only security guard on duty after the casino shut its doors at four a.m., June eighth. At some time between four and six a.m., two masked men entered the staff entrance at the rear of the Golden Sun Casino using keys. Eric claimed that he went downstairs to investigate a noise and that the two men overpowered him. He said they tied him up and coshed him over the head. Of course, none of this was recorded because the CCTV system had been sabotaged earlier in the day.

"The police commandeered the surveillance tapes from surrounding buildings after the robbery. I've got the tapes here, but I very much doubt they'll be of much use. The cops at Abbey Wood would have tried already."

"Typical," James tutted.

John continued his rundown of the facts. "The two masked men then used codes in their possession to open two safes and steal a sum of cash reported to be ninety thousand pounds, but now believed to be significantly greater, perhaps as much as six hundred thousand pounds. Eric claimed he regained consciousness two hours later and reported the robbery to the police as soon as he came around.

"Crisp was later treated in hospital for a minor head wound and rope burns on his wrists and ankles. The security guard is always the first person suspected in a big robbery, in the same way that a spouse is always the first person suspected in a murder. Eric was questioned extensively about the robbery, but as you'd expect from an ex-cop, he knew how to handle himself in an interview room and stuck to his story.

"In the months following the robbery, the behavior of our suspects was consistent with people who'd just come into a large sum of money. Eric Crisp sold his house in Battersea, quit his job in the casino, and moved abroad; we know not where. Leon Tarasov paid off his outstanding debts and purchased the Queen of Russia pub. Michael Patel paid off all his debts, took his wife on a luxury Caribbean cruise, gave his mother fifteen thousand pounds towards buying her council flat, and—this is my favorite detail—purchased a seventeen-thousand-pound BMW from Tarasov Prestige Motors."

Everyone around the table exchanged looks and smiles.

"Well, John, you've got me convinced," Dave grinned. "But would that stand up in court?"

John looked at the bearded man straddling a coffee table. "Mr. Schott, you're the legal eagle. Would you care to take that question?"

Schott leaned forwards, sucked in a lungful of air, and waved his hand in front of his face. "There's no clear evidence, like video or fingerprints, but the circumstantial evidence is strong. If we passed the information we've gathered to the Abbey Wood serious crime squad they'd pull Tarasov, Crisp, and the Patels in for questioning. Then they'd get search warrants and tear up their homes and workplaces.

"Patricia Patel would probably be the key to the whole thing. Michael, Eric, and Leon all know how the cops break a suspect down and won't play ball, but Patricia has never even had a speeding ticket. If you get the mother of a young child, scare the wits out of her, and then offer her a deal that enables her to stay out of prison and hang on to her kid, she'll usually crack."

"It's obviously good news that we've got a realistic chance of getting convictions for the robbery," John said. "The bad news is that three of our four suspects have no criminal record, one of them is an ex-policeman, and even Leon Tarasov only has a few minor blotches on his copybook. They didn't use guns and the only violence employed was when they duffed up Eric Crisp to make it look like he wasn't in on the deal. So, despite the large sum of money involved, none of our baddies would be looking at particularly long prison sentences. Four to six years would be my guess. With parole and remission, they'd all be out inside three."

James looked gutted. "Is that all they'd get?"

"Maybe a little more for Michael Patel because he's a serving police officer," Mr. Schott said. "Other than that, John is absolutely right."

"That's bull," Dave yelled furiously. "What about Will? The poor kid's dead."

John grinned. "Boys, keep your hair on and let me finish. I've studied the photographs of Will's body again and I can't help agreeing with your theory that Michael Patel touching an obviously dead body was a highly suspicious thing to do. He was tangled up in a robbery with Will and on the scene at the time he died. The data disk hidden inside the computer indicates that Will either wanted evidence against his partners if things turned bad, or he was trying to blackmail them for a bigger share of the loot. Taking all of this into account, I now think it's highly probably that Michael Patel killed Will Clarke. Are we all agreed on that?"

John looked to everyone in turn for confirmation. Lauren and Kerry both nodded.

"Ninety percent certain that he killed him," Dave said.

James shook his head. "Eighty percent, more like."

Chloe smiled. "Well, I'm not going to put a number on it, but I think he probably did."

Mr. Schott nodded.

John looked at Millie last. She seemed upset, and for a second James thought she was going to start blubbing again. Her eyes narrowed into determined little slits as she spoke. "I'd like to see Michael Patel go to prison for a *very* long time."

"So we agree," Dave said, looking at Mr. Schott, "but to get Michael convicted of murder, you've got to convince a jury of twelve people beyond *any* reasonable doubt. We don't have anything strong enough to do that, do we?"

Mr. Schott shook his head. "Not even close. We're all basing our presumptions of guilt on the fact that Patel touched the body, but a smart lawyer will defend Michael by claiming that he acted strangely because he was traumatized by what had just happened. Even if some of the jury members thought Patel was probably guilty, the judge would instruct them to find him innocent even if they entertained moderate doubts."

"We've all got doubts ourselves," Chloe reminded everyone.

"Does that mean we're bummed?" Lauren asked.

"There's little chance of turning up more evidence via conventional investigative methods," John said. "We're going to have to get a confession."

"You're tripping," James said, shaking his head. "Tarasov and Patel will never confess, not in a million years."

John smiled. "Credit me with *some* intelligence, James. I'm not planning to take Tarasov and Patel down to Palm Hill police station, make them a nice cup of rosie, and ask them to do the decent thing. I'm talking about a sting operation. We're going to have to devise a trap."

"How?" James asked.

"I've got a few ideas," John said. "But it's going to take time and a lot of detailed preparation to get all of the elements into place."

"How long?" Dave asked.

"Ten days, perhaps," John shrugged. "Maybe a fortnight."

"So what do we do until then?" Lauren asked.

"James and Dave stay at Palm Hill, keeping in with the Tarasovs and seeing what else they can dig up. I expect you and Kerry will be able to go back to campus until a day or two before we're ready to roll."

Kiss

The plan took much longer than expected to come together, not that James minded. He spent the nineteen days after John announced his scheme bumming around Palm Hill with Max and Charlie: playing football, riding bikes, cruising the shops, hanging out at the reservoir, and making out with Hannah, whenever her parents weren't keeping tabs. It wasn't as much fun as the CHERUB hostel would have been, but James was determined to enjoy himself because he knew it was the closest to a summer holiday he'd get.

TUESDAY, 20:58

What started out as a low-key mission had turned into the most technically complex CHERUB operation James had been involved with. The sting was going to be controlled from the suite adjoining the one John Jones had been living in.

James passed through the connecting door, stepping gingerly over a dozen tangled cables. There were three satellite dishes ripped up on the balcony. The beds had been put in storage and replaced by metal racks stacked up with computers, monitors, tape drives, telephones, backup power supplies, and two-way radio equipment. The only active screens showed Internet weather forecasts, one from the BBC and one from CNN.

Chloe was crawling behind the wire racks with a bunch of cables draped over her shoulder and she looked stressed out. James leaned over one of the computers and menacingly wiggled a finger in front of the reset switch.

"Here, Chloe, what would happen if I pushed this button?"

"Don't you *dare*," Chloe yelled. "Unless you fancy spending the next six months in traction."

James looked at the two weather forecasts. "Has John given the go-ahead yet?"

Chloe's voice strained from beneath a chipboard shelf as she reached for a power socket. "Not yet, but it looks OK. The BBC were saying rain earlier in the day, but they've changed their minds now."

"Why's the weather so important, anyway?" James asked.

"Some of our listening posts are using laser microphones and all our linkups are via satellite. If it rains heavily, especially thunderstorms, half of our signals will go down the toilet."

"Right, like when you're watching football on Sky and the picture freezes as Thierry Henry's running on goal."

"That's it exactly," Chloe said.

"I don't think I've seen so many wires before in my whole life."

"James, I'm trying to concentrate here," Chloe

said irritably. "I've got thirty-seven electrical devices going into four wall sockets, more than fifty cables to plug in, and a wi-fi network to set up. I don't mean to be rude, but can you *please* go next door and sit with Kerry and your sister."

"Sorry," James said, holding up his hands. "Give us a shout if you need anything."

James turned around and headed back through the connecting door. Kerry and Lauren had both been watching TV when he stepped out a minute earlier, but the set was off now and they'd both disappeared. James figured they'd gone into their bedroom. He sat on the sofa, hit the power button, and flipped until he found an episode of *Futurama*.

After thirty seconds, the lights went out. James felt the back of his T-shirt being grabbed, followed by a shower of popcorn going down his neck.

"*Aaagghh!*" James yelled, jumping up as Kerry switched the lights back on.

Lauren sprung from behind the sofa with a massive grin on her face. James ripped off his T-shirt and flicked away the bits of popcorn stuck to his back.

"You are *so* dead, Lauren."

Lauren grinned. "Gotta catch me to kill me."

James closed down on the sofa. Lauren was fast and could wriggle for England. James knew whichever way he moved, she'd dive out the opposite side. To get around this, he charged at the sofa and pushed it backwards. When Lauren realized she was about to get pinned to the wall, she scrambled up over the sofa and collapsed onto the cushions. James stopped pushing and dived onto his sister's back. She tried to break out, but James had enough of a weight advantage to hold her.

"I can't breathe," Lauren moaned as he squashed her.

James scooped a handful of the loose popcorn off the sofa with one hand and tugged the elastic of Lauren's shorts with the other.

"James *no*," Lauren squealed. "Not down my knickers. This is war, James. *LET ME GO.*"

21:06

John was seventeen floors down in a corner of the hotel bar, as far as he could get from the other guests. Two stocky men passed through a set of double doors, and John reflected that somehow, years of police and intelligence work had given him the nose to spot a plainclothes cop a mile off: jeans, beer gut, ski jacket. There was even something about they way they spoke.

"You must be John Jones," the older one said as he dumped an Adidas sports bag on the carpet.

John reached out to shake their hands. "Greg Jackson and Ray McLad, I believe. Grab a seat. What are you drinking?"

Ray and Greg worked for the Metropolitan Police Complaints Investigation Bureau. CIB officers specialize in dealing with corruption and allegations made against fellow officers.

"We were intrigued by your e-mail," Greg said as John returned, placing three pints of beer on the table and sliding back into his seat. "Not much in the way of specifics, but you're talking about a big collar:

bent cops, robbery, and murder all in one go. So what's the deal?"

"In a nutshell, my plan is to take our two main suspects, make them fighting mad, and set them at each other's throats. If all goes well, they'll end up in a confrontation, recounting past misdeeds while we've got a microphone aimed at them."

Ray nodded. "How come you wanted us involved? Intelligence usually likes to snaffle all the glory for itself."

"I've been working with a community police-woman called Millie Kentner, but the rest of my operatives are a bit on the unusual side," John explained. "They can't show their faces in open court without undermining the security of an organization that doesn't officially exist. So, if we pull this off, we'll package all the evidence up so it looks like everything was done by Millie herself and you two. I'd imagine a chief inspector's badge will be within easy grasp."

Both cops tried to act like they weren't impressed, but couldn't help smiling into their pint glasses as they drank.

"When you say your agents are unusual, are we talking about informants, or what?" Greg asked.

"Far more exotic than that," John grinned. "An old friend of mine recommended you two guys because you've worked with MI5 before, but I'm still going to remind you where you stand: If you ever disclose any information about the agents you'll be working with over the next couple of days, you'll be undermining dozens of undercover missions throughout the world and putting lives at risk. If you leave us in a position where we have to choose between your lives and the safety of our agents, you might find yourselves in some very hot water."

Greg and Ray exchanged a look, as if to say: *Is this joker full of his own important, or what?* John didn't mind; he knew the cops would take the threat seriously enough when they learned the truth.

"Finish your pints, then I'll take you upstairs to meet the cherubs," John said.

Ray scratched his nose. "Why bother with a cherub when he's out to lunch?"

21:11

Millie had worked out of the same cramped office since she first came to Palm Hill in 1996. For nine years she'd been dedicated to her job. She'd pulled twelve-hour shifts, attended community meetings that dragged into the early hours of the morning, and often came in on her days off to catch up with paperwork.

Discovering Michael Patel's criminal past had shattered Millie's confidence. How good a cop could she really be if she hadn't noticed that her right-hand man was a bully, a thief, and probably a murderer to boot? However the sting operation went, Millie had decided to quit the force as soon as it was over.

She had a mound of paperwork to deal with, but she'd spent the past half an hour brooding into the bottom of a coffee cup, with her black stockinged feet resting on her desktop. When the mobile in her top pocket started to vibrate it was Chloe back at the hotel.

"Sorry we kept you waiting," Chloe said. "The weather looks good for tomorrow. I called John for confirmation and he's cleared us to go."

"Got that," Millie said, breaking into what felt like her first smile in days. "I just hope this works out."

"Don't sweat it," Chloe said. "John really knows his stuff. He was running operations like this when you and I were in nappies."

Millie ended the call. She knew this wasn't going to be easy, but it was a relief to be underway after nearly three weeks of preparations. She slipped her feet back into her shoes, rolled her chair forward, and grabbed the receiver of the landline phone on her desk. Her finger tapped in memory seventy-three: Michael Patel's home number.

"Six-zero-three-one."

"Pat, is that you? Is he home?"

"Oh, hi, Millie," Patricia said. She yelled after her husband before putting her mouth back to the receiver. "You must come round to dinner again some time, by the way."

"That would be nice," Millie lied as she over-heard the Patels' three-year-old daughter, Charlotte, screaming in the background. "It sounds like the young lady doesn't want to go to bed," she added.

"She's been a pain all day. First she wouldn't get in the bath. Now she's refusing to get out." Patricia shouted out again, "*Michael,* are you going to take this call or not? I can't leave Charlotte alone in the water."

Patricia put the receiver down and dashed off. Michael picked it up twenty seconds later. "Sorry to keep you waiting, guv. What's up?"

Millie had practiced the lie a hundred times over the previous week. "Afraid I'm the bearer of bad news, Mike. Remember you pulled in a kid called James Holmes over by the reservoir a few Saturdays back?"

Michael nodded at the receiver. "Yeah, the tough little brat, turned over a couple of real hard cases. What about him?"

"I've got a heads up that Holmes's solicitor has filed a complaint against you. James claims you knocked his head against the roof as you put him into the car. You'll get the official two-eight-nine notification some time tomorrow. You'll obviously have to go over to CIB for an interview about it at some stage, but I thought you'd want to know now, so you can check your notebook and get your details straight."

"Appreciated, boss. Usual story I suppose: It'll be my word against Holmes's, but it's still a damned nuisance. It'll be half a day wasted dealing with CIB, when I've got a million better things I could be doing."

Millie turned the screw a little tighter. "I did get one other detail: James's solicitor reckons he's got hold of some CCTV footage of the incident."

"Oh," Mike said, audibly shocked. He missed a couple of beats before covering himself. "He can have all the CCTV he likes, boss, because nothing happened."

"Of course," Millie said. "I know you're whiter than white, Michael. You've got nothing to worry about and you know I'll be supporting you all the way. I just thought you'd want to know as soon as possible."

John snapped his mobile shut and tucked it into his jacket as he headed down the deserted seventeenth-floor corridor. Greg and Ray walked in step behind him.

"Good news?" Greg asked.

John nodded. "That was Millie calling. She's a good cop, but she's tearing herself apart over all that's been happening. She's just spoken to Patel. She reckons he swallowed her line about the phony complaint. He won't be sleeping easy tonight with that hanging over his head."

"So how old are these cherubs?" Ray asked.

"Dave's the oldest, he's seventeen. James and Kerry are thirteen and Lauren is ten. You've got to remember, though, they aren't ordinary kids. They're all intelligent, disciplined and highly trained. The things I've seen them accomplish in the year that I've worked for CHERUB have been astonishing."

John slid his key card into the lock and pushed the door open, revealing a scene of devastation. There were sofa cushions scattered about, dots of popcorn everywhere, streaks of water across the carpet, and puddles on the furniture.

James nearly crashed into John as he sprinted out of the toilet holding an ice bucket filled with water.

"Oh . . . ," James said, wilting under John's scowl.

John looked set to kill. "James, what in the name of *God* are you playing at?"

"We're just messing," James said, glancing around at the carnage. "I suppose we got carried away."

Kerry burst out of the bedroom, holding a plastic water bottle and using a pillow as a shield. "I'm gonna make you guys so wet . . . ," she said, tailing off abruptly when she spotted the three men standing in the doorway.

"You two stand over there," John yelled, pointing at the wall. "Where's the other one?"

Lauren meekly emerged from beneath a pile of sofa cushions in the far corner. She had a gigantic Coke stain down her T-shirt and significantly more popcorn stuck to her clothes than James or Kerry.

"This behavior is ridiculous," John screamed. "Millie has set off the sting operation, there's a room next door packed with tens of thousands of pounds' worth of electronic equipment, and you three are throwing water around and acting like a bunch of five-year-olds."

He pointed at Lauren. "*You*, get in the shower right now. The other two, I want you to straighten up, wipe up the puddles, and pick every piece of popcorn off this carpet. And be quick about it, because if this place isn't cleared up by the time Dave gets here, I'm gonna start dishing out punishment laps."

Ray and Greg were grinning at each other as they stepped into the lounge area and began brushing popcorn off a couple of the sofa cushions.

"Highly disciplined," Greg laughed.

John allowed himself to smile as everyone mucked in with the clearing up. "No matter how much we train 'em, they're still kids."

21:32
James returned the vauum cleaner to the house-keeping cupboard at the end of the hotel corridor. Now they'd finished cleaning up, he realized he needed a shower to get all the bits of toffee off his skin, but Kerry was queuing outside the door and Lauren was still in there.

He battered the door. "Get a move on, Lauren. Any normal person takes five minutes, not twenty."

"Use the shower in the other room," she yelled back.

"We can't," Kerry yelled. "Chloe's got cables running from the shaving socket. You can't close the door and the steam might blow everything up."

"OK," Lauren tutted. "I'll be two more minutes."

James and Kerry leaned against the wall near the entrance of the room, facing each other. John and the two cops were drooling over the surveillance equipment in the next room. Kerry's face was red from chasing around. She wore a giant T-shirt that almost went down to the bottom of her shorts and one lemon trainer sock. The other one had gone missing during the battle.

James suspected Kerry's feelings towards him were starting to mellow. They'd hurled abuse, popcorn, and cushions at each other, but still hadn't managed a normal conversation, except when they'd had to talk during mission preparations.

James looked up when he noticed Kerry smiling to herself. He tested the water with a single word. "What?"

Kerry's look stiffened when James spoke, but after a second she grinned and looked up at him.

"You look funny with all that popcorn stuck in your hair," she muttered, as if she didn't really want to say it.

James couldn't read Kerry's body language. Her expression seemed a lot like the way she used to look at him before they kissed. Or was it anger?

With Kerry's temper, James knew he'd wind up on the floor in an excruciating arm-lock if he got this wrong, but he fancied her so much it was making him loopy. He'd never wanted to kiss someone so badly in his life and she was standing less than a meter away with nobody else around.

James took a half step forward, so that Kerry was right in his face. Her dark brown eyes kept staring up, but refused to give any obvious signal. He kissed her on the cheek, then backed away, as if he'd jabbed a snake with a sharp stick.

Kerry's smile grew and James felt a massive rush as he realized his bravery had paid off. She grabbed James around his waist, pushed him back against the wall, and they started snogging. It lasted for about twenty seconds, when the latch clicked inside the bathroom door. Kerry stepped backwards and acted innocent as Lauren emerged, wearing an adult-length robe that dragged along the floor.

"Finished," she announced as she cut across the carpet towards the bedroom.

Once Lauren was out of sight, James moved in to start snogging again, but Kerry's expression had changed completely. She shoved him away.

"I'm still not talking to you," she said firmly as she slid into the bathroom and shut the door in his face.

Confusion

23:07

A gray VW van pulled up directly opposite the Patels' house. Dave switched off the lights and engine, climbed out of the cab, and walked around the outside to join James and Kerry in the back.

"All OK?" Dave asked.

James had never felt so confused in his life, but Dave was asking about the mission, not his relationship with Kerry.

"Yeah," James said. "Except it's boiling in here."

Surveillance vans aren't air-conditioned, because the noise it would make is a giveaway. The rear compartment contained three office chairs, which were bolted to the floor in front of a bank of monitors and VCRs. These were linked to hidden cameras and microphones built into the exterior and roof. The lack of ventilation, combined with the heat coming off the electronic gear, pushed the temperature into the forties on this warm August evening.

"Kerry, have you got the laser microphone lined up yet?" Dave asked.

"It's a bit cranky," Kerry said as she leaned over a console, adjusting a row of knobs beneath a small TV screen.

As she fiddled, the picture changed from white to black before settling into a steady bluish hue.

"OK," Dave said as he fed digital audio tapes into two recorders. "Now line it up on the house. You want to get a window dead in the center so that it picks up the vibrations when people speak."

Kerry tutted. "I know what I'm doing, Dave." She used a joystick to line up the image on a window. "Ready when you are, James."

James hit a switch to activate the laser. The invisible beam detected vibrations in the glass and relayed a crude impression of any noises or speech going on inside the house. The output was set to max volume and James lunged at the control to turn it down before it fried their eardrums.

"*The Israeli government says that it's trying to calm tension in the region following . . .*"

"TV news," James said.

Dave nodded. "Kerry, line that microphone up on some of the other windows. Then save the positions in memory and keep flicking between them."

Dave pulled a two-way radio out of his pocket. Its signal was digitally encrypted, so nobody could listen in. "Base, this is Dave inside unit one. We're in position and we have good sound, but Michael's still up watching TV."

"Roger that," Chloe answered. "John is in position at the railway arch. Tell us when you're ready to move in."

WEDNESDAY, 00:57

They'd been sweltering in the van for two hours. James had managed to nod off on the floor, while

Kerry and Dave took turns monitoring the sounds inside the house.

The TV went off at 00:22. They tracked the sound of Michael Patel walking upstairs, brushing his teeth, and flushing the toilet. Patricia woke up as her husband climbed into bed. At 00:30 Michael told his wife that he loved her and that he'd checked on their daughter. The microphone began picking up a gentle snoring sound at 00:37.

"They've been asleep for twenty minutes," Kerry said. "That's long enough, isn't it?"

Dave nodded as he pulled his radio out of his pocket. "Base, I think the Patels are asleep. We're moving in."

"Copy that, Dave," Chloe answered.

Dave pinched James's nose to wake him up. He gasped through his mouth before opening his eyes and shooting up from the floor of the van.

"Joanna," James gasped.

"Who's Joanna?" Dave said with raised eyebrows as James yawned and rubbed his hand over his face.

"I was having this weird dream. I was in a tent with this girl I met on my first mission. But Clint Eastwood and my nan kept flying over in a hot air balloon and dropping rocks on us."

"A dream like that probably means something really profound." Dave grinned.

Kerry couldn't resist chipping in. "It means he's an idiot and we knew *that* already."

"Are they asleep now?" James yawned.

Dave nodded. "You're going in."

James grabbed the backpack he'd been using as a

pillow. He pulled out his radio and fitted the ear-piece. "Testing, testing, James testing."

Chloe came back in his ear. "Hearing you loud and clear, James."

Kerry did a radio test, then she and James pulled on disposable gloves and baseball caps. Kerry fitted an attachment to the front of her lock gun and tucked it into the front pocket of her shorts. Dave checked all the monitors to makes sure nobody was walking along the streets outside, then switched out the lights so that James and Kerry weren't seen as they jumped out the back doors.

"Good luck out there," Dave whispered. "I'll radio right away if the mike picks up any movement inside the house."

Kerry led James across the road and up the Patels' driveway, passing their BMW. She pushed the lock gun into the deadlock and made easy work of undoing it, before swapping to a different-shaped pick and attacking the regular lock.

James whispered into his mouthpiece as they passed through the doorway. "We're in."

After pushing shut the door, they each grabbed cylinders—like mini fire extinguishers—out of their backpacks and pulled rubber gas masks over their faces. Kerry checked James's mask was fitted properly and James returned the favor. They were halfway up the stairs when Dave called through their earpieces.

"Back up, we've got movement in the bedroom."

James and Kerry hurried stealthily down the staircase as the light came on in the upstairs hallway. Patricia Patel stepped out of the bedroom. She checked on her sleeping daughter before cutting into the bathroom.

Kerry whispered into her mouthpiece. "Do we pull out?"

"Negative," Dave answered. "She'll probably go back to bed. Stay in the house unless she starts coming down the stairs."

Sure enough, Patricia flushed the toilet and wandered back to bed.

James peeled off his gas mask and spoke to Kerry. "We'll have to wait until she's gone back to sleep."

01:16
Fifteen minutes dragged by as James and Kerry sat against the wall at the bottom of the staircase, listening to their heartbeats. When Dave gave the all-clear, they refitted and rechecked their gas masks before heading up the stairs again.

The Patels slept with their bedroom door open, so they could hear if their daughter woke up and started yelling. James and Kerry ripped safety collars from the necks of the gas canisters as they entered and crept around to opposite sides of the double bed. James held up three fingers and counted down. They both moved on zero.

James positioned the white cup on the top of the canister a few centimeters above Michael's nose and mouth before gently turning a screw to release the gas. Kerry's task was more awkward, because Patricia slept with her face buried in a pillow. They each held the canisters in place and counted until their victims had inhaled seven times, enough gas to knock them out for two and a half hours.

Job done, they cut the flow of gas and backed out of the room. James ripped off his mask. Kerry did the same and they smiled at each other.

"Good job." James grinned. Then he pressed the button to speak into his mouthpiece. "This is James. We've done the sleeping gas."

"Copy that," Dave said through the earpiece. "I'll meet you on the doorstep."

"Drive safe, James," John added. "And try not to wake the little girl up."

John had checked out the Patel family's medical records and discovered that three-year-old Charlotte suffered from asthma. This made using sleeping gas unacceptably risky, so John had settled on a less than ideal solution: Kerry would have to sit with Charlotte. Hopefully the toddler wouldn't wake up. If she did, Kerry had a bottle of juice mixed with a mild sedative that would help her go back to sleep. If Charlotte mentioned what had happened in the morning, she was young enough that her parents would assume it was a dream.

While Kerry settled onto a beanbag next to Charlotte's little bed, James headed downstairs. He let Dave in the front door, then began searching for the car keys. Dave had a backpack full of listening devices and would spend the next hour wiring up the Patels' house so that no snippet of conversation got missed.

The keys were in Michael's coat pocket. Dave stood on the kitchen table, replacing the lightbulb with one containing a bug, as James made to leave.

"I'm off," James said. "Keep an eye on Kerry if the brat wakes up. She's hopeless with little kids."

"I will," Dave nodded. "Later, James."

James headed out onto the driveway and climbed into the Patels' car. He'd driven a few now, but he still got a buzz every time he lined up in front of a steering wheel looking at all the switches, knowing there weren't many kids his age that got to hare around in two tons of BMW. He pulled the seat forward so he could reach the pedals, belted up, and turned the ignition key.

It was a nice drive—the roads were empty and the car had plenty of grunt. Unfortunately it was only five kilometers. He pulled up a turning at the side of a bridge and crawled along an unlit, cobbled lane with a line of railway arches along one side. The arches were mostly used for storage, but he passed a plumbing suppliers and a couple of auto repair shops. The last one had a light shining out of its open doorway. James turned cautiously into a floodlit garage filled with equipment for respraying cars.

John and Greg were waiting. They opened the doors on the passenger side before James had even got out. He'd parked next to a BMW 535i that looked identical in every detail to the Patels' one. Not just in terms of model and color—it had the same number plates, a small amount of parking damage on the front bumper had been carefully replicated, and if you'd opened up the bonnet and done a detailed inspection, you'd have found the same serial numbers on the chassis and engine block. The only visible difference between the two cars was the personal effects inside the one that belonged to the Patels, and that was about to change.

John grabbed the rubber floor mats from the Patels' car and transferred them to the duplicate, Greg dealt with the contents of the glove box, while James clambered into the back, pulled out the child seat, and picked up dozens of Charlotte's toys and books from the surrounding area.

While James struggled to fit the child seat into the back of the duplicate car, Greg transferred the pushchair and junk in the boot. John even went as far as to move the sweet wrappers in the ashtrays and the dried-out orange peel in the center console. By the time they'd finished, there was no way the Patels would have been able to tell the duplicate car from their own.

"Can I drive the copy back?" James asked.

John shook his head. "No way. You need a bit of strength to drive this one, she's an absolute pig. Greg's gonna take you back to Palm Hill. You'll need your beauty sleep. It's gonna be hectic tomorrow."

02:17

John pulled the BMW into the front drive of the Patels' house, being careful to position it in the exact spot James had removed the original from forty minutes earlier. It wasn't easy because the power steering wasn't rigged up properly and the wheels were out of alignment.

After climbing out, John raised the hood. He slid a screwdriver out of his jacket and used it to lever the tops from the plastic compartment at the back of the engine bay that contained the engine management system. This consisted of a small blue circuit board with a row of microchips on it. John rocked the board loose from its socket and replaced it with an identical one that had been shorted out.

John got back in the driver's seat and turned the ignition key. Instead of the engine starting, he got crazy beeping sounds and the indicator lights on the dashboard flickering like Christmas decorations. Satisfied that the car wouldn't run, he locked it up and walked towards the house.

The front door was on the latch. After replacing the car keys in Michael's jacket, John found Dave sitting on the living room couch using a Palm Pilot handheld computer.

"All set?" John asked.

Dave nodded. "I'm running a diagnostic on the bugs. I've put in five altogether, which should cover the entire house. Chloe's getting a strong signal back at the hotel. Did everything go OK with the car?"

"Pretty much. You need to be a pro wrestler to steer that thing though."

Dave grinned. "Hardly surprising under the circumstances."

"You can head back to Palm Hill if you're done here," John said. "I know you've got to be in work early tomorrow."

"What about Kerry?"

"Oh, I forgot she's still up there," John grinned. "Do you mind dropping her off at the hotel on your way home? I'll have to sit it out here for at least another couple of hours. We can't have Charlotte waking up and roaming the house while her parents are unconscious."

"No worries," Dave said.

John reached into his trousers and pulled out a set of car keys. "I'll take the van, because we'll need it back here tomorrow morning. These are for a little yellow Mitsubishi; it's parked up the top of the road, about a hundred meters on the left."

"Cheers, John," Dave said as he swiped the keys and stood up. "So far so good, eh?"

"Touch wood," John replied as he leaned forward and tapped his fingers on the top of the coffee table. "Have a safe drive home and good luck with Leon at the car lot tomorrow."

Disharmony

07:59

Kerry woke up with bits of popcorn stuck to her legs. They'd tidied up, but she was still finding it everywhere, including between her bedclothes. She'd had less than five hours' sleep, but she wanted to know how the mission was progressing.

She looked across to the next bed and realized Lauren was already up, then slipped into the grubby jeans and T-shirt she'd worn the night before and scooted across to the bathroom. After a pee and a quick gargle of mouthwash, she found Lauren, Chloe, and John gathered around the surveillance equipment in the adjoining room. All three wore headsets.

"What did I miss?"

"Morning, Kerry." John smiled. "Nothing huge. We're just earwigging on some domestic disharmony."

Lauren pulled a headphone out of one ear and held it out for Kerry. "It's hilarious, actually," she explained. "Michael and Patricia and having a row over who takes Charlotte to nursery. Charlotte chucked a fit. She hurled her cereal bowl and called her daddy *a bum head*."

"Mike has mentioned Millie ringing about the

complaint," Chloe added. "He hasn't admitted any-thing, but it's definitely playing on his mind."

Kerry squeezed onto the edge of Lauren's chair and plugged the foam-covered loudspeaker into her ear. The sound from the bug Dave had fitted into the kitchen light was excellent: She could hear all the little details, like Charlotte murmuring to herself and the washing machine going around.

08:25

Over at Palm Hill, James and Dave sat at their dining table eating bacon sandwiches. James was finishing a long explanation about what had happened with Kerry the night before. Dave didn't exactly look fascinated.

"It was wild, Dave," James enthused. "I don't know where I found the guts to do it, but it was the best kiss *ever*. Like a million volts of electricity, or something. But now she's back to not talking to me again. Except she is, kind of, when she feels like it . . . What do you reckon I should do?"

Dave leaned back in his chair and scratched beneath the logo on his greasy Tarasov Prestige Motors polo shirt. "Tricky," Dave said. "I mean, she kissed you, which means she obviously still fancies you."

James nodded. "That's what I thought."

"And there's definitely no other boyfriend in the equation?"

"Not that I know of."

"And she dumped you and threw your boots at your head, then went really nuts when you battered poor little Andy?"

James nodded again.

"Sounds like more trouble than it's worth to me. What's wrong with Hannah, anyway?"

"There's nothing wrong with Hannah, but we'll probably be out of here in a few days, so I'm not letting myself get too fond of her."

"Sensible," Dave said. "What I don't get is, why are you so hung up about Kerry? I mean, she's nice, but there's nothing really special about her."

James bit the crust of his sandwich and shrugged. "I dunno. I just really like Kerry. Haven't you ever had one girl that you've really, really liked and you can't get her out of your head?"

"Nah." Dave grinned. "I can think of a couple of girls who've felt that way about me, but that's perfectly understandable."

"It could have been a one-off," James said. "You know? Like, she kissed me on the spur of the moment, but she really doesn't want to go out with me. Or it could be that she wants to get back with me and she's expecting me to make the next move. Do you think I should buy her a present, or try talking to her, or something?"

Dave leaned forward and pointed his finger. James got excited, expecting to hear the solution to all his problems.

"You see, here's the thing," Dave said, waggling the finger and pausing to build up the suspense. "I really don't give a monkey's about your love life."

James pounded angrily on the tabletop. "Thanks, *mate*. I thought with all the girlfriends you'd had you might help me sort this out."

Dave laughed as he crammed the last bit of bacon

sandwich in his mouth. "I'm off to work. I've got more important things to worry about than your train-wreck relationship with Kerry Chang."

08:27

Patricia Patel emerged onto the driveway holding Charlotte in her arms. She had no clue that a CIB officer was sitting inside the gray van parked less than twenty meters away, videoing her every move.

She put Charlotte down beside the silver BMW and gave the little girl a Tweenies lunchbox to hold while she adjusted the straps on the baby seat inside. They were all out of kilter for some reason. After her daughter was safely strapped in the back, Patricia belted up in the front and turned the ignition key.

There was a microphone inside the duplicate car, so everyone back at the hotel could hear what was going on.

"*Shit*," Patricia yelled as she banged her palm on the steering wheel.

"Mummy," Charlotte said, pointing an accusing finger. "You said a rudey word."

Patricia got out of the car and stormed back to the house. "Michael, can you come and look at this car? It's not starting."

Michael stepped out, dressed in boxers and carpet slippers.

"She used a rude word, Daddy," Charlotte said as her father got into the driver's seat.

"Sometimes grown-ups say naughty words when they're upset, sweetie. I think the car is broken and it made Mummy cross."

"Can you fix it?"

"I don't know about cars, Charlotte. We'll have to call the mechanic."

"What's mechanic?"

Michael ignored his daughter's question as he stepped out and confronted his stern-faced wife.

"I'll call out the Auto Club." Michael shrugged. "You'll have to wait in for them."

"Why *me*?" Patricia said indignantly. "I can't wait in. I'll have to take Charlotte to nursery on the bus and then I'm getting my hair done."

"It's your day off," Michael said. "I've got a neighborhood watch meeting in the bloody community center at half eleven."

"You just said they're a bunch of pensioners with nothing better to do."

"They *are*," Michael said. "But I'm a community police officer, it's part of my job."

"You've got nearly two hours. The mechanic should be here before then."

Charlotte whined from inside the car. "Mummy, I want to get out."

Michael grunted at his wife. "Fine. I'll wait for the mechanic. It's *your* day off, but you piss off and get your hair done. I guess the world would stop spinning if that didn't happen, whereas we don't need our car at all."

"Get me out," Charlotte screamed, kicking her pick trainers against the seat in front of her.

"It wouldn't kill you to get off your lazy backside and do something around here for once," Patricia yelled as she ducked inside the car and unhooked Charlotte's seatbelt.

Ray's voice came through to the hotel suite from his position inside the gray van. "Base, that's it. I can see Michael going into the house."

Kerry and Lauren were still squeezed up on the chair sharing the headphones as John grabbed a microphone. "Thanks, Ray, got that. I'll get Chloe to switch over the phone at the exchange."

"Been there, done that," Chloe said. "We've now got the option of answering any call Michael makes."

"CHERUB *has* the technology," Lauren said, deepening her voice to make herself sound like a movie trailer.

John looked at Kerry and Lauren. "You'd better keep the chatter down when this call comes through—in fact, scrub that order. Lauren, you're not even dressed, and Kerry, your hair looks like a bird's nest. We might need you for something later on, so get yourselves scrubbed. Then go downstairs and get breakfast before the buffet closes."

Lauren looked back at John. "Can't we *please* stay long enough to hear the phone call?"

"No," John said sternly. "This isn't Chat FM you're listening to here. This is a mission and we've all got jobs to do. Now scram."

The girls skulked out of the room and began rowing over who got first dibs in the shower.

"Keep the noise down," John yelled. "And you're not that big, you can shower together and save time."

"But . . . ," Kerry said reluctantly.

"Think of the water you'll save," Chloe laughed. "It'll be good for the environment."

A phone that was linked up to one of the computers started ringing almost as soon as the girls had gone. After three rings, Chloe let a call-center program on one of the computers answer it with a message she'd recorded a few days ealier.

"Hello, my car . . . ," Michael Patel spluttered, before he realized he was speaking to a machine.

"*Welcome to the Auto Club home-start hotline. We're sorry, but all our operators are busy at this time. Your call matters to us and one of our operators will take it as soon as they become available. For your convenience, please have your membership number ready . . .*"

"For *God's* sake," Michael yelled as light classical music broke out over the line. "Why can't anyone just answer a telephone these days?"

08:59

Leon had given Dave a set of keys for the car lot. As he undid the padlock on the gate, Dave looked over his shoulder at the orange Mercedes van parked across the street, knowing that the CIB agent Greg Jackson was watching him from inside.

Leon and Pete never made it to the lot much before quarter past nine, which meant Dave had a few minutes to run some final checks. He unlocked Leon's office and filled the kettle to brew up. Then he pulled the Palm Pilot out of his rucksack and ran a diagnostic on the five listening devices he'd set up on the lot over the previous week. He was a little perturbed when he entered the access code for the first bug, only to find that the signal was very weak. He flipped through the other four devices, and found that they were completely dead.

Dave felt a shot of panic. This was the most important location in the sting operation and one weak audio signal coming out of the tool shed wasn't going to cut it. He frantically checked out of the window to make sure nobody was approaching the cabin before grabbing the two-way radio out of his pack.

"John, Chloe, I'm in big trouble here."

John's voice crackled through the speaker. "Dave, what's wrong?"

"I'm not picking up a scrap of sound through the Palm Pilot. Can you double-check at your end?"

"Will do."

It took thirty seconds for John's reply to come through.

"They're all dead," John called anxiously.

"I've got a signal on one," Dave said.

"If they're all down, it must be a problem with the booster aerial that relays the signal up to the satellite. Where did you hide it?"

"On the cabin roof," Dave said.

"Is Leon there yet?"

Dave looked at his watch. "Not for eight to ten minutes, I reckon."

"Do you think you've got time to get up on the roof and have a go at fixing it?"

"I can try," Dave said. "But I'll have some explaining to do if he turns up early."

"We're dead in the water if we can't get Leon's conversations on tape. You'll have to risk it."

Dave anxiously checked his watch and tucked

the Palm Pilot and two-way radio into his shorts. He grabbed a dustbin from near the entrance of the lot and dragged it up to the cabin. He stood on the lid, then hauled himself on to the corrugated metal roof.

It wasn't a nice place to be, but as he clambered over the moss and bird droppings, he could at least identify the cause of the problem: some drunk had lobbed an empty vodka bottle onto the roof of the cabin, knocking the stubby gray booster aerial out of its mounting bracket.

Dave clicked it into place then pulled the Palm Pilot out of his pocket and scanned quickly through the five transmission frequencies. They were all back at full strength.

He crawled towards the dustbin to get down, but as he did he noticed Pete getting out of the passenger door of his uncle's Jaguar to open the gate. There was no way he'd be able to clamber down before being seen.

09:07

John was delighted to see the signal graphs from the bugs on Tarasov's car lot shook back into the green.

"Looks like he's fixed it," John said to Chloe. "Good lad."

Michael Patel had been on hold for nine minutes, getting more and more ratty as the calling system repeated its loop. Chloe finally decided to put him out of his misery and grabbed a telephone handset, which was rigged up to the computer in front of her.

"Good morning, this is Chloe speaking. Auto Club would like to apologize for the delay in answering your call this morning. Can I have your name and membership number please?"

While Chloe took down the details of the problem with Michael's car, John had moved into the bedroom. He unbuttoned his shirt, stepped out of his trousers, and grabbed a yellow and blue Auto Club uniform out of his wardrobe.

Pickle

09:11

Dave lay flat against the corrugated rooftop, with his nose uncomfortably close to a fresh splat of bird poop. Pete and Leon stood by the gate looking up and down the street.

"Dave must have unlocked," Leon said angrily. "Nobody else has keys. But where's the little idiot legged it to?"

Dave heard the conversation continue as Pete followed his uncle into the cabin.

"Look," Leon said. "The kettle's hot."

"I checked in the toilet," Pete said.

Dave couldn't climb down onto the bin without being seen through the cabin window. He realized his only chance was to drop off the back of the roof into the derelict builders' yard next door. He crawled furtively, knowing that he was only separated from Leon and Pete's heads by forty centimeters and a sheet of wobbly metal that amplified every noise he made.

When he got to the rear edge, Dave slid his legs over the side before dropping down into a tangle of weeds. He narrowly missed clattering into a set of rusted paint cans as he stumbled forwards, then swept most of the dirt off his clothes. He set off towards the street, keeping low to avoid being spotted through the wire by Leon or Pete.

There were a couple of missing planks in the wooden fence along the front of the yard. After checking that nobody was coming, he trampled down some stinging nettles, pulled in his stomach, and squeezed through the gap on to the street. Dave realized he needed an excuse for leaving, so instead of heading straight back he ducked into the newsagents and caught his breath as he queued up to buy a newspaper and a pint of milk.

He strolled onto the lot a couple of minutes later, trying to look innocent as Leon exploded out of the door of his cabin.

"Morning, boss," Dave said.

"What sort of prick are you?" Leon yelled as he stood in the doorway. "*Get* in here."

Dave acted dumb as he stepped into the cabin. "What?"

Leon slammed the door. "What? *What?* I drive in here and I find that everywhere's unlocked and you've legged it, that's *what*. There's over a hundred grand's worth of cars here. Are you off your head or something?"

Dave jiggled the pint of milk. "I thought we might run out later in the day."

"You mean to say we haven't even run out?" Leon shouted. "Did your mother drop you on your head when you were a baby or something? Give me your keys back, right now."

"Come on, Leon. I just got chatting to Mr. Singh

in the newsagents and lost track of time. The car keys were all locked in your safe and I was only gone for five minutes."

"Keys," Leon repeated.

Dave got the keys out of his shorts and dangled them in front of Leon. "I'm really sorry, boss."

"Count yourself lucky," Leon said as he snatched them. "You do something as dumb as that again and you'll be out of a job."

"You've been really good to me, Leon. I swear it won't happen again."

Leon flicked Dave away with his hand. "You'd better get out there and make yourself look busy before I *really* lose my temper. Start off with the Mini. That time-waster had his kids in the back yesterday afternoon. There's handprints all over the windows."

09:49

John pulled into the Patels' driveway and blasted the horn of his yellow and blue recovery truck.

"Hello, Mr. Patel?" John said, jumping down from the cab as Michael came out of his front door. "Is this the vehicle with the problem?"

Michael nodded. "Yeah, the wife was taking my daughter to nursery this morning and it wouldn't start. It's as dead as a doornail."

"Was there any sign of a problem before this morning: squeaks, rattles, high oil consumption?"

Michael shook his head. "I've had the car just over six months and this is the first glitch we've had."

John nodded as Michael handed him the car keys. "Nice cars, BMWs. All the fancy gizmos go wrong now and then, but we still don't get to see many of them."

John leaned under the steering wheel and popped the hood open. He spent a couple of minutes under the hood, waggling the dipstick and pretending that he knew what he was doing, before looking up at Michael.

"Was this car ever in an accident?" John asked.

Michael shook his head. "Not that I know of. What makes you ask that?"

"There's a lot of paint spattered inside here, like it's been resprayed. Did you get a mechanical inspection before you bought the vehicle?"

"I didn't think I needed one. The dealer that I got it from is an old mate of mine."

John smiled a little, knowing that the microphone in the van had just recorded Michael admitting his friendship with Leon Tarasov.

"This car has had a heck of a lot of repair work done on it," John explained. "Come and look here. You see those bolts in the bottom of the engine bay?"

Michael leaned under the hood.

"You see how the paint has pooled inside the heads? That would never happen in the factory, because the engine is fitted after the bodywork is painted. It means that a large area of the car has been resprayed at some point."

Michael looked shocked. "How much damage are we talking about here?"

"It's hard to be sure," John said. "But I can certainly see all the signs of a big smash-up. Do you mind if I look in the back?"

"Not at all," Michael said anxiously. "What for?"

"I want to see if there's any evidence of respraying at that end too."

John popped the boot and made an *ah-haah* noise.

"Mr. Patel, I have to say I'm starting to feel extremely concerned about the history of this car."

John tore up a corner of the carpet lining the boot, revealing patches of red paint.

"A silver car with patches of red paint in the boot," John said suspiciously.

Michael Patel had worked as a cop for long enough to know what this meant. "Are you telling me this car is a cut-and-shut?"

"Or something along those lines." John nodded as he ran his finger over a bump where the rear pillar joined the boot sill. "This weld looks more like the work of some bloke in a back alley body shop, instead of a high-precision robot in a BMW factory."

Michael Patel was breathing hard and his face looked gaunt.

"The front appears to have been heavily resprayed in its original silver and the back end clearly has parts that originally belonged to another vehicle that was painted red," John continued. "I'm afraid what you have is the front and rear portions of two different BMWs that were involved in serious accidents. The good bits from each car have been crudely patched together."

"I know what a cut-and-shut is," Michael said bitterly.

"It's an impressive piece of work," John said. "There's no obvious joins on the exterior bodywork.

Although if you jacked her up, I'm sure you'd find clues underneath. They tend not to be so thorough prettying up the bits that are out of sight."

"These things are death traps," Michael said, shaking his head. "My wife and daughter have been driving around in this crate. . . ."

"Absolutely," John nodded. "A cut-and-shut car has nothing like the structural strength of the original vehicle. If you'd been involved in an accident, this whole lot might easily have snapped in two. Do you have the details of where you bought it?"

"I've got a receipt inside the house. But, like I say, I bought the car off a man I thought I could trust. I can't *believe* that he'd do this to me."

"I'm going to have to inform the police about this," John said. "I could probably get the car running again, but I'm obviously not prepared to do that. This vehicle isn't fit to be on the road."

Michael suddenly looked even more stressed, which delighted John. His whole plan was based on the assumption that Michael wouldn't like the idea of the police coming between him and Leon Tarasov.

"No, no," Michael said, waving his arms and sounding panicky. "You don't need to call the police."

"I'm afraid I have to," John said. "I'm sure you're an honest man, Mr. Patel, but some people who've been caught out like this cut their losses by getting the car repaired and then selling it on to the next unsuspecting punter through a classified ad. It's Auto Club policy to inform the police as soon as we discover a potentially dangerous vehicle."

"No," Michael said, with a hint of desperation.

"You see, I'm a cop myself. I'll show you my ID."

Michael dashed into the house and grabbed his warrant card out of his jacket. By the time he'd got back, he'd thought up an excuse.

"You see," Michael said as John inspected the badge, "this will come through to the vehicle crime unit at my station. I'll be a complete laughing stock if this gets out. But I've got a mate who works in motor vehicles. He'll help me save my blushes, you understand?"

John scratched his chin like he was thinking it over. "Well, Mr. Patel, my obligation is to tell the police and I suppose you *are* the police."

"That's right." Michael looked relieved. "And I bet it saves you some hassle if it's done this way as well."

John grinned. "Yes, a bit."

"Great," Michael said.

"I guess there's no reason for me to stick around then," John said.

Michael reached out and shook John's hand. John headed back to his recovery truck. He grabbed his two-way radio off the passenger seat as he drove away.

"Did you catch all that, Chloe?" John asked cheerfully. "Do you think I pulled it off?"

Chloe came back laughing. "Yeah, bang-up job, John. I reckon our Mr. Patel is going to be out gunning for Leon Tarasov any minute now."

10:11
Lauren and Kerry stepped out of the lift into the seventeenth-floor corridor. Lauren was holding her tummy.

"I ate too much breakfast," she groaned. "One of these days I'm gonna work out that 'all-you-can-eat buffet' doesn't mean you have to eat all of it."

The girls had an air of excitement about them as Kerry grabbed a room key from her wallet. She tutted as she flicked away a piece of popcorn.

"How the hell did it get in there? That's James and his *stupid* popcorn fight."

"We started on him," Lauren reminded her.

Kerry grinned as she pushed the heavy room door. They kept the noise down as they stepped through to the adjoining room, in case Chloe was on the phone or something.

"Hello, girls. All washed and fed now?" Chloe asked.

"*Over*fed," Lauren said. "What did we miss? Has John gone out yet?"

"He's already on his way back."

Kerry looked at her watch. "That was quick. Did Patel buy the cut-and-shut ruse?"

"Hook, line, and sinker," Chloe grinned. "The duplicate car worked a treat. I just taped a phone call between Michael and Patricia's mobiles. She was in the hairdressers, so she couldn't go too nuts, but you could tell how mad she was. She was screaming at Michael, telling him to speak to Leon and demand their seventeen grand back. And listen to this."

Chloe hit a volume slider on her computer screen so that the sound from the Patels' house came out through the speakers.

"This is the live feed," Chloe explained.

Michael was pacing around, breathing furiously,

and occasionally pounding on something.

"Why doesn't he ring Leon, or go to see him?" Lauren asked.

Chloe shrugged. "I guess he's trying to work out what to say."

A red warning box popped up on Chloe's computer: *Wiretap Six: dialing.* The numbers appeared on screen a fraction of a second after Michael Patel hit them. By the time he'd dialed the area code and the first two numbers, they knew it was going to be Tarasov.

Kerry grinned at Lauren. "Stand by for fireworks."

Sparks

10:15

A couple of ex-fleet cars had come in from auction and Dave was vacuuming the interiors when Pete stuck his head out of the cabin holding a cordless phone to his ear.

"You seen Leon?"

Dave pointed towards the brick-built toilet. Pete walked over and slid the handset under the door to his uncle. Leon put down his *Racing Post* and picked the phone off the floor.

"Yeah, Leon Tarasov speaking."

"You're lucky I don't *kill* you," Michael screamed. "I just had the Auto Club out looking at my BMW and the mother is cut-and-shut."

Michael's voice was so stressed that Leon didn't recognize it. "Why don't you calm down and start at the beginning, chum? Who am I speaking to?"

"It's me, Leon, and I just became your worst nightmare."

"Mike, is that you? What the hell's the matter?"

"Like you don't know. That BMW you sold me is junk. The mechanic ripped up the carpet in back and it's full of red paint. The other end's been resprayed and there's botched welds all over the shop."

"Mike, do you think I'd be stupid enough to sell a cut-and-shut car to a cop? The Auto Club guy must have been a trainee or something. I got that car out of a BMW dealership that had too much stock on its hands. Corporate owner, full service history. The only reason I didn't have it for my own wife was because I knew you were on the lookout for a five-three-five."

"Don't *lie* to me, Leon. I have eyes in my head. I want my seventeen grand back."

"Are you in debt again, Mike? Because if this is some dumb attempt to shake me down, you can go and shove your thumb up your butthole. I ain't buying it."

"Don't wind me up, Leon. You charged me seventeen grand for a heap of crap and you damn well know it."

Leon couldn't believe the bizarre turn his day had taken, as he sat with his trousers around his ankles, grinding a palm against his head. "Look, Mike, I haven't got a clue what the problem is. So why don't you calm yourself down and talk me through it."

"I told you *twice* already. The Auto Club guy showed me inside the engine bay. He tore up the carpet and showed me red paint in the boot."

"Mike, I don't know *what* you've seen, but I swear on my kids' lives that I didn't sell you a cut-and-shut car. Now calm yourself down and let's try to sort this out. How long have you had the car?"

"Just under seven months."

"Have you had it serviced?"

"It's due, but I haven't got around to booking it."

"Right," Leon said, trying to keep himself from blowing his stack. "Technically you're out of warranty, but seeing as you're a mate I'll try and sort this out. I know a good guy who used to work for a main dealer. I'll send him over to look at your car and I'll even cover the labor and towing charges. You'll just have to pay for the parts."

"Have you heard *one* word, Leon? You can't pull the wool over my eyes. You've sold me two bits of junk welded together to make a death trap. My wife and my kid could have been *killed*. If it was anyone but you, I'd already have had the law out tearing apart every car on your lot.

"I've got to go to a meeting at the community center this morning. When I come out, I'm gonna head straight to your cabin. I expect my seventeen grand back and after that I never want to see you again. And don't go expecting any more favors from me, or any other cops at Palm Hill from now on."

"Seriously, Mike, are you having mental problems?" Leon yelled, finally losing his cool. "You're a cop. You've got a wife and a kid and you're acting like a *complete* nut. I thought you were gonna straighten yourself out after the casino deal."

"You'd better have my money when I come through that door, Leon, or I'm not gonna be accountable for what I do."

10:54

James was supposed to be on standby for any eventuality that arose, but Hannah's parents were at work and he couldn't turn her down when she arrived on the doorstep with freshly painted toenails and a tight black T-shirt. Hannah wanted to go swimming, but James said he was waiting for a call, to they ended up snogging on his bed while they listened to Dave's Rolling Stones CD.

"Don't answer," Hannah begged when James's mobile rang.

"Got to," James said as he untangled himself from Hannah. "It's probably my social worker. I'm a millimeter from getting busted back into a children's home after I got arrested the other week."

James snatched the ringing phone and walked out into the hallway.

"John," he whispered. "How's it going?"

"Really good," John said happily. "Patel made a call to Tarasov. They're at each other's throats and we've already got mentions of the casino and a virtual admission of corruption on tape. Mike says he's going over to the car lot for a showdown after some meeting at the community center. That gives the red mist a couple of hours to clear, which is the last thing we want happening. Chloe's gonna crank up the pressure on Tarasov. I need you to head over to the community center and wind up Patel."

"How?"

James was grinning after John explained. "That is *so* gross, John."

"What's funny?" Hannah asked as James came back into the room and shut his mobile.

"Nothing," James said tetchily.

"I thought your social worker was called Zara."

"She is."

"But you were talking to someone called John. And why did you have to leave the room?"

"I couldn't hear with the music on," James said.

"You'd better tell me what's going on, James. Are you seeing someone else?"

"Don't be daft . . . ," James said, wishing he'd made some excuse not to let Hannah in earlier on.

"You're lying to me about something, James, and I don't like it."

James turned back angrily. "Well, I don't like *you* spying on me. For your information, that was an old mate from when I was in foster care. I'm going out to meet him down the West End."

Hannah looked pissed off as she slid her feet into her sandals and set off towards the front door. "James, if you're gonna start treating me like an idiot, you can stick it."

James didn't want to upset Hannah, but he had to get rid of her fast. "Look, I haven't got time right now. I'll call you later."

Hannah stopped briefly as she stormed down the hallway. "Don't bother."

As the front door slammed, James raced into the kitchen and found a couple of Sainsbury's carrier bags. He grabbed his keys, mobile, and two-way radio before heading out on to the balcony. He caught a glance of Hannah, angrily fumbling with her front door key and disappearing into her flat.

James ran down to the ground floor, wondering if he'd blown it with Hannah Clarke. Two days earlier that would have made him sad, but the kiss off Kerry had changed everything.

Back in the hotel suite there'd been a scramble to make Chloe look like a police officer. They didn't have a uniform and even if they'd been able to get one of Millie's, they wouldn't have had time to alter it for Chloe's much shorter figure. Making a warrant card was easier. John had a shoebox packed with wallets and insignia that could turn you into anything from an emergency repairman for Thames Water to a captain in the Royal Marines.

Lauren snapped Chloe's photo with her digital camera, while Kerry typed a name and number into a warrant card template on one of her computers. By the time Chloe emerged from her room across the hallway, dressed in flat shoes and a plain blue skirt, John had printed, trimmed, and laminated her police ID, before slipping it into a foldout wallet printed with a Metropolitan Police crest.

Nobody had told Dave what was happening, so he was surprised to see Chloe pull on to the lot in the yellow Mitsubishi he'd used to take Kerry home the night before. Leon came down the steps of his cabin with his special customer grin.

"Good morning, my dear," Leon said as Chloe stepped out of the car. "How can I help you? If you're looking for something bigger than the Colt, I'm sure I could do you an excellent trade-in."

Chloe put her handbag on the roof of her car. She felt like an idiot as she rummaged for the warrant card. It didn't seem like the kind of thing a real police officer would have done.

"Sergeant Megan Handler," Chloe said as she

flipped open the warrant card. "Vehicle inspectorate, Bow Road."

Leon's expression drooped. "What can I help you with, officer?"

"A little bird told me that some of the cars you're selling here might not be kosher," Chloe explained.

"Did he now," Leon said, shaking his head knowingly. "I wonder who might have done that."

Dave smiled discreetly as he overheard. This hadn't been part of the original plan, but he immediately realized that it was a neat way of making Patel and Tarasov even madder at each other.

"Do you mind if I have a little look at your stock?" Chloe asked.

"Have you got a warrant?"

"No, but if you make me get one I'll come back with three uniformed officers and I bet you won't sell a single car while they spend half a day poking around."

Leon stepped back and spread his arms out wide. "I tell you what, sweetheart: Go ahead, knock yourself out. You'll find nothing out of order here."

"Thank you, Mr. Tarasov," Chloe said. "I appreciate your cooperation."

Leon kept the false grin stretched over his face as he walked back towards the cabin. Once the door was shut, he crashed at his desk and glowered at Pete, who was doing the accounts on the computer.

"Patel must be losing it," Leon said. "That piece of skirt was a cop. Says she's had a tip-off."

Pete looked away from the screen. "There was nothing wrong with that BMW, Uncle. It came from the dealer without a scrape on it. I can't work out what kind of scam Patel's trying to pull."

Leon shrugged bitterly. "Join the club, nephew. Join the sodding club."

11:24

James hurried towards the community center, searching in the gutter as he walked. He spotted what he was looking for behind the rear wheel of a scaffolder's truck. After putting both Sainsbury's carrier bags over his left hand, he looked up and down the street to make sure nobody was coming and tried not thinking about what he was going to do.

He put one trainer in the gutter and crouched down low. A dozen bluebottles whizzed away as he put the covered hand over a giant pile of dog mess and picked it up. As it squished nauseatingly between finger and thumb, James used his free hand to turn the bags inside out, so that the turd was in the bottom.

Stink

12:08

While Chloe took her time inspecting the cars at Tarasov Prestige Motors, John was running the show back at the hotel. He left Lauren and Kerry in charge of the computers for a couple of minutes, taking advantage of an apparently quiet moment to go into his bedroom and strip off the garish Auto Club uniform.

Not long after John closed his bedroom door, a red warning box popped on to the screen in front of Lauren: *Mobile 3—incoming call.*

Lauren panicked. "Shall I call John?"

"Let him change," Kerry said calmly. "Just double-check the communications properties to make sure the call is being recorded."

Lauren right-clicked the mouse and a list of parameters popped up on screen. Kerry pointed at one of them.

"There, it's automatically being recorded onto tape drive number five. Now, all you have to do is write the start time and details into the manual ledger."

"Chloe makes it look really simple when she's running this," Lauren said as she fumbled for a pencil.

12:09

There were fifty chairs set out in the main hall of Palm Hill community center, but less than a dozen were occupied. Millie sat next to Michael Patel in the front row, while a man from the council stood up in front giving a speech about an *exciting initiative* to improve street lighting around Palm Hill.

"Sorry, Mil," Michael whispered as he grabbed the vibrating mobile out of his pocket and saw it was his wife. "I'd better take this."

Michael answered his mobile as he scurried through the double doors at the rear of the hall, stepping into a corridor that smelled of floor polish. "Patricia, hi."

"So, what did Leon say?" she asked anxiously.

"He tried to fob me off with some bullcrap about sending out a mechanic."

"I want to see *all* of that money back, Michael."

"I'm going over there after this meeting. I've told him I'm expecting the full whack."

"Don't let him knock you down, Mike. We know enough about that sod to have him sent to prison for a very long time."

"I know we do," Michael said. "But that cuts both ways, doesn't it? We've got to handle this delicately."

"Charlotte could have been *killed* in that death trap," Patricia steamed. "I can't believe our baby was going round in a car that could have broken apart. I swear, if I got my hands on Tarasov right now, I could happily take a knife and stick him."

"Pat, you know I feel the same as you," Michael said. "But that kind of talk get us nowhere."

"So when does your meeting end? When are you going over to Tarasov's?"

"It's really dragging. We're not even halfway down the agenda."

"Can't you make an excuse?"

Michael thought for a couple of seconds. "Yeah . . . I suppose I could."

"I think you should get over to Leon's and sort this as soon as you can."

Michael nodded. "You know what, Pat? You're right. I can't think straight while this is going round in my head. I'll tell Millie you called to say that Charlotte's sick and I've got to pick her up from nursery."

12:13

Kerry burst into John's bedroom. "Michael Patel's gonna make an excuse and head over to Leon's right now."

"Balls," John gasped. He rushed into the adjoining room with no shoes on and his shirt buttons undone. "Lauren, call your brother on the two-way and tell him it's action stations. Kerry, contact Dave on his mobile. I'll call Chloe and tell her to clear out of the lot sharpish, then I'll contact the cops in the vans."

12:14

James was in the gents' toilet at the community center when Lauren called to say that Michael was on the move. He dried his hands rapidly and stepped out into the corridor as Michael jogged past without recognizing him. James followed him around a corner, then held back as he pushed through a set of doors and out into the car park.

Michael pulled out the keys for a police Astra and unlocked. As he grabbed the handle to open the door, he felt the tips of his fingers glide through something soft. He pulled his hand away sharply, then stood stunned as he caught the smell and it dawned that he'd just stuck the fingers of his right hand into dog mess smeared under the handle.

James watched through the doors as Michael pounded on his car and screamed a torrent of foul language. It felt like sweet revenge for banging his head against the car. He pushed the door open and stepped out into the sunshine.

"Something the matter, officer?" James grinned, keeping a safe distance.

"*You,*" Patel snarled, glowering at James. "You did this?"

"Me, officer?" James said, acting all offended. "I don't know what you're talking about."

"You *wait,*" Michael shouted. "I'm not having you now, 'cos I've got to be somewhere else; but you'll be coming home from school one night and I'll have a couple of my mates throw you in the back of a van. We'll wipe that smile off your little face; mark my words, James Holmes."

James was struggling not to laugh. "You'd better make sure it's not being videoed this time, officer. My solicitor says you'll be kicked off the force when they show the tape of what you did to my head. And I'm gonna be up for a few grand's worth of compensation."

"You think you're *smart,*" Patel foamed, with

veins bulging in his neck and eyes set to explode out of his head.

"Well, I might not be smart," James shrugged. "But at least I'm not the dude with dog crap all over me."

12:33

Michael had used the community center toilets and doused his hands with about twenty squirts of soap, but he still didn't feel properly clean as he swung the police car violently into the lot, going way too fast. The sight of Leon's XJ8 was more than Mike could take. He bumped it at low speed, nudging the Jag into the brick toilet and shattering a front indicator light.

Leon bowled angrily out of the cabin as Michael opened the car door.

"You dumb prick," Leon screamed. "What do you think you're playing at?"

"Have you got my money?" Michael steamed. "Cash or check, I don't care how it comes but I want it *now*."

"What money, Mike? I sold you a good car and suddenly you're trying to pull some scam—asking for money and grassing me up to the vehicle inspectorate."

"I didn't grass anybody up."

"What? You expect me to believe it's coincidence that this is the morning a policewoman just happens to turn up asking to look at my stock?"

"That's nothing to do with me, Leon. I want my seventeen grand, then I want you out of my life."

Leon aimed his finger at the gates. "Get off this lot, Patel. Cop or no cop. I don't know what your game is, but you're not scamming me for seventeen grand. You're not getting seventeen pence."

"My family could have *died* in that car," Michael screamed. He swung a punch, but his fist plunged harmlessly into a layer of fat. Leon grabbed Michael by his lapels, slammed his back against the police car, and planted a gigantic fist in his face.

Leon looked worried as he held up the dazed police officer by the scruff of his shirt. Pete was at lunch so Dave was the only one around, but the lot was on a busy street and it was pure luck that there were no other witnesses.

Leon dragged Michael the short distance from the car to the cabin while Dave looked on, horrified.

"Help me get him up the steps," Leon shouted urgently.

"Leon, this is bad," Dave gasped.

"Come *on*, don't stand there like a lemon."

Dave grabbed Michael's ankles.

"By my desk," Leon said, straining under the load as they carried the policeman into the cabin.

Leon dumped Michael into a swivel chair. He used all his strength to straighten him up, then turned and spoke to Dave.

"Make yourself scarce, son."

"You're not gonna kill him, are you?" Dave asked as he backed away.

"I'm not the murderer in this room," Leon said angrily. "We'll just be having a little talk. Take your lunch break and lock up the gates on your way out. I don't want customers wandering in."

Michael's eye flickered open and he made a sudden

lunge at Leon. The big man shoved him back into the seat as Dave headed out.

"That temper's gonna wreck your life, Mike," Leon said as he grabbed a handkerchief out of his trousers and threw it across the desktop.

Michael used it to mop the streaks of blood running out of his nose.

"Seventeen grand, Leon."

Leon smiled. "Remember during the Cold War, Mike? Remember *mutually assured destruction*?"

Michael looked bewildered as he spat a mouthful of blood into the handkerchief.

"The Russians and the Americans had so many nukes pointing at each other that neither side dared use them. If the Yanks nuked the Russians, the Russians would nuke 'em back. It's the same with you and me, Mike. We know too much about each other. If we start slinging mud and threatening each other with the law, it ends up with us both going down. So whatever scam you're trying to pull with that car, I suggest you drop it."

"Charlotte could have died," Michael screamed. "She's three years old."

"Don't start that up again," Leon shouted, putting his hands on his head. "I don't understand how you've got yourself worked into this state over the car, Michael. But whatever's behind this, you've got to learn to control yourself. The last time you lost your cool like this, you ended up throwing Will Clarke off a rooftop. I don't know how you've got the face to come in here trying to scam me after that. You'd be doing life if I hadn't got Falco to deal with the witness statements."

Mike waved his hand dismissively. "Falco wasn't your personal property. That old fart's taken more bribes than he's had hot dinners."

"Not for you he wouldn't have," Leon said. "Falco hates your guts."

"What happened to Will Clarke has got *nothing* to do with the car," Michael spat. "You ripped me off."

Leon bunched his fist in Michael's face. "You say one more word about that car and I swear I'm gonna knock every tooth out of your head. That BMW was *pristine* and now it's out of warranty. I want you out of here, Mike. Get in your little white *nee-nah* and don't ever come back. And if you feel like sending any more of your police buddies over here, remember what I said: If you bring the law into this, you'll be on the chopping block too."

Falco

"Rewind it. I want to hear that bit again," John ordered.

Lauren twirled the jog/shuttle controller built into the keyboard and Leon Tarsov's voice came out of the loudspeakers.

". . . *trol youself. The last time you lost your cool like this, you ended up throwing Will Clarke off a rooftop. I don't know how you've got the face to come in here trying to scam me after that. You'd be doing life if I hadn't got Falco to deal with the witness statements.*"

"*Falco wasn't your personal property. That old fart's taken more bribes than he's had hot dinners.*"

"*Not for you he wouldn't have. . . . Falco hates your guts.*"

"*What happened to Will Clarke has got nothing to do with the car. . . . You ripped me off.*"

Lauren hit the stop button. "I wish he'd admitted it, instead of saying about the car."

John smiled. "Lauren, by the time you've been in this game as many years as me, you'll have given up expecting it ever to be *that* simple. Leon's accusation is still powerful evidence, and Michael did nothing to deny it."

"The name Falco sounds familiar," Kerry said. "I'm sure I've seen it on a document somewhere."

John shrugged. "If you think you can remember something, go have a look in the files. I'll ring and check with Millie."

John grabbed a telephone, while Kerry dashed into the other room to rummage through the filing trolleys.

"Millie," John said when she answered. "What does the name Falco mean to you?"

"Hang on, I'm still in the community center," Millie said as she crept out of the meeting and into the hallway. "Alan Falco worked on the serious crime squad at Palm Hill. Not the greatest cop in the world, but he was a nice old stick. He retired before Christmas."

Kerry dashed up to John holding an open folder. John moved the phone away from his face. "What?"

"It's on here," Kerry said. "Alan Falco must have been the second cop on the scene after Michael Patel. He took this witness statement from a girl called Jane Cunningham and a couple of people who were inside the flats."

"Leon said he paid Falco to deal with the witness statements," Lauren said.

"Maybe he had them altered," John said. "Or just removed certain ones that contained incriminating information."

John put the telephone back to his face. "Thanks, Millie. I've got to go. It looks like we're on to something here. We'll be in touch."

"Look, look," Kerry gasped, tapping on the folder. "In Jane's statement it says a group of boys had nicked Hannah Clarke's sandal and were throwing it around."

"So what?" Lauren asked.

"Well, where are their statements?"

Lauren leaned over Kerry's shoulder and pointed at the next paragraph. "It says the boys all ran away when the body hit the ground."

"Yeah," Kerry said. "But they were local kids and they probably had a better view of what happened than anyone else. Wouldn't someone have found out who they were and asked them what they'd seen?"

John nodded. "I think you're spot on, Kerry. We need to find out who those boys were and what they saw."

14:21

The elderly lady put the security chain on before opening her front door to the policewoman.

"Mrs. Cunningham?" Millie asked, flashing her warrant card. "I'm looking for your granddaughter, Jane. Is she home?"

Mrs. Cunningham looked pale and her hands were shaking out of control. "Jane's popped out to the shops," she wheezed. "I shouldn't think she'll be much longer. Would you like to come in and wait?"

"Yes," Millie said.

"She's not in trouble, is she?"

Millie shook her head and smiled reassuringly as she stepped into the hallway. "I'd like to ask her some questions about the incident last August."

"The boy on the roof?" Mrs. Cunningham asked.

Millie nodded as she stepped into the living room. The old lady settled into an armchair. There was an oxygen tank at her side and dozens of pill bottles on the table.

"You're welcome to make yourself a cup of tea, officer. I'm afraid I'm not up to much. Not in this heat."

"Does your granddaughter look after you by herself?"

The old lady smiled. "I don't know what I'd do without her."

Jane came home a few minutes later, looking haggard and carrying three Sainsbury's bags. She wanted to get the food in the fridge, so Millie spoke to her in the kitchen while she unpacked the shopping.

"This is the statement you made a year ago," Millie said, setting a photocopy on the dining table. "You mention that there was a group of boys playing football. How many do you think there were?"

Jane shrugged. "Seven or eight, I guess."

"You said that they ran off, but did you see any of them giving statements later?"

"I think they all did," Jane nodded. "One of them—a little skinny guy—got knocked flying somehow and ended up with a bloody nose. The others were all around him for a bit. Then they gave statements to a cop, for sure."

"Michael Patel?"

Jane shook her head. "Patel stayed with my friend, Hannah. Will was her cousin and she was hysterical. How come you're digging this all up again? It's like a *year* ago."

Millie knew how fast rumors could spread, so she didn't tell the truth. "It's a routine audit. We like to dot the *I*s and cross the *T*s before we send our files off to be archived. I couldn't work out why no statements had been taken from the boys. Based on what you're saying, the statements were taken but then lost. You wouldn't happen to know any of the boys' names, would you?"

Jane shrugged. "Sorry. I mean, they're all kids who hang around this part of the neighborhood, but I don't actually know them."

"Have you got any idea where they live?"

"Oh, now you've said that," Jane nodded, breaking into a smile. "One of them was Kevin Milligan. He lived above our old flat in block six. He used to wind my nan up, filling balloons with water and dropping them down to our balcony."

14:50

"Oh, Christ," Kevin Milligan's mum said as she opened her front door. "What's he gone and done now? *KEVIN*, get out here."

"He's not done anything wrong," Millie said as a worried looking ten-year-old emerged from his bedroom dressed in an England rugby shirt.

"Hello, Kevin." Millie smiled, stepping into the hallway. "Do you mind if I ask you a few questions about what happened last year, when you saw Will Clark fall off the roof? You don't find it upsetting, do you?"

"No," Kevin said, resenting the suggestion that he might be squeamish.

Millie noticed another boy had his head sticking out of the bedroom.

"That's Adrian, his partner in crime." Mrs. Milligan grinned as she pushed up the front door shut. "He was there as well."

"Excellent," Millie said. "I can ask you both. It shouldn't take long."

Kevin led Millie into his bedroom. The boys had snacks and a Scalextric set spread over the carpet. Millie sat on the edge of Kevin's duvet, while Mrs. Milligan stood in the doorway.

"We seem to have lost the statements you gave," Millie explained. "I wanted to know if you'd remembered seeing anything."

"I never saw anything except the boy hitting the ground," Kevin explained. "I legged it and this cop came charging round the corner and knocked me flying."

"Which officer was that?"

"The Indian one."

"Sergeant Patel?"

Kevin nodded. "Yeah, he was running off the staircase."

Millie realized this was significant: Michael had always claimed that he'd just arrived on the neighborhood and was getting out of his car when he heard Hannah scream out.

"What about you, Adrian? What did you see?"

"I saw the boy falling. Then I looked up and I thought I saw another man up there."

"Really?" Millie said.

Mrs. Milligan looked mystified. "Are you sure you saw someone, pet? Only all the papers and that said it was an accident."

"Well, I wasn't *really* sure, because I only saw it quickly. But it *was* like there was a man or something up there."

"And what about your friends?" Millie asked. "Were you the only one who thought you saw something?"

Adrian shook his head. "No, miss. Robert did as well. Me and him both thought we saw something."

15:18

James asked if he could come to the hotel, where he'd get a much better idea what was going on, but John told him to stay put at Palm Hill in case anything unexpected cropped up.

He crashed on his bed listening to the messages going back and forth on the two-way radio and he rang Lauren a couple of times for an update. She told him about Alan Falco losing the boys' statements and that John and Ray McLad were driving out to his house.

James felt down, lolling around on his own while things spiraled off in all kinds of exciting directions without him. He realized that the mission was drawing to its end and he wondered if Kyle and the others were still going to be blanking him when he got back to campus.

Then he remembered Hannah and sent her a text saying that he was sorry about the way he'd behaved earlier on. She didn't reply.

After retiring, Alan Falco and his wife had moved out to Southend on the Essex coast. John and Ray had taken forty minutes to drive out from east London.

"Nice house," John said as they walked up a row of steps to the front door.

Ray pointed out the sticker in the back window of Falco's car: Another Satisfied Customer of TARASOV PRESTIGE MOTORS.

When nobody answered the doorbell, John went up on tiptoes and peered into the back garden. The next-door neighbor gave John a fright as he shouted over the wall. "The old boy's a bit deaf. He's out in the greenhouse."

"Thanks," John smiled.

He opened the wooden gate into the back garden. Ray followed him across a neatly mowed lawn and into a huge greenhouse stuffed with flowers.

"Mr. Falco?" John asked.

Falco was in his late fifties, but looked older. The gray beard, open-necked shirt, and braces fitted Millie's description of him seeming like a nice old stick.

"Beautiful plants," John said. "Must take a lot of work."

Falco smiled. "I have a lot of time on my hands, Mr. . . . ?"

John left Ray to flash his warrant card. "I'm Inspector McLad, CIB. My colleague is Mr. Jones."

"CIB," Falco smiled. "Have I been a naughty boy?"

"Statements relating to the death of Will Clarke," McLad said, cutting straight to the point. "Do you remember taking any?"

"Or taking bribes from Leon Tarasov to lose them?" John added.

The old stick's face tightened up. John pulled a cassette recorder out of his pocket and pushed the play button.

"I don't understand how you've got yourself worked into this state over the car, Michael. But whatever's behind this, you've got to learn to control yourself. The last time you lost your cool like this, you ended up throwing Will Clarke off a rooftop. I don't know how you've got the face to come in here trying to scam me after that. You'd be doing life if I hadn't got Falco to deal with the witness statements."

Falco didn't know where to put his face.

Ray broke into the evil smile of a man who knows he's got his victim by the balls. "Mr. Falco, we've gathered some good evidence that Michael Patel killed Will Clarke. Probably enough to secure a conviction. But if you stand in court and admit that you took money from Leon Tarasov to cover for Michael Patel, our case will be rock solid."

Falco realized he was being offered a deal that might save himself from spending the remainder of his life in prison. He phrased his words carefully, in case John or Ray were covertly recording the conversation.

"Hypothetically, *if* there was a way I could help you two gents, I'd want *complete* immunity from prosecution. Not just for this, but for any other stuff that came to light as a result of a CIB investigation into corruption at Palm Hill police station."

16:18

Millie Kentner and Greg Jackson headed into Palm Hill police station. They were confident that they'd gathered all the evidence they needed:

(1) The two boys who claimed they'd seen a man on the roof.

(2) Another boy who'd bumped into Michael Patel coming off the staircase.

(3) Michael's suspicious handling of Will's obviously dead body.

(4) Recorded conversations where Michael and Leon openly talked about the murder.

(5) Most importantly, Alan Falco's willingness to testify that Leon had paid him to destroy the statements taken from the boys after Will's death.

The pair headed up to the community policing office on the second floor and found Michael standing by the photocopier.

"Michael," Millie called, breaking into a friendly smile. "Would you mind stepping into my office for a moment? I've got Greg Jackson from CIB with me."

"James Holmes and CIB," Michael groaned. "That's *just* what I need after the day I've had."

"What happened to your nose?" Millie asked as she led the sergeant towards her office.

"Walked into a door."

Millie sat in her chair as Greg pulled a set of handcuffs off his belt and spoke.

"Michael Patel, I'm arresting you on suspicion of

the murder of Will Clarke. You do not have to say anything, but whatever you do say may be taken down and used in evidence against you. . . ."

Michael looked aghast as Millie checked the time on her watch. Over at Palm Hill, two uniformed officers were driving onto the car lot to arrest Leon Tarasov.

Heart

20:30

James and Dave's stuff was going back to CHERUB campus in the gray surveillance van. John was helping James carry everything downstairs when Liza Tarasov bumped into him on the balcony.

"What's going on, James?"

James was holding a portable TV. "The cops arrested Dave at the same time Pete and Leon got nicked, so I've got to go back to the children's home."

"Permanently?"

"I guess." James nodded solemnly. "My social worker just blew her stack. I was only allowed to live with Dave if we behaved ourselves, but we've been here less than a month and we've both been arrested. Dave's already on parole, so he won't be coming out in a hurry and I can't live here on my own."

"That's really sad," Liza said sympathetically. "It was nice having you two around. You livened the place up."

The TV was straining at James's arms, so he put it down on the ground between his legs. "I think I upset Hannah this morning. I sent her a text, but she didn't reply."

Liza nodded. "Hannah phoned me. I got the whole story and you'd better *not* be cheating on her. She's been through a lot this past year."

James shrugged. "She'll be better off with me out of her life."

"I think she still likes you."

"Yeah, but I'll be in a children's home. A few weeks after that they'll ship me off to a foster home and that could be anywhere. It's better just to leave it—you know, fond memory and that."

John emerged from the flat, holding a sports bag filled with Dave's clothes.

"Come on, James. Help me out here."

James looked at Liza and felt sad. "I'd better go. Tell Hannah that I said I'll always remember her, OK?"

Liza nodded as James picked up the TV. "I will."

"So is Max about?" James asked. "Do you reckon I should stick my head in your flat and say good-bye to him?"

"I wouldn't," Liza said. "It's a nuthouse in there. Max is sobbing his little heart out about Uncle Leon and Pete getting nicked. Auntie Sacha's really upset, because bloody Sonya started a big row with her, blaming Uncle Leon for everything."

James smiled a little. "That explains why you're out here. I'm sorry about your uncle."

"Sonya's right about one thing," Liza shrugged. "Uncle Leon's like Teflon: Nothing ever sticks to him. He'll probably be home in a few hours."

"I hope so," James lied. "Anyway, I'd better carry this downstairs before I do myself an injury."

"Yeah, later James," Liza said as he waddled towards the staircase holding the TV.

James was heading up the M11 in the van when his mobile rang: *Hannah calling*. He stared at the display, picturing Hannah on her bed, lit up by lava lamps with her orange toenails. He wondered what kind of mood she'd be in and what she wanted to say, but he didn't answer. When the phone stopped ringing, James slid off the battery, pulled out the SIM card, and snapped it in two.

"That's another phone number I don't have to remember," James said, grinning at John but feeling sad inside.

John nodded, without looking away from the gloomy lanes of traffic. His eyes looked puffy, like he needed a good night's sleep.

James slid a nylon wallet out the back of his jeans and ripped the Velcro apart. He went down the little zip-up pocket, took out the SIM card he used on campus, and slotted it into his phone. After turning it on and looking at the intro message—which Lauren had changed to *U*Suck* months earlier—he flicked through the saved numbers and gave himself a shock: *Bruce, Cal, Connor, Gab, Kerry, Kyle, Lauren, Mo, Shak*.

Apart from Lauren, nobody on the list was speaking to him. He flicked up to Kerry's number and thought about sending her a text. The kiss had worked two nights earlier, so he figured he should try. But what should he write?

He typed SORRY, deleted it, then typed it again. After deleting again he got halfway through I APOLOGIZE before deciding that sounded too pompous. James wanted to tell Kerry how she made him feel special. How she wasn't the fittest or most beautiful girl in the world, but that he wanted to be with her more than anyone else.

James realized what he really wanted to say and typed it out: KERRY, I LOVE U.

He spent a full minute with his thumb over the send button before he felt brave enough to press it.

00:18
James's phone beeped. There was an envelope on the screen: *1 SMA from Kerry.*

WE NEED 2 TALK :)

CU AT BREAKFAST. K.

Epilogue

The Cops

The end of the CHERUB investigation into Leon Tarasov was just the beginning for RAY McLAD and GREG JACKSON of the Complaints Investigation Branch (CIB).

It took six further months of investigations for their team to root out and gather evidence against fifteen corrupt officers who had been based at Palm Hill police station over a twenty-year period.

Five of the fifteen officers were forced to resign. Nine others were arrested and charged with serious corruption offenses, such as taking bribes, tampering with evidence, and running a protection racket in association with Leon Tarasov. One of these officers was acquitted of all charges. The other eight were successfully prosecuted and received prison sentences ranging between two and nine years.

The final corrupt officer, ALAN FALCO, was not charged with any offense. His testimony was instrumental in successfully prosecuting his former colleagues. Falco was forced to move from his Southend home following a series of anonymous threats, an arson attack on his car, and waking up to find the word "grass" spray-painted on his greenhouse.

Disillusioned with her police career, MILLIE KENTNER took a two-month leave of absence. After considering her options—including an offer to become a handler at CHERUB—Millie decided to continue working for the Metropolitan Police. She successfully applied for a transfer to CIB and is now in charge of an undercover squad that specializes in rooting out corrupt police officers.

The Robbers
LEON TARSOV and MICHAEL PATEL faced charges relating to the Golden Sun Casino robbery and the subsequent murder of Will Clarke.

Shortly before his trial was due to start and in the face of overwhelming evidence, Leon Tarasov pleaded guilty to all of the robbery charges against him and to three others relating to covering up the murder of Will Clarke. He was sentenced to twelve years in prison.

Michael Patel maintained his innocence. Following a three-week trial, an Old Bailey jury found him guilty of both the casino robbery and of murder. The judge described Will's murder as "The most repugnant act committed by a serving police officer we are ever likely to encounter." She recommended that Michael not be considered for release until he had served at least eighteen years of his life sentence.

The recordings made during the CHERUB sting operation were used during the trial, but they were presented as evidence collected by Millie Kentner and the CIB team. The role CHERUB played in the operation was never revealed. Leon and Michael both suspected that they had been manipulated on the day of their arrest, but were unable to prove anything.

It was suspected, but never proven, that PATRICIA PATEL was an accomplice in the Golden Sun Casino robbery. She did face charges relating to the laundering of 220,000 pounds in cash—her husband's one-third share of the robbery proceeds. In the light of her young daughter and previous good character, Patricia received a two-year suspended prison sentence.

Her BMW miraculously returned to full working order while the police were questioning her and her husband.

PIOTR TARSOV (PETE) was briefly questioned about the robbery and released without charge. He decided not to go to university and now runs the Tarsov family businesses, with his Aunt Sacha.

The whereabouts of suspected third robber, ERIC CRISP, have not been traced. Police have issues a warrant for his arrest and are optimistic that they will eventually catch up with him.

The Rest
The bugs placed in GEORGE STEIN's car and office by James Adams and Shakeel Dajani have provided some insight into the terrorist organization known as Help Earth. It was a small part of an ongoing investigation involving dozens of intelligence agencies from around the world.

JAMES ADAMS's return to campus marked the beginning of a thaw in his relationship with his friends. Kyle and Bruce—no strangers to being in trouble themselves—broke the ice. Most of the others started speaking to him again over the weeks that followed.

KERRY CHANG is back on good terms with James, but she's decided that she doesn't want him back as a boyfriend—at least for now.

CHERUB:
A History
(1941-1996)

1941 In the middle of the Second World War, Charles Henderson, a British agent working in occupied France, sent a report to his headquarters in London. It was full of praise for the way the French Resistance used children to sneak past Nazi checkpoints and wangle information out of German soldiers.

1942 Henderson formed a small undercover detachment of children, under the command of British Military Intelligence. Henderson's Boys were all thirteen or fourteen years old, mostly French refugees. They were given basic espionage training before being parachuted into occupied France. The boys gathered vital intelligence in the run-up to the D-Day invasions of 1944.

1946 Henderson's Boys disbanded at the end of the war. Most of them returned to France. Their existence has never been officially acknowledged.

Charles Henderson believed that children would make effective intelligence agents during peacetime. In May 1946, he was given permission to create CHERUB in a disused village school. The first twenty CHERUB recruits, all boys, lived in wooden huts at the back of the playground.

1951 For its first five years, CHERUB struggled along with limited resources. Its fortunes changed following its first major success: Two agents uncovered a ring of Russian spies who were stealing information on the British nuclear weapons program.

The government of the day was delighted. CHERUB was given funding to expand. Better facilities were built and the number of agents was increased from twenty to sixty.

1954 Two CHERUB agents, Jason Lennox and Johan Urminski, were killed while operating undercover in East Germany. Nobody knows how the boys died. The government considered shutting CHERUB down, but there were now over seventy active CHERUB agents performing vital missions around the world.

An inquiry into the boys' deaths led to the introduction of new safeguards:

(1) The creation of the ethics panel. From now on, every mission had to be approved by a three-person committee.

(2) Jason Lennox was only nine years old. A minimum mission age of ten years and four months was introduced.

(3) A more rigorous approach to training was brought in. A version of the one-hundred-day basic training program began.

1956 Although many believed that girls would be unsuitable for intelligence work, CHERUB admitted five girls as an experiment. They were a huge success.

The number of girls in CHERUB was upped to twenty the following year. Within ten years, the number of girls and boys was equal.

1957 CHERUB introduced its system of colored T-shirts.

1960 Following several successes, CHERUB was allowed to expand again, this time to 130 students. The farmland surrounding headquarters was purchased and fenced off, about a third of the area that is now known as CHERUB campus.

1967 Katherine Field became the third CHERUB agent to die on an operation. She was bitten by a snake on a mission in India. She reached hospital within half an hour, but tragically the snake species was wrongly identified and Katherine was given the wrong antivenom.

1973 Over the years, CHERUB had become a hotchpotch of small buildings. Construction began on a new nine-story headquarters.

1977 All cherubs are either orphans, or children who have been abandoned by their family. Max Weaver was one of the first CHERUB agents. He made a fortune building office blocks in London and New York. When he died in 1977, aged just forty-one, without a wife or children, Max Weaver left his fortune for the benefit of the children at CHERUB.

The Max Weaver Trust Fund has paid for many of the buildings on CHERUB campus. These include the indoor athletics facilities and library. The trust fund now holds assets worth over one billion pounds.

1982 Thomas Webb was killed by a landmine on the Falkland Islands, becoming the fourth CHERUB agent to die on a mission. He was one of nine agents used in various roles during the Falklands conflict.

1986 The government gave CHERUB permission to expand up to four hundred pupils. Despite this, numbers have stalled some way below this. CHERUB requires intelligent, physically robust agents who have no family ties. Children who meet all these admission criteria are extremely hard to find.

1990 CHERUB purchased additional land, expanding both the size and security of campus. Campus is marked on all British maps as an army firing range. Surrounding roads are routed so that there is only one road on to campus. The perimeter walls cannot be seen from nearby roads. Helicopters are banned from the area and airplanes must stay above ten thousand meters. Anyone breaching the CHERUB perimeter faces life imprisonment under the State Secrets Act.

1996 CHERUB celebrates its fiftieth anniversary with the opening of a diving pool and indoor shooting range.

Every retired member of CHERUB was invited to the celebration. No guests were allowed. Over nine hundred people made it, flying from all over the world. Among the retired agents were a former prime minister and a rock guitarist who had sold eighty million albums.

After a firework display, the guests pitched tents and slept on campus. Before leaving the following morning, everyone gathered outside the chapel and remembered the four children who had given CHERUB their lives.

About the Author

ROBERT MUCHAMORE is a London-based private investigator. He likes Las Vegas and chocolate, and he hates fantasy books. CHERUB: *The Recruit* is his first novel. For more about Robert and his books, visit www.cherubcampus.com.

Want more

 ?

Don't miss
Mission 5:
Divine Madness,
by Robert
Muchamore.

James sat facing Rat, with bowls of frosted cereal and beakers of orange juice on the table between them. The two boys had wet hair from the shower and were still puffed from morning exercises.

Rat's expression suddenly wilted. "Oh, crap."

"What?" James asked, but a glance over his shoulder answered the question before Rat got the chance. Georgie was steaming their way.

"Why do you do it, James?" Georgie asked.

"Do what?" James asked defensively.

"I'm talking about your friendship with Rat. It does you no credit. It will lead to trouble, and when it does, I'll be on you like a rottweiler."

There was nothing James could say without

upsetting either Georgie or Rat, so he diplomatically crammed a spoonful of cereal into his mouth and crunched.

"I got a message from the office," Georgie said. "Ernie's taking the truck out for a special delivery run this morning. He reckons there's going to be some heavy lifting, so he wants you along for the ride."

"Bless you for passing on the message," James said politely, doing his best impression of a good little survivor.

But Georgie didn't appreciate the sentiment. "Finish your breakfast and get over to the vehicle compound. Chop, chop."

James smiled at Rat once Georgie had walked off to intimidate someone else.

Two thousand kilometers north, Dana, Eve, and Nina sat around a molded plastic table with cutlery laid out in front of them. Barry Cox wore a white vest and a pair of swimming shorts as he cooked up a breakfast.

"Get your stomachs filled," Barry said cheerfully. "Today's really gonna be something. If it goes to plan, our masters will be very happy."

A CHERUB agent always has to be careful about how much they pry, but Brian's comment seemed like an invitation to inquire.

"You're not wearing a leather necklace," Dana said. "So who is your master?"

"I'm an environmentalist," Barry said. "The planet is my master. I assume you've all heard of Help Earth?"

Eve shook her head, so Dana explained to her. "They're a terrorist group that targets the oil industry. If you'd seen a newspaper or the TV news over the last three or four years, you'd have heard of them."

"I most certainly *haven't*," Eve said indignantly. "The lives of devils are not my business."

"Haven't you even heard it mentioned at school?" Barry asked.

"If they talk about things like that, I do a chant in my head to block it out," Eve said. "We mostly hang out with the other Survivors, anyway."

Brian smiled as he turned around from the hob and began dividing a saucepan of scrambled eggs among four plates. "We prefer not to think of ourselves as terrorists. But the traditional environmental groups are constantly outmaneuvered by corporations and governments with billions of dollars in their pockets. We can't fight back effectively unless we're prepared to use extreme methods."

"But you're not angels," Eve said suspiciously.

Nina broke into a big smile. "Eve, darling, you know Joel Regan and his wife are extraordinarily passionate about environmental issues. The request to send you girls up here came from Susie Regan herself. What we're going to do today will be historic. This is an opportunity for us to strike a blow for the environment as well as raising a significant amount of money towards building more arks."

Eve smiled excitedly. "Does Joel Regan know we're doing this? I mean, will he have heard my name and everything?"

Nina smiled. "Of course, sweetheart. I wouldn't be surprised if there was some sort of reward in this. A personal presentation, maybe even a platinum bead for your necklace."

The prospect of a platinum bead—the highest award a Survivor can receive—had Eve bouncing in her chair with excitement.

"I can't believe this is happening to me," she squealed.

Dana faked a grin and patted Eve on the back. "You haven't earned the bead yet, mate," she said, before looking across at Barry, who'd finished dishing up and was taking his seat to start breakfast. "So what have we got to do?"

Barry smiled. "Nothing too tricky: just blowing up a couple of supertankers."

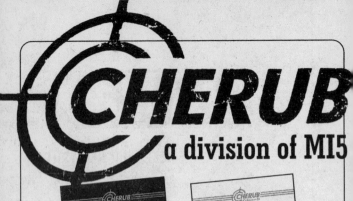